Unfinished

Business

Gemma Lubbock

In honour of the people of Hawick, whose bravery, pride and
camaraderie still abounds today.
Never forget.

"Hawick they left in ruins lying,
Nought was heard but widows crying.
Labour of all kinds neglected,
Orphans wandering unprotected.

All was sunk in deep dejection,
None to flee to for protection,
When some youths who stayed from Flodden,
Rallied up by Teri Odin.

Armed with sword and bow and quiver
Shouting "Vengeance now or never!"
Off they marched in martial order
Down by Teviot's flowery Border.

Teribus ye Teri Odin,
Sons of Heroes Slain at Flodden,
Imitating Border Bowmen,
Aye Defend your Rights and Common."

Taken from the traditional song *Teribus* by James Hogg, 1819.

Chapter One

The young girl danced under the rays of flashing coloured lights in the club and cast her spell over him in the early hours of the night. She caught his gaze only once but it was enough, he fell in love at first sight, feeling the exact moment the arrow pierced his heart. The girl was slim, she wore a sparkling white dress with long sleeves with lace cuffs, and danced in a slow rhythm than the faster beats of the song.

The noise of the music reverberated around them, softened only slightly by the high backs of the raised booth seats they were sitting in. The bass rythm vibrated round the floor.

"I'm going to marry her." Colton said.

The older man that was with him, Thomas followed Colton's gaze to the dancing girl and laughed at him, "That girl right there? She's untouchable Colton, she belongs to the owner of the bar. He's one of the Alessi brothers. You ain't going anywhere near her."

Thomas had seen a lot more in his time than young Colton. Thomas' face showed lines of wrinkles from scowling too much at everything life threw at him, and it was as if his grey hair was born of worry rather than his age. This night was no different. He didn't enjoy sitting in the nightclub, he felt static and out of place.

"All the same, I know my wife when I see her."

"Okay, Mystic Fucking Colton with your spaced out turban on your head, lose the daydream. Vivienne is already engaged to be married to the richest gangster in town, Marius Alessi. You aren't good enough for her buddy, you'll never even come close." Thomas was quick to nip Colton's ridiculous drunken notion before it went any further.

"I wasn't born to be a good guy." Colton turned to Thomas to reply, "But I know she was born to be my wife."

"Written in the stars is it Colton?" Thomas laughed, "Out of your league son. What are you going to do with a lass like her anyway? Offer her a life filled with worrying about where you are, whether you've been murdered or arrested? Growing old waiting for you to serve your prison sentences? She's got a better life lined up where she is, leave her be."

Colton gripped his pint glass, staring at the thin layer of froth, dissolving near the bottom, "The glass is half empty, the glass is half full." he said.

Just then Aubrey walked over to them, and sat down at the table, "The glass is refillable." Aubrey said, laying three new glasses filled with various poisons on the table.

Aubrey was a little older than Thomas, though his demeanour expressed a younger spirit, he didn't wear the same worn out look about him. Grey streaks ran through his wavy dark hair, the lines on his face only expressed wisdom, and complimented his handsome features. His eyes glistened and danced, giving the impression that he was always taking in everything and everyone around him. He sported an immaculate tailored black suit, the jacket of which was folded on his seat, while he wore a white shirt finished with gold cufflinks.

Colton too, bore strikingly handsome features, only he wasn't quite grown into himself yet, his dark hair was cut badly and his cheekbones still needed to mature. Colton only met Thomas and Aubrey for the first time in a bar earlier that night, and got on with them, they were full of stories and made him laugh. Colton's friends were away on stag weekend that he couldn't afford to go on, but he'd come out anyway, bored of his mum's television watching at home. Aubrey explained to Colton that they were from Hawick too, though they'd been away for a while, they were back on unfinished business. As the night wore on, Aubrey insisted on buying more and more rounds, resulting in Colton having far too much to drink. He felt like he'd made two new friends as they decided to go the club together.

Colton looked at Aubrey and took inspiration from him, "I'm not going to serve any prison sentences, I'm not going to get caught doing anything wrong. I haven't ever done anything wrong enough to get arrested."

"Not yet." Thomas laughed.

"Ah Colton, you're doomed just by associating with the likes of us now my son." Aubrey picked up his brandy, "Associating with known felons."

"Do you mean you?" Colton asked Aubrey, who nodded into his brandy glass in response, "But you told me you've never been to jail?"

"No, I have not been to jail. But that's not for lack of trying!" Aubrey laughed, "The police are desperate to frame me for something Colton, they've just never been able to yet."

But Aubrey lost Colton's attention, as his head was turned back to his beautiful Vivienne, who was finished her dance and now making her way across the crowded tables to the bar.

"I'm going to speak to her." Colton said, instantly knocking his pint glass all over himself as he tripped over his own feet in the process of standing up to leave the table.

"Not with stinking wet pants you're not!" Aubrey laughed.

"Maybe you can ask her to help you get out of your wet clothes, that's bound to work!" Thomas chortled.

"Well done Colton." Colton sighed, he sat back down again, "Goddamn it you're such an idiot."

"That's fate telling you that you and her just ain't meant to be!" Thomas laughed.

"Who are we talking about here?" Aubrey asked, as he was busy buying the drinks during Colton's arrow through the heart moment.

"Colton has fallen in love with the lady Vivienne Cowbridge." Thomas advised Aubrey.

Aubrey looked across at her, seemingly unimpressed.

"Thomas go an' lend me your trousers?" Colton asked.

Thomas spluttered on his pint, "I'm not walking round the bar in my underwear for you to go chasing a bit of tail who'll no' come near you anyway, Colton, no way."

"But you'll have trousers, I'll give you my jeans. And you can keep them, designer label these, better than the trousers you're wearing." Colton pleaded.

"I'll bet they're not better than mine," Thomas growled, "and they're covered in drink! I'll look and smell like I've pissed my pants." Thomas shook his head and crossed his arms.

"I'll give you twenty quid as well." Colton pleaded.

"This woman's costing you already, that's what they do, women, they just eat your money." Thomas warned.

"Give the lad your trousers Thomas." Aubrey commanded Thomas sternly, who unfolded his arms aghast, then stood up.

"Fine, Colton, but I'm no' getting naked for you here, you'll have to take my trousers off in the gents."

A couple walked past the table at that moment and the girl gave them a strange look. She was wearing a bright yellow dress and wore plaited round braids in her auburn hair. She whispered in the man's ear and pointed at Colton and Thomas making their way to the toilets. The man glanced over at them and frowned. Colton and Thomas did not notice this, as their backs were to the couple, even the usually sharp Aubrey missed this interaction between the couple as he was laughing to himself at Colton's desperate attempts to speak to a girl out of his league.

In the gents toilets there were two chambers, firstly a washroom area, with gold coloured taps and fixtures, leading to an inner room with a urinal and private individual cubicles. The walls were decorated lavishly in yellow and golds. It seemed overly decorated for a set of toilets in a small town club.

Thomas leaned against one of the washroom sinks and took his trousers off, holding them out to Colton. Colton removed his jeans and said, "Hold on Thomas, I'll try and get these a bit drier for you."

Colton held his trousers underneath the hand drier, he realised his bright yellow boxers were also suffering from some spilled pint so he stood with his legs parted widely so his boxers received a blast of hot air. Thomas laughed at him.

"I dunno if it's wrong, but this feels kind of pleasurable." Colton said over his shoulder to Thomas.

"Hold on I gotta try this." Thomas chortled, moving to the hand driers so that his groin area was directly under a hand drier.

"Here, try moving about a bit, get that warm air flowing through your balls." Colton laughed.

"Mm mm, that does feel sorta good." Thomas agreed.

They forgot momentarily why they were even there, languishing the warm air.

"I think I'm getting a semi." Colton laughed, and checked, "I am!"

Thomas caught sight of Colton swaying his hips out of the corner of his eye, but also the sight of the main toilet door opening and three burly suited men walking into the room accompanying a smaller man in a black suit. He wasn't a small-framed man himself, but the sheer size of the other three men dwarfed him. He was the man who had walked through the tables only moments earlier with the girl in the yellow dress.

"Shit." Thomas said.

Colton spun round, all four men's sets of eyes were immediately drawn down to Colton's tent shaped boxer shorts.

"Just what the hell do you think you're getting up to in here?" The smaller man in the suit asked icily.

"Not what you think we're getting up to." Thomas tried to begin to explain.

"Indeed." The man sniffed, "We don't condone any form of sexual activity in our washrooms, or in our club for that matter."

"Sexual?" Colton frowned, "But we were just trouser swapping."

"Disrespectful rat!" The smaller man said.

One of the large brutish men punched Colton square in the jaw, he spun round and hit the floor of the washroom. Colton opened his eyes momentarily to see a boot heading for his face. He curled into a tight ball and waited for the impact, then the world went black.

Thomas was grabbed by the other two large men who held his hands behind his back and led him through the washroom door.

The other brute picked Colton up by his feet, his white trainers and white socks making his pale white hairy legs almost luminous as they were lifted in the air and he was dragged across the washroom floor. His head was unceremoniously bashed against the door frames which made him regain a hazy consciousness. He was aware of being dragged past the tables and his heart leaped as he recognised the shimmer of a white dress near him, he looked up, and there she was, standing over him like his guardian angel. A woman in a yellow dress was holding fearfully on to Vivienne's arm and talking in her ear.

Colton flashed a blood filled smile at Vivienne. She caught his gaze and her hand went up to her mouth at the sight of him. His eyes closed again, his angel saw him, he would return for her, he knew, as he was picked up roughly by the men and thrown through the door of the fire exit.

Thomas was pushed out after him, followed by two pairs of trousers which landed on top of Colton. Thomas walked over to Colton and slapped his face. Colton came round again.

"I'm going to get those bastards." Colton said, rolling over to pick himself up and go back into the club, but finding himself caught in a tangle of trousers he couldn't get out of.

"No you're not, you'll bring nothing but trouble to yourself chasing after them." Thomas said, bending down to help Colton get out of the mess of trousers, "Know how to pick your battles Colton, this is definitely one where we just dust ourselves off and walk away."

"How will she know I'm not a homosexual if I don't go back in there?" Colton said, standing up and dancing around on one leg trying to put his jeans back on.

"Are you serious? You must be concussed. You and her, it's not going to happen. Both the Alessi brothers and their crew are in there tonight. There is no way you can go back in there, you'll just disappear and no one will ever find your body."

Cooper groaned, "Was that one of the Alessi's in the washroom?"

Thomas nodded, putting his pair of trousers back on.

"Was it the one Vivienne's engaged to?"

Thomas shook his head, "I don't know. Aubrey will though."

"I saw her, as I was leaving." Colton murmured, "She looked right at me."

Thomas laughed, "Oh my lord Colton, if your face wasn't bleeding all over the place I'd hit you to try and knock some sense into you. Just look at the trouble you've got yourself into already over her. She will bring nothing but more trouble to your door, leave it well alone kid!"

"As long as she comes to my door Thomas, I can handle the trouble she brings with her."

Thomas groaned, "Boy have you got it bad. Come on, let's find Aubrey."

They walked out of the small alleyway and round to the street where the main entrance to the club was, Aubrey was leaning with one foot resting against the wall, a little further up from the entrance away from the queue of people waiting to go in,, coolly smoking a cigarette.

"Holy hell, we can't send you home to your mum looking like that, she'll kill me." Aubrey exclaimed, "Back to my house we'll get you a new shirt and get your face cleaned up."

They walked along the street and to the taxi rank, where two cabs were waiting. It was a ten minute ride through the main street and up a hill to Aubrey's house. The taxi pulled into a private driveway with a 'for sale' sign at the entrance, and Colton was awed at the house that came into view round a corner. It was made of sandstone, with large bay windows at either side of the pillared entrance, and even featured a turret on the upper left corner. The three men stepped out of the cab.

"You live here?" Colton was impressed.

"Temporarily." Aubrey smiled and paid the driver.

"As you're selling it?" Colton asked.

Aubrey ignored him, lifted the doormat, found the key and opened the front door. Once the cab driver was away and out of earshot, Aubrey said, "I'm looking after it while the owners are away, don't make a mess of their clean carpets by bleeding all over the place, take your shoes off, and the bathroom to use is on the first floor, second door to the left."

Colton wandered up the stairs, running his hand up the smooth wooden rail. The house was beautiful, he imagined his beautiful Vivienne walking down the wide staircase in her white dress to meet him. "How much are they selling it for?" he called down to Aubrey who was making his way along the hallway.

"Too much for you kid." Aubrey called back.

Colton stopped in the middle of the stairs and turned to look over the rail at Aubrey, "Will you teach me what I can do to afford a place like this?"

Aubrey called back, "Go get cleaned up kid."

Colton sighed like a child and marched up the stairs.

When he came back down Aubrey and Thomas were sitting in a kitchen, at a large oak dining table, smoking cigarettes and supping drinks. They poured Colton a drink mixed with coke.

"You look a bit better." Thomas remarked.

"Thanks." Colton said.

"You'll hopefully not bruise too badly, not so much that your mum will notice, she'll think it was me." Aubrey remarked.

"This place is great." Colton smiled looking around at the kitchen.

"Do you even know how to change a plug, Colton?" Aubrey asked him, "Or let's make it even simpler, can you change a lightbulb?"

"Well, it's not rocket science, is it?"

"Hah-hah! That answers that question! I know you're an honest lad, and you're not wanting to lie to me and tell me you do, when you clearly don't even know how to change a lightbulb." Aubrey inhaled his cigarette, "That's the trouble with the youth of today, no common sense for the practicalities of life. The basics. The fundamentals. You are simply not equipped to survive."

"Changing a lightbulb isn't exactly a life or death situation." Colton remarked.

"You've not travelled anywhere either I take it? Not seen anything of the world and all of its cultures?"

"Mum says to tell people a day out of Hawick is a day wasted when they ask me things like that."

"But you live in Denholm." Thomas pointed out.

Colton shrugged and looked away from them.

"Thomas, let's not make the boy feel too uncomfortable. You think very highly of your mother?" Aubrey commented.

Colton took some of his drink, "She's my rock. She's worked hard my whole life to make sure we get by. But god, she's annoying."

"What was your dad's name?" Thomas asked.

"Jack Cooper."

"Jack Cooper." Aubrey repeated, "Well Colton, when we take you home I'd quite like to meet your mother and apologise to her for kidnapping her son, do you think I could do that?"

"Yes, no bother, she leaves for work at about seven thirty in the morning though."

"Early doors then. Thomas you'll need to stop drinking so you're fit to drive us there tomorrow." Thomas nodded, "In fact, let's call it a night here, I need to replenish these old bones." Aubrey stood up from the table, "Colton take the room next to the bathroom you were just in."

The next day arrived, Colton was woken up by Thomas shaking his shoulder at six in the morning. Colton's head hurt and he took a while to remember where he was.

Down in the hall, Aubrey was pacing the carpet, waiting for them to come down, "Good morning Colton, I must apologise for the early start, I had forgotten that the car was left down in the Common Haugh car park last night and we need to walk down to collect it. But please, have a coffee first before we go."

Colton groggily acknowledged Aubrey, supped on a quick coffee in the kitchen, then they left the house to walk the mile or so to the car park. The men spoke very little on the way down, the air was bitingly refreshing, barely anyone else was walking about, only two work vans past them on the road. Aubrey's car was a black mercedes. The men got into the car, Thomas turned the ignition key, but nothing happened. He tried again, then swore, got out and flipped the bonnet. He scratched his head, then walked over to Aubrey's side of the car, who opened the door.

"What's the problem?" Aubrey asked.

"I can't really tell, the whole engine's hidden away under a heap of plastic, but I think the battery is flat." Thomas shrugged.

Aubrey slapped his hands off his legs, "Well, we'll walk then, it's a fine day for a walk."

Colton raised his eyebrows and widened his eyes, "Denholm's five miles away!"

"Well, we'll miss our appointment with your mum, but we'll see her when she gets home from work." Aubrey said, "It's a grand day for it. Keeps you fit."

Colton sighed and got out of the car.

"Would you sooner be sweating away in a gym, or walking in the fresh air on a day like this?" Aubrey asked.

"Neither." Colton mumbled.

"Well you aren't ever going to build muscles to take on gangsters with an attitude like that, are you? Pick your feet up, and get walking." Aubrey frowned.

But the three men were not destined to make it to the village of Denholm that morning.

Chapter Two

Aubrey, Colton and Thomas were walking along the main road, heading out of town, they kept a steady pace for about five minutes, along Commercial Road heading towards the outskirts of town and the road to Denholm. Colton's head was pounding in time to his footsteps.

The plaintiff melody of a nursery rhyme jingle burst into their eardrums directly behind them and then stopped quickly, played specifically at that moment to make the men jump.

They looked at each other, "Bit early in the morning for ice cream?" Colton said, "But I could murder a can of juice if it's stopping."

The Ice Cream van cruised passed them at ten miles an hour. The driver looked out at them and scowled, they could make out a familiar face with Italian dark skin and heavy set eyebrows.

"Isn't that one of the Alessi's? The one from last night?" Colton asked, "What's he doing up so early?"

Colton could feel Aubrey beginning to bristle with rage, but he said nothing and stared straight ahead, watching the lights of the ice cream van trundle slowly past them.

"He's got it coming to him." Colton muttered bitterly, "Him and his brother."

Aubrey looked across at him, "The occasion will undoubtedly present itself in due course."

They continued walking for about twenty minutes. Colton knew a shortcut, he went straight over the roundabout, walking past the iconic red-bricked leisure centre, following the river Teviot along Mansfield Road towards the rugby grounds.

He led them past the rugby pitches, where the road curved, and ended in a turning area, surrounded by poorly growing scrub and thick trees.

"This is where people park to go dogging." Colton told them knowingly.

"And you would know that, how?" Thomas asked.

Colton stammered and blushed in response.

Parked at the end of a road, right round the corner away from the view of the road, was the same ice-cream van, parked up.

They walked past it solemnly, waiting for the Alessi to step out of it. But the ice cream van was empty. Aubrey tested the door, it was unlocked.

"What chance is this?" Aubrey asked, as if he knew.

"Where's he gone?" Colton looked around, peering into the foliage, "Do you think he's taking a shit? Or is it some sort of trap?"

"There's no way he would know we were going to come past, he probably thinks the van is well hidden here." Aubrey surmised, "He's lucked out. Get in lads, and be quick about it."

Aubrey stepped into the van and into the driver's seat. Colton sat next to him while Thomas clambered into the back.

"No keys." Aubrey muttered. He pulled down the sun visor and the keys for the van fell down onto his lap, "Bingo."

"Who does that?" Colton asked, "Who leaves their keys in their van, on the sun visor?"

"Perhaps the Alessi brothers think no one would be foolish or brave enough to steal one of their vans." Aubrey raised his eyebrow, flicked the key into the ignition and started the ice cream vans engine, "They guessed wrong now I'm back in town."

As the engine came to life, Aubrey, Colton and Thomas scoured the landscape around them, trying to spot the elusive Alessi.

"I think I see him, or at least his naked behind, boss!" Thomas laughed from the back, "He's got himself a bit of fluff out in the undergrowth and is a bit too preoccupied to notice his van is going to go walkabout!"

Aubrey giggled a high-pitched laugh, "Can you get a decent photo on your phone?"

"I'll try." Thomas grinned, pulling out his smartphone and clicked away, zooming in, "Yup, got his face and everything, looking a bit puffed! And that's definitely not that lass Vivienne he was with last night, this one's blonde."

"What?" Colton exclaimed, "How dare he! What a waste! He's got the woman I want, and he's cheating on her!"

"Right time to leave." Aubrey swung the giant steering wheel and the ice cream van floated along the thin road.

"He's not even noticed the van's gone." Thomas shook his head, watching out the back window.

"Boy is he going to be in trouble when his girl finds out." Aubrey giggled again, "Send me the photos onto my phone."

They drove past the rugby grounds, and took a right, up through the Burnfoot Industrial estate and out into the countryside onto a B-road, which snaked round bends and up hills until Aubrey slowed to a crawl at the entrance to a hotel.

"This wasn't here when I was last in town." he said.

"Its no' long been open." Colton explained.

"Let's go take a look." Aubrey said, turning the steering wheel to guide the van down the driveway.

They pulled into a carpark, in a secluded space hidden from view of the main building by the wall of an outbuilding. Aubrey stood up and climbed through into the back of the van.

"Let's see what these Alessi boys are getting up to so early in the morning then shall we?" Aubrey said as he slid open the freezer lid. He pulled out a layer of ice cream tubs and underneath were sealed cardboard boxes. Aubrey pulled one out, shut the freezer lid and rested the sealed box on top. He pulled a penknife from his pocket and slit open the box. Inside were heaps of small plastic bags smaller than the size of a cigarette box, containing loose brown powder.

Aubrey opened one of the packets, licked his finger and dipped it into the powder, taking the lightest sample he could with the tip of his tongue.

His face turned dark, "The little bastards." he glowered.

Colton and Thomas looked at him.

"Its heroin." Aubrey explained, "Mixed with God knows what, it's definitely not the pure stuff."

Aubrey packed up the box and put it back away into the freezer. He looked about the space and pulled down an open chocolate flake box from a top shelf above the freezer and the window. He opened it, to find it was filled with syringe needles.

"Christ almighty." Thomas whistled.

"Should we call the police?" Colton suggested, "Got all the evidence here to convict them?"

"No." Aubrey frowned thoughtfully, "We have our fresh fingerprints on the van and we don't involve the police in these matters. No, this is something we deal with ourselves. My way."

"What's 'your' way?" Colton asked.

Aubrey put the box back on the shelf and grimaced, "We are going to start making things a little uncomfortable for the Alessi brothers. Firstly, we need a way of getting rid of this van."

He looked around, and stared out of the window panel, "Come, into the hotel, I need to have a think and a refreshment."

The three men stepped out of the van and dusted off their suit jackets and trousers. Aubrey locked the ice cream van and they walked through the car park to find the hotel entrance.

Once they rounded a corner, there was no mistaking the entrance. A roofed promenade let to a set of twenty wide thin steps swept up to twin revolving doors. The promenade was decorated with flying banners. A concierge could be seen standing inside waiting to greet people on entry.

"Very fancy for Hawick." Aubrey whistled through his teeth.

"Must be some something going on today." Colton remarked.

"What do the flags say?" Aubrey asked, looking at the banners fluttering in the breeze.

"Man-a-tou." Colton frowned.

"Never heard of it. Could be interesting, could be dull as dishwater. Let's see what the crack is." Aubrey said.

The concierge pushed the revolving doors for the three well-dressed men, greeting them warmly. Colton raised his hand as if tidying his hair to hide the bruising on his face from the concierge.

Colton and Thomas walked out into the foyer, where they turned to look for Aubrey and noticed the concierge's smile freeze a little, with that tight awkwardness that expressed something was amiss that couldn't be addressed. They turned to see Aubrey still walking round and round in the revolving doors. He waved at them then stepped out and giggled.

"Gets me every time." Aubrey smiled.

The concierge raised his smile again and straightened his tailed waistcoat with his white gloves.

"Nice gloves." Aubrey remarked.

"Thank you sir." The concierge replied.

"We're here for the 'manitou' convention." Aubrey said.

"Ah yes, it is just down the hallway there sir, you are a little early they are still just setting up, but you should be able to pick up your welcome pack at the table just outside the hall. May I suggest that you sample a drink at the bar which is just a little further down the hall on the left?" The concierge explained in one fast exhaled breath.

"That is a great help, thank you my man." Aubrey fished in his pocket and handed the concierge a couple of coins. The concierge puffed up proudly.

Aubrey, Colton and Thomas made their way along the elaborately decorated hallway. Colton and Thomas kept quiet, while Aubrey hummed a little happy tune. Aubrey striding business-like along the hall, which widened a little to make room for an entrance doorway decorated in gold. A little table was just outside. On it were white paper bags with the word "Manitou" emblazoned diagonally on the side, small plastic badges that were blank, and a clipboard with a list of hand written names on.

Quickly and smoothly, without looking round, Aubrey picked up the pen and added three names onto the bottom of the check sheet. He popped the pen down and walked into the hallway, still humming his little tune. Colton and Thomas stepped after him.

Inside the hall was more dimly lit than the hallway, their eyes took a moment to adjust to the a black and grey walled room. It was a vast space, near them were rows of marketing stalls, with people mingling about with a quiet buzzing hum of putting the finishing touches to their stalls, while others were wandering around chatting to other people that they recognised from other conventions.

Aubrey kept walking with purpose, past the stalls, nodding to some people as if he knew them and was experienced with these sorts of events to the point of being bored by them. Colton and Thomas took his lead and donned the same expressions. Aubrey wandered round the pathway of stalls, which broke out in a central bay where there was evidently going to be teas and coffees on offer, as waiters were readying the tables with tea cups and biscuits. Aubrey grabbed a biscuit, and wandered on.

After passing more stalls they reached the end of the hall, where all the pathways were leading to, which was set up as a stage area. Spotlights and strobe lights were glinting off a shining white forklift, with huge rutted tires and a black sticker which had the word "Manitou" along the side.

"So that's what a Manitou is." Colton whispered.

"Indeed." murmured Aubrey, whose brain was beginning to tick over, "Time for a drink."

They wandered their way back through the stalls, Aubrey pocketed a pen or two from the unmanned stalls on their way. Not to be outdone, Colton eyed up a clear tub of round silver keyrings which he reached for and grabbed one successfully.

They made their way to the bar room, which was an ornate purple, silver and velvet affair, and took their standing positions next to two men who were seated on silver stools at the bar. One man was rather rotund, having taken off his suit jacket and draped it over his lap, it revealed his sky blue shirt which already bore small sweat patches around the arms and down his back. The other man was of average build, with mousey thinning hair and wearing a pair of black framed spectacles. He was holding a clear wallet from which the top sheet of his paperwork inside could be read, Colton could make out the words "Manitou convention" clearly at the top of the page, then the barman asked him what they were drinking.

Colton ordered three coffees, and looked at the two men, catching the rotund man's eye.

Colton smiled and nodded, "Are you here for the Manitou convention?" he asked pleasantly.

The man nodded, "Yes, just arrived. Bit early, had to catch the first train then a taxi to make sure we got here, bit of a remote place! This is my first convention. My boss usually comes to these things but he's away on holiday to Mauritius."

Colton looked at the other man, who chipped in with: "Mine too, never been to one, hope it's exciting."

Aubrey leaned over, "Our boss decided it was about time we came along. Do they do demonstrations? We saw the brand new machine in the hallway back there, it's a pretty impressive beast."

The two men nodded with recognition, the thin man said dreamily, "Ah yes the MT 007, so much power. It says on the schedule there will be an outdoor demonstration at four o'clock."

"I think most people will be away by then though, to beat rush hour." the rotund man sighed, "I have to miss it, I was really looking forward to it, it was going to be the highlight of my day, I've got a four hour journey to get back and the in-laws are coming round for dinner this evening."

"You've come quite some way." Aubrey remarked, "Could your boss not put you up in the hotel?"

The rotund man laughed, "No, I've got to be back at work first thing tomorrow, hit the road, targets to meet. You know the pressures we're under."

"Yeah." Aubrey nodded sympathetically, "I used to work for JCB, and they were even meaner on sales targets."

"Ah the opposition!" the thin one exhaled, "You've come over to the dark side!" he laughed.

Aubrey laughed as well.

The barman placed the three coffees on the countertop, Colton paid for them and Aubrey picked up his cup and made his way to a table well away from the two business men, Colton and Thomas followed him. When they sat down they noticed that Aubrey's eyes were alight with mischief, "I have an idea." he smiled, taking his spoon and heaping sugar into his cup from a bowl on the table.

"Oh?" asked Colton.

"Just how deep would you think a hole would have to be, to bury, say, an ice-cream van? And how long would it take a state of the art Manitou to dig out such a hole?" Aubrey pondered.

"You're going to steal the JCB?" Colton replied.

"Colton, please, don't mention the opposition to me." Aubrey said super seriously, "Oh no, we're not going to steal it, we're just going to borrow it for a little while. About as long as it takes to dig a hole I would think."

Colton took a drink of his coffee and set it down, holding the cup to warm his chilled hands, "Can you drive a digger?"

"No, but I'm going to get lessons at four pm." Aubrey leaned back and put his arms behind his head, "Let's get comfortable and enjoy the convention."

They ordered three english breakfasts at the bar, after which the three men returned to the now-manned table outside the hall, where a young girl with hair tight in a bun, in a crisp navy skirt-suit checked her clipboard for their names, which were of course, right there, and they were given hand-written name badges and a gift bag each. They milled around the stalls, pocketing more freebies on their rounds. Colton discovered his silver keyring was a miniature screwdriver set, and nabbed several more of them.

They enjoyed coffee with the other members of the convention, and even sat in the back of the auditorium to listen to some of the guest speakers, nodding at the appropriate moments and clapping with the crowd.

The minutes eventually struck quarter to four, those who were standing drinking their coffees were invited by a female voice over a loudspeaker to gather around the Manitou. They all hastily finished their coffees to gather round the Manitou, the whole crowd carrying an air of excited anticipation.

A man in a pair of green overalls and rubber welly boots stepped into the cab, the door swung silently shut behind him. Then the engine started. It didn't roar into life as Aubrey, Colton and Thomas expected, but hummed and purred like a washing machine beginning its first load. The people at the convention looked at each other, confused.

The female voice on the loudspeaker started up again, "Ladies and gentlemen, may we introduce to you, the Manitou MT 007! The very first hybrid Manitou of its class, in fact, the very first industrial vehicle to embrace this newly emerging technology. You will hear no familiar rumble of a diesel engine starting up, there isn't a drop of fossil fuels to be found. This Manitou runs on electricity and hydroelectric fuel cells." the voice paused for dramatic effect, sure enough hushed gasps emitted from the now enthralled audience.

"This manitou can dig six times faster than her competitors in her power class. If you don't believe us, follow Tony and the beautiful MT

007 out to the grounds for our final demonstration of the day. You will not believe what this girl can do, a true feat of remarkable design and the height of top secret patented technology, she was really worth waiting for. No one will be able to compete with her on the open market, or on the job. Okay, so if we're all ready? Simon, Jake?"

Two men opened huge doors which led out into the hotel car park, allowing a rush of cool late afternoon air to reach the crowd. There was a four-by-four parked up just outside the hall, with a long trailer attached to the back of it, a set of steps led up to the back of the trailer leading to uncomfortable looking metal seats. The crowd gathered onto the trailer, filling the seats and standing, while a privileged few got into the back of the four-by-four. Aubrey, Colton and Thomas stood, staring out onto the car park and were motioned by the woman to load onto the trailer. The engine of the four-by-four started and drove them away from the hotel.

The Manitou could be seen behind them, moving off the stage, down the ramps and out of the doorway, following the four-by-four. It was slick and almost silent, which seemed unnatural in a vehicle of its size. The group were driven out of the car park, but instead of following the drive to the right, the vehicle did a left turn down a dirt-track. This went on for some way, leading down past the hotel which was no longer visible through thick trees and foliage, and then round to the left the track then ran parallel with the flowing river Teviot, and was met on the other side with a steep cliff. The track ran along some way along to the left, and ended at a field enclosed by thick woodland. The four-by-four pulled into the field and drew to a stop, where the guests were asked to disembark using the steps that were pulled down for them from the back of the trailer by Simon as the Manitou pulled into the field behind them. Tony drove the Manitou round past the four-by-four and down a banking back towards the river side of the field. Murmurs of "That's too quiet for a Manitou," and, "God look at the speed she's going," emitted from the people disembarking.

The crowd were guided to the top of the banking, someone muttered about the wet grass spoiling their leather shoes.

A woman emerged from the four-by-four and walked to the front of the group, she was dressed immaculately, like the girl at the meet-and-greet table, in a navy blue skirt and suit jacket, an outfit finished off with a neck tie, neat navy hat and bright red lipstick, and a pair of shiny black wellington boots, "Well folks, here it is, the long anticipated demonstration by the MT 007, boy did we have some job keeping her under wraps, we have all just been so excited to reveal what she is capable of."

The woman paused, turning to Tony inside the cab she gave him a thumbs up sign and a great big smile and turned back to the crowd, "Let her rip Tony!"

The Manitou almost inaudibly raised its digging arm into the air and the crowd waited with baited breath for its first teethy reach into the grassy ground. Down went the arm, effortlessly scooping a clod of earth into its bucket with relative ease. The arm was lifted back up and the Manitou was reversed away from the hole. An intermittent beep emitted from the machine while it was moving backwards. The machine paused to allow the woman a chance to speak again.

"Did you catch the speed the arm lifted the earth out of the ground? It is unbeatable by anything currently on the market! The MT 007 arm is easily interchangeable to forks and other equipment, it has its own modern lightweight forks, and though the older heavier accessories can be used it is not really recommended. Tony?" she signalled the driver to continue.

Aubrey walked back from the front of the crowd to find Colton and Thomas, chuckling to himself, "The fastest digger known to man." he pointed across at the Manitou, now on its third round of digging, "Can you believe that?"

"Pretty impressive." Colton replied, standing with his arms crossed, resting his hands on his elbows, still being careful to maintain his business demeanour.

They waited around and watched till the demonstration was over. The crowd was loaded back onto the trailer and returned to the hotel, while the Manitou was driven round to the far side of the hotel, and parked directly next to the ice cream van, in order to be cleaned and polished for day two of the convention the next day. This, Aubrey learned from a particularly chatty Tony, who was in charge of cleaning the MT 007, and who was more than willing to discuss the various aspects of the new machine. Some way into the conversation, Aubrey dropped the actual question he was looking for an answer to, "So Tony, just how long do you think it would take this MT 007 to dig a hole deep enough, say, for that ice-cream van parked there?" Aubrey gestured nonchalantly towards the van.

Tony looked across at the van, then across to the digger, then placed his hand on his chin and rubbed it thoughtfully, "I'm no mathematician, but I reckon an ordinary Manitou would dig a hole that size in six hours and this machine can do it in three."

"Wow, that fast huh? I'm really going to have to ask my boss to get me one for the farm. Is it easy to drive? What's that lever for, that looks like a new addition?" And then Aubrey was sitting up in the driver's cab, getting driving lessons from the proud and kindly Tony.

Colton signalled to Aubrey that he was heading back to the bar, there was little point in Thomas and him hanging around looking like spare parts. Colton ordered a drink for themselves and one for the absent Aubrey and like creatures of habit, they chose to sit at the same table as earlier in the day.

Aubrey eventually walked through the bar across to the table looking pleased as punch with himself. He sat down and smiled into space.

"Care to enlighten us?" Colton asked.

Aubrey picked up his drink, "Gentlemen, our lady awaits us." he took a grateful sip and smacked his lips gently together, "Ah nothing tastes quite as good as a plan being put in action."

Aubrey leaned forward and encouraged Colton and Thomas to do the same, "Our friend Tony clocks off in ten minutes after he's finished cleaning the Manitou. After that, we are going to take the Manitou for a little test run and bury that ice cream van out there where no one will ever find it, and we're going to return the Manitou and no one will ever be any the wiser."

Colton frowned at the lack of forethought and detailing with this plan, "Can you remember how to drive it?" was his first question.

"Not entirely, but I have Tony's step by step instructions recorded right here on my phone." was Aubrey's confident reply.

"Where are we burying the van, boss?" Thomas asked.

Aubrey took another sip of his brandy, "Right under their noses Thomas. Where they were doing the test digging earlier on down by the river."

"Someone will notice an ice cream van driving down to the river." Colton warned.

"Who's going to see?" Aubrey asked, "The car park is hidden from view of the main hotel, the track is hidden from the view of the hotel, the field is hidden from view of everyone, we could barely hear the digger going and we were standing right next to it, it's perfect!" he calmed down enough to soothe Colton's steadily increasing nerves, "Listen, the hotel staff have nothing to do with the conventions that go on here, besides which they'll be changing staff to the evening shifts soon enough, I asked that Concierge about it earlier. We borrow the digger on the end of the day shifts and the evening staff won't even notice it's missing until it's returned, and then, it's just being returned from its test run anyway."

"Not tempted to just take the Manitou, boss?" Thomas asked him, "Sell it on?"

Aubrey looked at him and nodded approval, "I like your thinking there Thomas, but I haven't got a buyer and it would make a slow getaway vehicle, too risky. Safer that the machine doesn't leave the hotel grounds.

Colton looked at the two of them, "Given that I'm new to all of this, can you explain to me what I should do?"

Aubrey tilted his head thoughtfully, "Just keep your mouth shut kid, follow Thomas' lead and let him do all the talking. If anyone asks, you are from Russia and can't speak a word of English."

"He doesn't look very Russian boss." Thomas pointed out.

"What? Okay, Ukrainian then, how's Ukrainian to you Thomas, does that fit with you?" Aubrey said, "No one will ask questions anyway, this isn't the sort of establishment that has things out of the ordinary ever happened to it."

Aubrey looked at his watch, "Almost clocking off time, drink up boys, game's on."

The three men stood up and walked out of the bar at a steady pace. Aubrey stared straight ahead and walked with intent towards the hall.

Colton attempted to don the same air, though there was no need to, the entrance table was vacant, as was the entire hall. No one wanted to stay late that evening it seemed.

Aubrey strode over to the Manitou and jumped into the cab, finding the keys where he watched Tony leaving them in the cab earlier on, "God bless you Tony, son." Aubrey muttered.

The engine started like a delicately bred lady clearing her throat at an opera concert, almost completely inaudible.

"That just sounds wrong." Thomas said as he strode over to the big double doors and played with the latch, "These machines are meant to roar into life. Next it will be a robot machine that won't even need a driver at all. Give me a hand with the other door Colton."

Colton was watching the skill that Aubrey used in navigating the Manitou, but jumped to life, stepping quickly across to the other door. He opened his door and the Manitou drove almost silently out of the hall, leaving Thomas and Colton to close the hall doors.

"Now what?" Colton asked.

"We go back to the bar, and we wait." Thomas explained, frowning, pulling his phone out of his pocket to check it, "I'm not hanging around in the freezing cold waiting for him to dig a great big hole in the ground, he can do that part himself."

They strode out of the hall and back to the bar, passing one member of hotel staff as they did so. She was young with dark hair in an unkempt ponytail, carrying clean white towels, looking to be in a hurry, barely acknowledging them as she walked briskly passed.

Colton's hands were shaking a little, adrenaline finally beginning to make him nervous. Thomas noticed this change in him.

"Cool it down kid," Thomas said, "We'll order something to eat, it'll help your nerves, and I'm pretty hungry."

The two men walked to the bar, and much to Colton's relief, he saw a different barman waiting to serve them. Thomas ordered two drinks and asked to see the food menus.

"Aubrey was right about the staff changeover." Colton muttered to Thomas once they were seated at what was now their usual table.

"You aren't going to talk nervous chit-chat the whole way through the meal are you? How about you keep up your appearances and act all Ukrainian by staying quiet?" Thomas was smiling when he spoke, but Colton realised he was being careless with his conversation now that the plan was underway.

Colton nodded and picked up the menu, while Thomas tapped out a text message on his phone. Thomas put the phone away and picked up the other menu.

Moments later, a waitress came over, a young girl with dark hair in a long ponytail, "Can I take your order?" she asked politely in her lilting local accent.

Thomas looked up and smiled pleasantly but tapped a toe against Colton's leg as a gentle reminder for him to stay quiet, "Yes I'll have the venison steak, with chips, and my friend here will have a homemade double cheeseburger with the curly fries."

"Is that everything?" she scribbled into her notepad and smiled at them.

"Yes, thanks." Thomas replied.

The waitress took their menus off the table and walked quickly away.

"You best text your mum and tell her you'll be late home." Thomas suggested quietly to Colton.

Colton's eyes widened, "Hell, I forgot about mum, she'll have made my tea for me." he said a little too loudly for Thomas' liking.

"Colton I'm only gonna ask you one more time to keep quiet then I'm going to punch you in the face and shut your mouth for you." Thomas warned.

Colton nodded and lowered his head, pulling out his phone from his pocket he saw three missed calls from his mum. He wrote her a text message saying not to worry but he would be late back, though his hand shook a little while he was typing. He put his phone away and started biting his nails. Thomas glared at him and Colton put his hand back down by his side. Colton pulled his phone back out and saw that his mum replied with the dreaded question, "Where are you?" Colton never lied to his mum. Thomas leaned over and took the phone from Colton's hand, reading the message.

"Tell her you're with your friends and everything's fine." Thomas said, handing the phone back to Colton.

Thomas leaned back into the seat and looked out at the bar around them. Colton typed the words in and clicked send. He held the phone in his hand and in a moment the reply came back from his mum, "Names please?" Colton felt a pang of guilt mixing up with the nervousness inside him. He sent the reply with the first names of his two new friends, as that was all he knew of them, then put his phone away into his pocket.

The waitress came over to the table with their cutlery and napkins, she laid them out and Thomas thanked her. Thomas got up and found a newspaper, and took to ignoring Colton for the ten or fifteen minutes it took for the food to arrive. Colton listened to the bar man talking to their waitress about the Manitou convention, gossip he'd been passed on from the barman earlier, referring to guests who had stayed for a meal and were now getting a bit too drunk in their restaurant. Colton didn't realise how hungry he was until the meal arrived, he bit eagerly into the burger.

"Slow down kid, you'll give yourself heartburn." Thomas said, cutting at a bit of his steak with his knife, "Aubrey wouldn't like to see you eatin' like that. Food is meant to be savoured, and enjoyed. Chefs have trained for years and slaved in that kitchen for hours to bring you that meal, an animal has lived a life and died to bring you that flavour, a farmer has got up at five o'clock in the morning to feed that animal. Take your time, and appreciate all of that." Thomas took his steak chunk delicately from his fork with his teeth.

Colton looked at the burger, he wanted to swallow it whole he was so hungry, but he took smaller bites at Thomas' instruction. Sure enough, the flavours began to drift into his taste buds. He realised it was the best burger he ever tasted. It had been a long day, he thought about it with his next gratifying chew of delicious burger.

Colton finished before Thomas and sat in respectful silence. When Thomas finished his steak the meal was done. Thomas ordered one more round of drinks at the bar, where he paid the tab.

They sat for perhaps another half an hour, then Thomas got up and gestured for Colton to follow him. Colton picked up the white convention bags full of freebies and they walked out of the bar, along the hall and out of the revolving front doors of the hotel, where a different concierge acknowledged them as they left.

Thomas walked Colton round to the back of the hotel, to the parked up ice cream van, and stepped into the driver's seat. Colton sat next to him. Thomas drove the ice cream van out of the hotel car park and down the dirt track, Colton glanced nervously up into the woods that screened them from view, making sure there was no way anyone could see them. Thomas parked the van outside the field, on the dirt track. "Its gonna need a straight run in that field, the ground's soft, it'll get stuck otherwise." Thomas explained, killing the engine and stepping out to find Aubrey.

Aubrey was in the cab of a filthy Manitou, so covered in mud that the white paintwork was barely visible, he was stripped down to his white vest, his suit jacket and shirt were hanging up in the cab. A hole was dug at the bottom of the banking, down at a steep angle it cut into the banking itself. He raised his hand in a little wave as Thomas and Colton walked up to the hole.

Thomas whistled, "Phew, that digger can shift some soil."

Colton looked at the hole, it was vast and huge, and big enough to fit an ice cream van in. Aubrey backed up the machine and jumped out, walking up to them rubbing sweat from his hands, "I've got to get me one of these." Aubrey smiled.

"There's just one thing." Colton said, "How do you get the ice cream van into the hole if it's going to get stuck in the field when it comes to a stop? We'll not be able to push it into the hole."

Aubrey looked at the van parked outside the gateway, then at Colton, "You're a smart kid. I'm glad we brought you on this unusual outing. What would you suggest we do to solve that little problem Colton?"

Thomas grinned wickedly, already anticipating what needed to happen.

Colton thought about it then answered, "Can the Manitou lift it into the hole?"

Aubrey shook his head, "That would cause damage to the van and potentially leave shards of broken ice cream van everywhere, or damage to the digger and we don't want that either as it would rouse too much suspicion."

Colton thought some more, "Someone would have to drive the van towards the hole, set it running, then jump out at the last minute." he suggested.

"Bingo!" Aubrey said, "And you're just the kid to do it, light and agile enough that you won't break any bones on the landing."

Thomas laughed at the expression that appeared on Colton's face.

"But, I…" Colton stammered.

"Colton, you're either with us, or against us, and if you're against us, I'll have to shoot you and bury you in this hole myself. So what is it to be, kid?" Aubrey folded his arms.

Colton inhaled, turned and walked towards the ice cream van.

"Do you know how to drive the van into the hole, kid?" Thomas asked him.

Colton shook his head in response, Thomas sighed, jogged after him and explained to him how to drive the van at the right speed and leave it in gear then jump out.

"Won't it explode if the engine's left running as it lands in the hole?" Colton asked.

Thomas shook his head, "Nah, it'll stall itself somewhere in the fall. You get one shot at this, you better get it right."

Colton stepped up into the driver's seat and gripped the wheel to steady his hands which were trembling almost uncontrollably now. He took a few deep breaths, looking at Aubrey and Thomas, who were standing talking together, looking at the ice cream van. He started the engine and slowly drove the van into the field, feeling the van change responsiveness beneath his hands as it drove onto the deep grass of the field. His breathing grew increasingly unsteady as he steered the van left towards the steep banking and guided it down the hill, feeling gravity desperately trying to pull the van more quickly down the slope. The hole was increasing in his view, it was a mass of a dark hole in the remaining daylight diminishing in the evening sky. Colton opened the driver's door and jumped for his life.

He landed on the grass, rolled several times and turned to see the van cruising slowly towards the ditch. The van almost successfully drove itself directly into the hole, but then decided to do a part nosedive leaving part of its back end in the air.

"Shit." Colton swore, jumping up and running back to Aubrey and Thomas, "I did everything right Thomas, I swear."

The three men looked at the ice cream van on its end in the great big hole.

"Yes, you did." agreed Aubrey.

Then, just like that, there was a lurching groan of protesting metal to be heard from the hole, and the back end of the ice cream van dropped down into the hole and out of sight.

"Well, would you look at that." Aubrey exclaimed, "The gods are smiling on us today. Right, no time to waste, let's bury this thing."

Aubrey ran back to the Manitou, jumped into the cab and swung the arm back in action, moving it back and forth across the mounds of dirt, dragging soil over the ice cream van and into the the hole around it.

The hole was filled in, Aubrey then tried his best to flatten the huge mounds of dirt that were left over.

It was dark and Colton was shivering by the time Aubrey was finished. The air was damp and the alcohol from earlier was wearing off. He was cold, with sore legs from standing watching the ice cream van being buried, but he didn't dare complain to Thomas, who stood steadfast the whole time.

Aubrey opened the cab door, "Well?" he called.

"It's not a neat job, but it will do boss, it's a bit dark to tell." Thomas replied.

Aubrey gave them a thumbs up. The field was a slightly different shape from when they first visited it, but Aubrey was confident no one from the convention would notice as they would be watching the digger, and the landowner would just presume it had been the convention people getting carried away.

"Come on kid, get the hall opened up again." Thomas tapped Colton on the shoulder.

Colton bent down, picked up the damp bags of freebies and strode after Thomas. They set off at a brisk walk to the hotel, heading purposefully towards the hotel entrance. They pushed the revolving doors themselves, there was no sign of the concierge nor was there any sign of the girl at the reception desk.

"Guess what that pair are up to when the place is quiet for the evening?" Thomas raised his eyebrows suggestively.

They didn't see another soul walking through to the hall where they opened the double doors where they could see Aubrey outside giving the Manitou a once over with the power hose, like he'd watched Tony do hours earlier. Then the Manitou was driven into the room, Aubrey taking his time to drive back into position on the stage in the semi darkness.

Aubrey picked up his jacket and silk shirt, which he then used to clean the keys and steering wheel of his fingerprints. He cleaned the door handle and jumped down to them.

"Job well done boys." Aubrey smiled, putting his shirt back on and buttoning it up, "Let's get out of here."

The three men walked out of the large hall, leaving the resting Manitou back on its centre stage for tomorrow's convention.

As they exited the hall and turned to walk down the hallway the girl from reception jogged along, a little rosy cheeked, "Are you all okay there?" she asked them smiling breathlessly.

Aubrey smiled at her, "Yes thanks, just took a wrong turn, these hotels are like rabbit warrens."

She nodded and smiled back and wandered on, in a rush to get back to the reception desk.

The men walked slowly back towards the reception and exit, but they were then overtaken by a briskly walking concierge, also rosy-cheeked, who then opened the swinging doors for them on their way out.

"What did I tell you about that pair, Colton?" Thomas grinned.

As they walked down the large steps and made their way out of the car park, a jingling tune drifted across the night air towards them.

"Is that what I think it is?" Colton asked with a panicked look upon his face.

Aubrey and Thomas stopped walking to listen. Sure enough, it was the same plaintive melody that their stolen ice cream van played.

"That, my son, is not our problem anymore." Aubrey said, smiling, "The battery will run itself flat before morning."

"How are we going to get back to town?" Colton asked.

"We're not, we're still on our way to your place, come on quick quick." Aubrey said, "I want to be there in time to meet your mum before she goes to work."

Chapter Three

The three men trundled along the roads and eventually reached the village of Denholm in the early hours of the morning. Colton put his key in the door and was immediately greeted by his mother's angry tones.

"I don't want you going about with anyone called Aubrey and Thomas." were her first words echoing down the hallway of the ground floor flat.

She was sitting at the kitchen table, he could tell by the way her voice was carrying through the hallway. Colton took his shoes off, his feet ached and sent shooting pains up his legs when he placed his damp socks on the soft green carpet. He put the freebie bags down next to his shoes and walked gingerly through the small duck-egg blue hallway, past the living room door and into the kitchen, leaving Aubrey and Thomas removing their shoes in the hallway.

"Oh my god you look like you've been dragged through a hedge backwards. Has he kept you up all night? Look at the state of you!" his mum got to her feet and began to fuss over him, touching his shoulders, his hair, his crumpled suit jacket, which she pulled at knowing it didn't belong to her son. She was wearing her nurse's uniform and her dark hair was neatly tied back in a loose bun, she was evidently about to leave the house for a long shift.

"Mum, it's okay." Colton began to say.

"It's never okay with Aubrey, Colton, he brings nothing but trouble to the door."

Colton cleared his throat awkwardly, "How do you know who he is? I mean, well it's funny you should say that, as he's actually at the front door just now."

"What?" his mum put her hands to her face, "he's here?"

Colton nodded, "His car broke down. His driver's with him too, Thomas."

"I know who Thomas is, don't you tell me he's Aubrey's driver don't you dare start telling those small white lies to me Colton." his mum suddenly threw a voltage of anger at her son, "Don't you ever lie for him, Colton, not to me."

"Sorry mum, its what he told me to tell you."

His mum looked so hurt at that moment, "And he should know better than to lie to me too." she ran her hand across her face, brushing loose strands of hair behind her ears, "Well go on then, you'd better show him in. And make sure he takes his shoes off."

Colton's mum paced around her small kitchen nervously while her son closed the door behind him, walked through the hall and gestured to Thomas and Aubrey to make their way into the kitchen.

Aubrey and Thomas's feet were clearly just as aching as Colton's, for they did the same ginger walk through to the kitchen. They could see the silhouette of Colton's mum pacing back and forth through the cloudy glass panelled door.

Thomas was about to head into the kitchen, when Aubrey stopped him, "Colton can you and Thomas go into the other room for a moment, let me try to talk with your mother?"

Colton shrugged, thinking little of the request, and showed Thomas through to the living room, where Thomas promptly collapsed into a soft grey heavily cushioned sofa, sighing gratefully to be off his weary feet.

Aubrey knocked at the kitchen door and opened it slowly. He looked into the room and saw Colton's mum standing with one hand holding the kitchen counter, the other held in mid-air.

"Hello June." Aubrey said, stepping into the room and closing the door quietly behind him, "It's been a long time, how've you been?" his heart was beating as if it would burst through his chest, it really was her. It was his June standing looking at him.

June took an intake of breath, trying to hold back a rush of emotions inside her. She was unsure of herself, not knowing the right words to say to the man standing in front of her, "It has been a very long time, Aubrey Delaney." June chose carefully to say as her reply.

Aubrey closed his eyes ever so slightly, hearing his name on her lips was a sweet sound that his ears hadn't heard for many years, it was a sound he yearned for and missed with each passing day, he lingered on her words. She was just as beautiful as ever, hardly a line etched her smooth heart shaped face it seemed, but she carried a weariness about her, the weariness of working every day god sent to make ends meet for her son.

June stared at Aubrey, he was just as handsome as ever, with the same hair style as when they first met, only slightly greying round the edges and thinner on top, still in the same smart black suits and crisp, albeit slightly creased shirt, he never changed. But he was still a rogue, he was the one who left without a word of goodbye eighteen years previously.

"I see you've met our son." June said with an air of demanding to know what was going on,

Aubrey broke out of his spell, "Yes, he was in a rather bad fight in a bar in town," Aubrey started to explain.

"My Colton can usually handle himself." June sniffed, hearing a slight lilting American accent in Aubrey's voice.

"Yes, but not against five men with iron bars he can't. Thats who were heading his way when I stepped in." Aubrey embellished the events from the night club a little.

"And just what were you doing there?" June asked, "Last I heard you were in America, lost in Las Vegas."

Aubrey looked at her, the absolute love of his life, standing opposite him. She always wanted the truth from him, "I was doing my time." Aubrey bowed his head, "I went from there to Spain. But I'm done with all that now, I've come home."

"And you just happened to bump into Colton and thought you'd pay me a visit?" June's face turned to anger, "Well that's rich. Eighteen years without a word from you, and you just get yourself an open invitation to my home from our son."

"I didn't know who he was when we met," Aubrey lied, "I was saving the boy's life, and then I found out who he was. I wanted to see you again."

"You destroyed my life, and you left me alone here, expecting your child, without anything in the world!" June raised her voice.

"I'm sorry." Aubrey murmured and looked forlornly at June, trying to reach for her hand.

"Don't you touch me you son of a bitch." June whipped away from him, "I want you to leave and I want you to stay away from me and stay away from my son."

Aubrey furrowed his brow, "I can't leave June, I want to be part of his life."

June laughed, "Excuse me? You want to be part of his life now? Where have you been for the last eighteen years?"

June's eyes widened with disbelief and she wavered on her legs. Aubrey grabbed her and guided her to the chair. June put her head in her hands, her hair fell out of its clip and covered her face.

"I thought you were dead." tears rolled down June's face, "Haven't you done enough damage already?"

"I'm here now." Aubrey placed his hand on her arm.

June raised her face and stared fiercely at him, "For how long? And what trouble are you bringing with you? That boy through there is *your* son, you left me three months pregnant without having any way of reaching you. Why would I want you to be any part of his life now, you were a liar, a cheat and a snake!"

Aubrey sat down at the chair next to June, his legs would no longer hold him.

"You had to come back didn't you, you couldn't just stay away. And you sit there at my kitchen table and tell me you want to be part of our lives? Why? What happened to maybe saying eighteen years ago 'hey June, here's a heads up seeing as how you're pregnant with my child, I'm jetting off to Vegas as I owe some gangsters a massive debt and you'll never hear from me ever again?"

"I did it to protect you, to keep you both safe. I knew one day I'd be able to come back, I just didn't realise it would be this long."

"Don't you dare lie to me Aubrey! I can see through your lies, I know you plan everything down to minute details, you planned to come here and wreak your bitter twisted plans on me and my son and lead him into a whole heap of trouble."

Aubrey looked at June then looked down at his hands, June leaned back, "Yes you've had years to plan it haven't you, the big moment where I'm down on my knees with gratitude that you've returned home, you telling me some speech you've committed to memory, and then the police will arrive at my door with my son's body in their arms."

It was Aubrey's turn for anger to flash through his eyes, "What ever happened to you loving me? You knew who I was when you went with me, it didn't bother you then! I want to make it up to you, and be a father to Colton."

"So you're here to take my son away from me?" June cried, "That makes it so much better, coming to my door with that smug look on your face to tell me that. Well guess what, I've got news for you, you can't have him! You'll have to kill me first!"

"June, it's not like that." Aubrey murmured, his face contorting with confusion, the conversation clearly not going the way he had hoped it would.

"You're a liar!" June shouted, struggling to hold back eighteen years of built up anger that she thought she'd put away for good.

"I'd never lie to you!" Aubrey shouted back, "I had to leave to protect you and our son!"

"You didn't leave, you ran away from me after you went with another woman!"

Colton and Thomas looked at each other as the voices became increasingly raised in the kitchen. Colton stood up, feeling protective over his mum, Thomas raised an arm to stop him, "Don't you worry about her Colton, she can hold her own with Aubrey, they go back a long way."

Colton grimaced at the sound of his mum's voice shouting, he'd not heard her lose it like that since he was much younger. Then the sounds of crockery smashing careened into the living room. Colton was on his feet again, but Thomas barred his way, "Sit back down, and leave them to work through it." Thomas requested.

Thomas leaned over and picked the television remote from Colton's clenched hands, and pushed Colton back down onto the sofa. Thomas then sat next to Colton and turned the volume up, though it didn't muffle the high pitched noises of further smashes coming from the kitchen.

Then there was absolute silence. Even Thomas raised his eyebrows and turned his head in the direction of the kitchen.

"Fuck this." Colton growled, jumping up and striding past Thomas through to the kitchen.

He opened the glass panelled door, catching his socked feet as there were shards of glass and crockery all over the floor. He took two steps into the kitchen so he could see round the door. His mum was grasping Aubrey in a choke hold over the cooker, with a knife to his throat.

Colton leaped over to her, "Mum!" he shouted, "What are you doing? Let go of him!"

June looked up at her son and loosened her grip on choking Aubrey, who stepped away from her and caught his breath.

"Mum?" Colton asked her, "Put the knife down?"

Aubrey stood up and held out his hand, "It's okay, it's okay." he said, "I deserved that."

June held the knife still in her hands, staring at Aubrey.

Aubrey laughed, "June, you're the only woman in the world who could ever get the upper hand over me like that."

June raised her eyebrows at him, "I should have slit your throat."

"Right, Mum, give me the knife, please." Colton asked her, his voice too high-pitched.

Thomas stood in the doorway and also started chuckling at the scene in front of him, "Just like old times." he laughed.

"It's not funny Thomas." June scowled at him.

"Mum! Can you tell me what is going on?" Colton asked, exasperated and confused, "Why are you trying to kill each other."

"Yes June, why are you trying to kill me, would you like to tell your son?" Aubrey piped up.

June turned on him again and pointed the knife his way, Aubrey stepped back again.

"Thomas you get over there and stand with Aubrey." June ordered, "Colton, get out of the kitchen."

Aubrey nodded at Thomas to do as he was requested.

"If either of you move, I will kill you." June said.

June stepped backwards away from them, out of the kitchen door. She shut the door behind her and drew a bolt across the door, that she used to use to stop their old family dog from raiding the kitchen while they were out of the house.

"Colton, go upstairs, and pack a bag please, we're leaving." June said to her son.

"What?"

"You heard me. Pack your things. We're leaving."

"For where?"

"No more questions Colton! Pack your bag! Be quick with it!"

Colton sunk his head and ran upstairs.

Aubrey tried the door, "June! June let me out!"

"You shut up and you wait in there!" June ordered.

Thomas could be heard laughing in the background.

"Thomas this is not a laughing matter! Will you get the door please?" Aubrey asked him.

"Thomas don't you dare break my kitchen door I will cut your head off with the shards!" June shouted, running up the stairs behind her son.

"You heard the lady, boss, I'm not going to get stabbed, she's on the wrong side of crazy right now."

"Well, this is just getting better by the minute isn't it." Aubrey muttered, sitting back down at the kitchen table.

June grabbed a holdall from under her bed and threw some spare clothes into it. She found their passports, stuffing them into a pocket of the bag. She grabbed her savings from above the wardrobe, threw them into the bag, grabbed some toiletries from the bathroom and marched into her son's room, "Are you packed?" she asked breathlessly.

"Yes mum." Colton replied.

"Then get downstairs and get in the car. No questions!" she ordered.

Colton opened his mouth to protest then thought better of it, his mum was the only person he knew to trust above anyone, he couldn't go against her for the sake of his new friends.

June ran back down the stairs and glanced at the kitchen door.

"Don't leave without saying goodbye June!" Aubrey called through to her.

"Fuck you, asshole!" June shouted, throwing an ornament from her hall table at the kitchen door, it shattered into tiny china pieces on the hall carpet.

As the front door slammed behind June and Colton, Aubrey looked at Thomas, "God I've missed that woman." he said.

"Can we leave through the back door now boss?" Thomas asked, indicating the door behind them, in the corner of the kitchen with the keys dangling in the lock.

"Give her a minute, if we go straight after her, there's every chance she will run me over in the car. I'm not as agile as I used to be, there's every chance I might not be able to get out of her way in time." Aubrey smiled.

June struggled to put the keys into the ignition of her little blue Renault Clio. Her hands were shaking, but she managed. She reversed quickly out of the driveway and fought to get the car into first gear. The flat was situated on the edge of the village in a small cul-de-sac, she drove onto the main road.

"I've worked hard my entire life to build this little life of ours, God knows it's not much Colton, but I'll be damned if he's marching in here and taking it all away from us." June said to her son who was sitting silently in the passenger seat.

"Where are we going mum?" Colton asked.

"I haven't got that bit figured out yet." June replied.

"How do you and Aubrey know each other?" Colton asked.

June bit her lip and stared straight ahead, "He was a friend of your fathers."

Colton looked at his mum. Worry lines etched her face, she looked terribly old all of a sudden, as if a hundred burdens had just been placed on her shoulders, "I don't think that's true." Colton murmured.

"Well you're not getting to know what's all true right now till I figure out where we're going and maybe we'll sit down and I'll tell you all about it when we get there." his mum replied, then calming slightly, she added, "Sorry that you saw me like that Colton, that man brings out the worst in me."

"He's been nice enough to me."

His mum went, "Hmm" angrily and drove silently on.

Colton stared out of the window. They drove past the lucky house with painted windows on the beginning of the tight corner bends and Colton looked up at Fatlips Castle on the wooded hillside beyond it. His mum drove them along the road and out onto the main A68 trunk road. To break the silence his mum put the radio on. Colton pulled his phone out of his pocket and swiped the screen, there were two missed calls from Aubrey and a text message, "Sorry about that. Hope she's not taking you far, we have a lot to talk about."

"Is that him?" the tone in his mum's voice was filled with tension.

"Yes." Colton mumbled.

"Give me your phone." his mum reached her left hand out, palm held upwards.

"No, mum, why?" Colton whined.

"Now, before I crash the car trying to get it from you!" June commanded.

Colton reluctantly handed her his phone and she passed it to her other hand and then popped it into the side pocket of her door.

"Because he is not to know where we are. You are to stay away from him. Please Colton, you're too young to understand, please just trust me."

Colton didn't understand. His mum was starting to annoy him with her over-reactions, and confuse him too with her utter hatred of Aubrey, and how dare she take his phone off him. Aubrey was mad, but harmless enough. Colton saw first hand Aubrey's reaction to the heroin on the ice cream van and knew he was a good guy. Why would his mum put a knife to his throat when he'd come to meet her?

His mum pulled into the hospital where she worked, "I need to go and speak to my boss. Wait in the car." she stepped out and looked him right in the eyes, "I'll be as quick as I can."

Colton watched her walk into the hospital. She'd forgotten about his phone. He leaned over and grabbed his phone back. Another missed call from Aubrey, then the phone started ringing in his hands.

"Colton, lad, are you okay?" Aubrey's voice came down the phone.

"Yes, but mum's gone nuts." Colton replied, scratching his head.

"I know. Are you hurt? Are you safe?"

"Yes, I'm in her car, she's gone in to speak to her boss."

"Sounds like she's planning on running away, Colton, do you want to run with her?"

"What? No, not really. What's going on?"

Colton looked around him and saw a bus pull into the hospital turn-off, it was headed back towards Denholm.

"You can come and stay with me." Aubrey's voice suggested sweetly in his ear.

It was all it took. Young Colton leant round, grabbed his bag from the back seat and jumped out of the car. He ran to catch the bus just as it was pulling away from the bus stop, Aubrey still on the line on his phone clenched in his hand. The driver looked at him, slowed back down and opened the doors. Colton fished in his suit pocket for some change, surprised at how many coins he found there, then took a seat. A noise from his hand caught his attention, it was Aubrey on the phone, Colton brought it back up to his ear,

"What's happening I heard running are you okay, Colton, tell me you're okay?"

"I'm on the bus back to Denholm." Colton said victoriously, "Where can I meet you?"

"Clever lad! Well done! He's on the bus back to Denholm Thomas! Where can we meet him? What? Thomas says we can meet you in the Cross Keys."

"Okay see you soon." Colton hung up.

Colton's mum stepped out of the hospital fifteen minutes later, puffy eyed. It was not easy revealing her past to her employer, no one knew of her connections to Aubrey in her job. But having heard only a brief account of an abusive ex-partner back on the scene, her boss authorised her special discretionary leave to give her the chance to find a new place to live and agreed to help her with a job relocation to another hospital. Her heart skipped a beat when she walked to the car to see the passenger door hanging open and an empty passenger seat where her son should have been. She stopped walking and raised her hand to her heart and tried to steady her breathing.

"My boy, where have you gone?" she whispered.

Chapter Four

Colton stepped off the bus at Denholm and said cheerio to the driver. He slung his holdall over his shoulder and sauntered into the bar door of the Cross Keys Inn.

The bar was straight ahead of him, and the room opened out to the right, with tables, a large screen television that was playing football silently in the background, and a pool table. The walls were wood panelled adding warmth to the room. A fire was just beginning to burn in the fireplace right next to the door, hitting Colton with a nice heat as he stepped into the room.

Aubrey and Thomas were playing a game of pool, "There he is!" Aubrey said cheerfully as he saw Colton, "What happened to you then?"

"I left my mum at the hospital. I don't know what's going on with her she's gone mental." Colton shrugged.

"Well, give her a bit of time to cool off and calm down. She'll be fine. Meanwhile, do you want a drink? You look like you could do with one." Aubrey looked at Thomas who put his cue down walked to the bar and rang the bell to attract the attention of the bartender.

Aubrey played the situation down to Colton, choosing not to reveal his past relationship with June just yet. He wanted to savour the time to get to know his son, and utilise it to make sure June couldn't sway Colton away from him so readily. His one offering of respect towards June's wishes were that he chose not to reveal to Colton that he was his father that morning. Aubrey walked round the pool table to Colton and put his arm round his shoulder and hugged him briefly, "It'll be fine. Don't worry, I'm here for you. Have you told your mum you're okay?"

Colton shook his head, pulling out his mobile he grimaced at the six missed calls from his mum. His battery was pretty low, "I don't know what to say, she's going to go nuts whatever I tell her."

Aubrey thought for a moment, "Then don't say anything at all." he shrugged.

Colton smiled a little at Aubrey's suggestion, but sent a text to his mum saying, "I'm not going to run away." Colton and June had their fallouts as any family does, but this was the first time Colton went so opposedly against his mum. He put the phone away in his pocket and didn't check it again.

When Aubrey and Thomas finished their drinks they left the bar, taking the next bus back into town. Aubrey sat on the back seat quietly for a few moments then announced he was going to open a training club in town, "Are you up for helping me manage it Colton?" Aubrey asked him.

Colton opened his mouth to speak, but no words came out. He couldn't tell if Aubrey was being serious or not.

"He's lost for words boss." Thomas laughed.

"It's a good opportunity, and you're a good kid. I like what I see in you. I've already looked over a place in town that's sitting empty, there's space upstairs for an office, and also space for you to have your own room. We can put a bed in there, you can stay there, work on your body, get fit, and learn about running a legitimate business from me. What do you think?"

"Wow, are you sure Aubrey, I mean, we've only just met, I hardly know you."

"I have my own reasons for wanting a young man such as yourself on board, but I think it would be good for you specifically, given that your mum is working really hard to keep the both of you, and you're a young man now, with a mind of his own. I mean I could go and pick any lad off the street and offer them the same position, they'd be jumping at the chance." he paused and placed his hands together to his mouth, in thought, "In fact, that's where we'll go right now, we'll go to the solicitors and pick up the keys. No time like the present to start this new venture."

"Don't you need a business plan and investment and things? And to check out the market to see if there's someone else running a club in town already?" Colton asked him, in awe at the speed Aubrey seemed to be able to make things happen.

Aubrey waved his hand as if he were swatting a silly suggestion away like an irritating fly, "No, not me. That's not the way I do business."

They stepped off the bus at the bottom of the high street and wandered casually up the left hand side of the street until they arrived at the entrance to the office of Solomon's Solicitor's. As they walked through the door a secretary looked up and acknowledged them, she was about the same age as Colton though he didn't recognise her. The room was small, just enough space to house a desk and some waiting chairs, there was an archway leading through to a hallway of back rooms. Through the archway, in the hallway a round little man in a suit was walking towards a photocopying machine. He was unshaven, with round rimmed spectacles and a close haircut on his dark grey hair. He wore a light blue shirt and a dark blue tie, with loose baggy trousers despite his size. His cheeks were rosy and his nose tinged with a purple hue, indicative that the man liked to keep his nose in a glass of whisky of an evening. The man glanced up from his paperwork at the sound of the door jingling open, and almost dropped his papers as he saw who walked through the door. The man scurried away into a back room.

"Good morning." Aubrey greeted the secretary, "I'd like to speak to Carl please."

The secretary looked at him with a pleasant smile on her face, "I'm sorry I'm afraid Carl's not in today."

Aubrey laughed, "I just saw him walk, or run rather, into that back office, I know he's in, which means you're lying for him. How much does he pay you to lie for him?"

The girl's smile broke just a fraction, "Sorry, I meant he's not able to see anyone today, he's busy with case paperwork."

"Tell that man Aubrey Delaney wants to see him, if you don't mind, and we'll take a seat right here until he's ready to see me."

Thomas and Aubrey sat down on the uncomfortable horse-hair waiting chairs, Colton did the same.

The secretary picked up her phone, "Carl, there's some man called Aubrey Delaney here who would like to see you, I have advised him you don't have time in your schedule today." There was a pause as the secretary listened to the man on the other end of the line, "I would but he said he's going to wait until you are free." there was another gap and then the secretary hung up.

The back office door opened and the portly man walked down the hall to them, his face perhaps more flushed than it was earlier. "Aubrey, it's been years, how are you?" Carl held out his hand, Aubrey stood up and shook his hand.

"It has Carl it has, but I'd like to talk to you in the office if you don't mind."

"Certainly, come on through."

Colton leaned forward to stand up, Thomas held out an arm to refrain him, so he sat back down. Thomas and Colton waited about thirty minutes, flicking through tired magazines that were a couple of years out of date, until Aubrey walked back through to them with some paperwork tucked under his arm and sets of keys jingling in his hand.

"Thank you, as always, it's a pleasure doing business with Solomon's." Aubrey said to the secretary as they walked out of the door.

Colton flashed a look at the secretary who gave him a warm dazzling smile in return, 'Not as pretty as my Lady Vivienne, sorry.' Colton thought as he left the office and walked out to the street to catch up with Aubrey.

"It's just up here and round the corner." Aubrey said to Colton, handing him a set of keys, "They're your set. Don't lose them."

"Thanks." Colton's voice was hoarse, he was overcome by the gesture of being gifted the keys.

"We're going to do great things together you and I, Colton, great things, this is only the beginning." Aubrey smiled.

They walked to the end of the high street and took a left turn, and then Aubrey quickly took another left turn through a sandstone archway leading them away from the road, into a vennel which opened out into a cobbled courtyard. Aubrey walked over to a set of large weathered green doors, with a smaller more manageable sized door cut into the left door. Above the large doors in faded flaking paintwork were the words "Armstrong's Abattoir".

"I'll let you do the honours, Colton." Aubrey indicated at the small door.

Colton fished in his pockets for his newly acquired keys, having already forgotten which pocket he'd placed them in. He found them and approached the door, jangling the keys to try to find one that would match the lock. It was an old mortice lock, Colton found the longest key on the chain and tried it. With a little maneuvering, the bolt clicked and he opened the door. It was dark inside. He pulled his phone out of his pocket and unlocked the screen, holding it in front of him he stepped through the door, he looked to the inside wall to the left of the door frame and found an old fashioned light switch. The plating was made of brass and the switch itself was a small bobbly knob. He flicked the switch. Initially nothing happened, then an overhead strip light flickered reluctantly into life. Colton turned to take in the room in front of him.

Thankfully, nothing remained as a reminder of the building's former life except for the sign outside. It had already been cleared of its deathly devices. It was one large open space, with a staircase on the left leading to the upper floors and doorways at the back of the main room.

"What do you think?" Aubrey said stepping into the room.

"It's a bit grim." Colton sniffed the dusty stale air.

"Not for long Colton, with a lick of paint, a bit of heat, we can make it work. We can use one of the rooms through the back for changing rooms to start with, put a boxing ring here, some punch bags here, and we'll make money off the business to fix the other rooms up over time."

"How much are they asking for to rent this place?" Colton asked.

"It's mine. I own it."

"What? How?" Colton asked.

Aubrey smiled, "I made Carl an offer he couldn't refuse."

"I don't understand." Colton replied.

"What do you mean you don't understand? It's *The Godfather* movie? You know, an offer he couldn't refuse?" Aubrey said.

"I've never seen it."

"You've never seen *The Godfather*? Are you kidding me?" Aubrey asked.

Colton shook his head. Aubrey turned to Thomas who was closing the door behind them, "Can you believe this kid? He's never seen *The Godfather*. First thing we're getting you Colton, is a copy of that movie."

Chapter Five

Aubrey roped in a few local lads that he met in the pub to help with the clean up of the Abattoir, with the aid of cash in their hand and a few drinks on Aubrey's tab at the bar, they worked like troopers to get the training club looking good. Layers of pigeon droppings were scraped back to reveal a stone floor, which was scrubbed and cleaned, then painted gloss white. Which looked great until a stray cat wandered into the open double-doors and put a set of complementary paw prints around the entranceway while it was drying.

"We're not redoing the floor, the pawprints can fucking well stay there." said Thomas as they returned from buying lunch to find the prints in question gleaming at them.

The rooms on the first floor were mostly cleared out, in that all of their contents were relocated to a large back room on the second floor, which was became the store room. The front most room which was situated above the double doors became Aubrey's office. Next to that was a small waiting area, with a low table and chairs in it, a kitchen area on the right, a bathroom on the left, then there was a corridor through to the back rooms. Three of which were initially used as sleeping quarters by Aubrey and Colton, rather than tackle the second floor. Initially they showered and washed in the facilities at the local swimming baths, and ate their meals at different restaurants on the high street, until the bathroom and kitchen were ready with new plumbing fixtures. Thomas removed himself to his house on the Silverbutthall estate, but Aubrey would not venture up there to clean, nor did he return to the large house up the hill which he initially entertained Colton in, stating that the residents were back and no longer required him to look after it.

Colton text his mum to let her know he had somewhere to stay. She took two days to reply with the word, "Okay." he didn't try to contact her again. She wasn't even worried about him, that's the effort she went to, what did he care. He had new friends and a new life to look forward to. He was going to make something of himself and he didn't have to justify any of it to his mother.

There were young lads knocking at the double doors before the place was anywhere near finished, wanting to join the new trainting club, word of mouth on the street spread quickly. On Aubrey's instructions, Colton signed them up for club memberships, which was set at an affordable price, and set them to outdoor training, running a circuit round the town's Wilton Park until the club was closer to being ready for them to actually train in.

Aubrey instructed Colton on how to lead the boys out on the circuit, what warm-ups to do and the pace to set. He insisted Colton run with them to get fitter. Aubrey bought Colton a tracksuit and trainers, refusing to take money for them. Colton almost passed out on the first few runs, the pace was too fast for him, but he gritted his teeth and kept going, determined none of the other lads were going to take his privileged position in the club.

Aubrey didn't allow him to socialise much with the other lads, Aubrey shook his head when Colton was getting ready to go for a few drinks indicating he wasn't to go, "These boys, they're the punters, the riff-raff, the money generators. You are with me now. You learn from me how to behave, how to act, how to speak, and eventually how to think, from me, not from hanging around with them every night."

Colton reluctantly accepted this, as Aubrey did say it was okay to go out on Saturday nights, and he felt he couldn't risk angering him.

A team of tradesmen built the fight ring up out of nothing in a matter of hours after it rolled off a delivery lorry, after which the smaller items were installed, such as the lockers, punch bags, and weights. And then, the club's main room was ready for training.

Aubrey wore a look of triumph on his face when Colton appeared up the stairs from one of his runs the day before official opening, "We've got ourselves a television, son." Aubrey grinned, "Tonight, Thomas and I are going to give you an education. Sit down, and learn from The Godfather himself."

They walked through to Aubrey's upstairs office, which now housed comfortable second hand oxblood leather chairs and a matching couch, sourced from a second hand shop just down the road, and carried to the Abattoir by the boys with the promise of another pint at the pub. Thomas handed Colton a can of beer, Aubrey closed the blinds, and the movie began to play. Colton was enthralled, but still couldn't stop his heavy exhausted eyes from closing when the movie wasn't even halfway through, opening them again at the end credits.

Aubrey and Thomas weren't in the room. There was a knock at the double doors, Colton stood up and peered through the blinds to see if he could see anyone but all he could make out were two shadowy figures. He thought Aubrey and Thomas must have locked themselves out so he jogged out of the office and down the stairs to open the small door, but it wasn't the faces of Aubrey and Thomas looking back at him.

It was the Alessi brothers, Dreyfuss and Marius. Colton's stomach sunk.

"Is your boss here?" Marius, the one who was engaged to his temporarily forgotten Vivienne asked him.

"I'm the boss here." Colton replied.

The Alessi brothers looked him up and down, then laughed at him.

Dreyfuss took a step towards him, grabbed the collar of his rugby top and hauled him out of the doorway. Colton was thrown to the ground, kicked in the chest and face. With the final blow to his head he felt something snap and give in his face.

"Tell Aubrey we're looking for him." Marius said, "We want to have a word with him about the whereabouts of a missing ice cream van."

With that, they walked away, leaving Colton in a crumpled heap on the cobblestones outside the building. Colton spat blood onto the cobbles and felt a fire of rage ignite in his being before he passed out in pain.

Chapter Six

Colton didn't open his eyes for a while. His ears tuned in to an unfamiliar noise, he breathed in an unfamiliar warm air which wasn't his skinny single bed at the Abattoir. He felt like he was floating. That feeling lasted for about a minute then the pain hit him, nerve endings he never knew existed were set off in his jaw. He opened his eyes and realised he was lying in a hospital bed. His first thought was that if his mum saw him at her place of work, she would kill him.

But of course June was already standing at the foot of Colton's bed, reading his notes from a clipboard. She saw that he was awake, but said nothing for a time, allowing his thoughts to process. He tried to open his mouth to speak but winced with pain.

"You have a broken jaw, you need to stretch your muscles and build up to speaking slowly otherwise you'll just burst your stitches open. And it's going to hurt when you do try to talk." June put the clipboard down and looked at her son.

Colton looked away from her and out of the window by the side of his bed.

"What the hell has he got you into?" she sighed, walking to him and brushing his left hand with hers. He pulled it away. She bit her lip.

"The other nurses had to tell me my son was in here, do you think I don't care about what happens to you?" June walked over to the window, playing with a gold chain around her neck, "Colton, you're everything I have in this world."

Colton cleared his throat and slackened his jaw as best he could, "He didn't get me into anything." he said hoarsely.

June placed her free hand on her hip and continued to play with her chain, "Really Colton, you never got your jaw broken until he walked into our lives again, and all you can do is defend him."

"Why do you hate him so much, why all the secrecy mum? Why won't you tell me anything?" Colton tried to say, but instead, he just made a series of noises that ended with a lot of pain.

June stared out of the window, her chest heaving with worry and upset, "Who was it who did this to you?" she asked him.

"Alessi's." Colton managed to whisper.

"Jesus God." June gasped.

"It's okay."

"They're only after you because you're associated with him!" she said, "You can put a stop to all of this right now, come home with me Colton?" his mum pleaded, "Stop now, you don't know what you're getting yourself into."

"I'm okay." he said.

"Really? Do you even know why they're after Aubrey? Isn't it time you started asking him some questions Colton?"

At that moment, the ward door swung open and in walked the man himself, Aubrey, "Why doesn't he have a room on his own?" Aubrey announced as he walked past the other beds in the room.

"Stop making a scene Aubrey, or I'll have you thrown out." June snapped.

"Oh I forget I've got to be on my best behavior since this is your establishment." Aubrey replied sarcastically. He sat down in the chair next to the bed and sniffed, "I'm getting him a bigger room this is too cramped and he's got no privacy."

"Well thankfully you're not having to stay in the hospital bed yourself then Aubrey. No, no, you always make sure it's someone else, don't you." June replied bitterly, "And this time it's my son lying there."

"June this is all a big misunderstanding, the boy wasn't meant to get hurt at all." Aubrey raised his hands in defence.

"Wasn't meant to get in the way of them hurting you no less!" June sniffed.

"He's old enough to make his own mistakes, and his own choices. As far as I know, he's chosen to stay with me." Aubrey said.

"Because he doesn't know who you are and what you're capable of!" June hissed.

"Maybe it was you who never knew what I was capable of, sweetheart." Aubrey said.

"Oh don't you sweetheart me!" June stepped away from the window, hackles evidently raised.

"Mum!" Colton rasped.

June turned to look at her son with tears in her eyes, "I'm leaving, I have to start my shift. You sort this mess out Aubrey, and if you dare get my son into anymore trouble, I swear, I'll come after you myself."

"I'd love that darling. We will finally get to dance together under a starry night." Aubrey smiled as June walked past him with tears slipping down her face.

She turned as she reached the ward doors, an inner strength reaching her again, "You're right Aubrey, this is my establishment. And we have incinerators here, they'd never find your body."

Aubrey turned to Colton as the door swung shut behind June, "She's always got to have the last word, your mother, god but I love her."

Aubrey made himself more comfortable in the chair, shrugging off the threats to his life that were made by June, "We're getting CCTV cameras put up outside The Abattoir, Thomas is doing that right now. I can't believe those two Italian nutjobs came to the door and did that to you. Don't worry Colton, we'll get them. But I need you back on your feet, and I need you stronger than you've ever known you could be."

Colton nodded, Aubrey took Colton's left hand in his, "I'm creating an army here Colton, and you are going to lead them, long after I've gone. I know you've got it in you, you've just got a long way to go before you get there, but I'll be with you every step of the way kid, if you'll stick with me."

Colton wet his mouth to speak, "I'll do it." he rasped.

"Then let's get it done!" Aubrey smiled that infectious smile, "Get yourself back on your feet and lets start shaking things up around this town! We're gonna take them by surprise Colton, we're gonna be unstoppable, we'll be like bullets in the night, you and I, and they won't even know what's hit them."

He laughed to himself, "Then, after that, your mum can stick me in the incinerator. I ain't done till then though." he got up and patted Colton's shoulder, "Get better kid, get better quick, we got shit to do."

Chapter Seven

Six weeks later, Aubrey and Colton were sitting in the warmly lit Turnbull's cafe, situated at the bottom end of the High Street next to the infamous Horse monument, in commemoration of the brave youths who defended the town against English soldiers in 1514.

Turnbulls was tastefully decorated with vintage posters and exquisitely detailed Art Deco wallpaper. Aubrey and Colton were sitting on cushioned benches in the far corner, tucked away from the large front window and the view of passers by.

The training club was up and running, Colton was toning up along with the other local boys, and he was starting to feel strong for it. His jaw was healing well and he remained in touch with his mother a little bit better than before, partly due to Aubrey reminding him every couple of days to stay in touch with her. There were no further run-ins with the Alessi brothers, nor did Aubrey appear to be taking any obvious action against them.

Aubrey ordered two coffees which were placed on the table by a friendly young waitress wearing a white and black uniform. Colton was hungrily eying up the plates of fresh meats and salads on the delicatessen counter they walked past to reach their table, there was a smell of freshly baked bread in the air which made his stomach ache for a bite of something.

Aubrey stared intently at a man three tables away from them, but as the cups were placed down, the motion broke his gaze and he started speaking quietly to Colton, "Look at him, see the way he reads his paper? He folds it, he turns each page to perfection so that not a single sheet falls out of place. He sips his coffee and places it quietly back on the saucer so as not to disturb his bubble of peacefulness in the cafe

Or our bubble. He is so unobtrusive, no one notices he is here. That is an undercover detective, right there, he's the one we have to watch out for. He is meticulous. He makes all of these movements subconsciously without a second thought, it's his second nature now, to be meticulous with small details."

Aubrey picked up the teaspoon and delicately took a spoon of sugar from the bowl, "If there's a mistake, it will be that man right there who will spot it, and no one will know he's found it until he's back at the police station and you're in handcuffs in the cells." he placed the teaspoon of sugar into his coffee and stirred slowly.

"Do you know him?" Colton asked.

"Oh yes." Aubrey smirked, "I went to school with him. I saved his ass many times, took the brunt of the blame for all the mistakes he made as his parents would have beat him up, as when I got in trouble mine just shouted at me. He went on to be the success and I went to the underground."

"Then why's he stalking you in a cafe?"

Aubrey tapped his teaspoon loudly, too many times on the side of the cup and placed it to the side, making the man flinch ever so slightly, "He's doing his job. The cops know I'm up to something, they just can't figure out what. Don't worry, I'm smarter than them, I've never been caught yet."

Aubrey called the waitress over to their table and asked her to send the man a slice of their finest carrot cake. The waitress smiled and went to the counter, lifting the clear lid from the cake stand and slipping a slice onto a plate. She walked over to the man and Colton watched her excuse herself and place the plate over the newspaper and onto the table. The man looked at the cake, then looked up around at his surroundings in a confused fashion. He spotted Aubrey looking at him, Aubrey raised his coffee cup at the man in acknowledgement. The man's face flushed pink and he ducked his head back down and raised his newspaper up so they could no longer see his face.

The newspaper was raised just enough off the table that they could see a hand use a silver fork to take a chunk out of the slice of carrot cake. The man put the fork down on the plate, then lifted it back up again, twice. Aubrey laughed.

"What does that mean?" Colton asked him.

"It means he's not the only cop watching us today. If Magnus was on his own he'd have come over and asked how my beautiful wife is."

"So if he was on his own, stalking you, then he'd come over and say hello to you, but instead he's pretending not to see you, but, you're not married?"

"No kid, there's only one woman ever came close and she wouldn't have me. It's a code for telling me he's on duty. He knows I ain't got a wife, but if he's working he's going to have a recording device on him, so doesn't want the station to know he's speaking to me directly, that's why he's tapping his fork, to let me know."

"I see. And we know he's not just sitting in a cafe reading the paper on his day off because?"

"Magnus is holding *The Guardian* in his hand, Magnus never reads *The Guardian*. Always keep a step ahead Colton, always keep a step ahead."

"Well right now I feel about three steps behind." Colton said, rubbing his forehead.

"Waitress! Another coffee for my man here please!" Aubrey called.

The waitress smiled and nodded. When she came over with the fresh coffee Colton asked for a Full English Breakfast.

"We don't do those here." The waitress smiled apologetically, "But I can get you a great home-reared pork sausage and brie sandwich on fresh seeded bread, baked here this morning?"

"Sounds delicious. I'll have one." Colton thanked her.

"Make that two?" Aubrey added, "And a dish of potato salad, and some olives, and a couple of slices of your quiche. I'm in no rush this morning, a leisurely breakfast is just in order."

Aubrey stood up from the table, "Excuse me for a moment Colton, I'm off to buy the paper."

The waitress and Aubrey walked to the counter at the same time, Aubrey struck up a whistle as he walked past Magnus reading his Guardian newspaper. Colton watched as Magnus lowered his paper to observe Aubrey leaving the tearoom. Was Aubrey right, was he being watched by the police? Colton wondered. As Aubrey left the tea room and took a left turn along the street, a man subtly strode past with his eyes intently fixed on Aubrey, Colton guessed it could be another tail on Aubrey. Magnus was waiting in the cafe for Aubrey's return. Colton frowned at his coffee.

Four minutes later Magnus carefully folded up his newspaper, paid his tab at the counter and left the cafe. Aubrey walked back in with a newspaper tucked under his arm shortly afterwards, and sat back down just as the waitress brought their lunch.

"Excellent" Aubrey smiled, "We now have the place to ourselves. Gave them the runaround, they've no idea where I went to."

Chapter Eight

Aubrey and Colton enjoyed a fine filling lunch without any further suspected spying, Aubrey called in at the off-licence on the way back to the Abattoir, stocking up on brandy and beers, which he placed in his office for later. They spent the afternoon on the second floor, beginning to sort out the rooms up there.

At about five o'clock, they showered, then sat down in Aubrey's office for a drink.

Aubrey was sitting behind his desk, while Colton was lying opposite him staring at the ceiling, on the sofa. Aubrey always insisted on topping up his decanter to drink brandy from, explaining that for him to truly savour the experience, the pour must be perfect, he didn't want to be distracted by the label, and the decanter aerated the brandy to his taste. The first bottle from the off-licence was poured into the decanter which was about a third full.

Aubrey brought up the subject of how Colton felt about the Alessi brothers.

"I want them dead." Colton said to him, gripping his mouth together and inhaling, holding his anger inside him.

"Killing is a tough game Colton, a tough game. You're dancing with death, disrupting the natural order of things." Aubrey sighed.

"Well with those two, you know, I wouldn't mind if they died. It might stop them beating me up every couple of months for no reason." Colton said.

"If you're going to play God you have to choose pretty wisely my son. Poor decisions will haunt you for the rest of your life, literally, ghosts breathing over your shoulder, every single moment of every single day." Aubrey placed his hands upon the desk and leaned forward, "When people die in real life, that's it, they're gone, no second chances, nothing. Time's up, and you'll never have it back again. That time with them, that's all there was, and that's all you'll ever have. Until you lose someone close to you, Colton, I don't know how to explain it any other way."

"They deserve it." Colton grimaced.

Aubrey reclined into his leather chair, "And what do you think would happen to Vivienne if you were to kill off her fiance? Do you think she'd come running to you with open arms?"

"Well, I was kind of hoping that." Colton smiled.

"She'll run a hundred miles from you. No, my son, you don't get your revenge by killing your enemy outright, no." Aubrey drifted off into thought and went silent, waiting for Colton to speak.

Colton sighed impatiently, "Well what would you suggest I do? Let him marry her and fuck other women and watch from the sidelines as she gets pregnant to a monster and ruins her life when she could be with me?"

A smile began at the edges of Aubrey's mouth, "Now that sort of long term misery filled life time would be a good suggestion if you wanted to play out some sort of vengeful vendetta against our lady Vivienne, rather than want to marry the girl yourself. No, I have a grander plan than that. We're going to destroy them from the inside out."

Colton swung his legs down off the sofa, got up and paced about the floor, "You always talk in riddles!" he exclaimed, "you might know what you're talking about, but really, Aubrey, I'm lost here. You're going to have to help me out. I want to go round and beat the crap out of the guys who keep trying to ruin my life and you won't let me. Why?"

"Because Colton, revenge is a dish best served cold, when the enemy thinks everything has settled back down and has gone back to normal, when they think that their little posturing threats have done the trick and scared you into submission. No, you don't even strike out then. You wait. You wait and you wait. You go underground. And you only strike, when they are on top of the world. Then, you destroy everything, their lives, their businesses, everything, and leave just a shell of a man. And at that point, you will own him."

Aubrey leaned forward, lifting the round lid from the glass decanter he lifted the vial and poured it, topping up the brandy in his glass, "I am in the business of revenge Colton, I have been for many years, I know it very well."

"Have you killed people before?" Colton asked, sitting back down on the sofa and picking up his drink.

"What would you think of me if I had killed people, and what would you make of me as a man if I hadn't killed people in my line of work?"

"Did that actually answer my question?" Colton frowned.

"It's not a requirement for me to answer, and it's not a necessity for you to know right now." Aubrey lifted the glass to his mouth and his eyes widened, his face went pale.

"Are you alright Aubrey? You don't look well" Colton asked him.

"Just know, with people like the Alessi brothers, that when the bullet leaves the gun, you better be aiming straight for the head. Otherwise you're the one that's dead." Aubrey slurred his words, and gulped the last of his brandy.

"I don't think I've ever seen you like this before." Colton said.

Aubrey bowed his head and chuckled into his chest, unable to keep his head upright.

"Are you okay?" Colton stood up and walked over to Aubrey, while at the same time, Aubrey slumped forward and passed out onto his desk, "Shit, Aubrey?" Colton shook Aubrey by the shoulders, nothing happened.

He pulled out his phone and dialled Thomas' number, "Thomas, Thomas, there's something wrong with Aubrey. What? Well," Colton leaned over Aubrey, "Yes, he is still breathing. Shouldn't I call an ambulance? What? Where are you I can't hear you? Okay, please hurry!"

Colton rung off the phone, placing it in the back pocket of his jeans. He pulled off his jacket and placed it over Aubrey's slumbering shoulders, sat back on the desk next to him, and waited for Thomas to arrive.

Colton heard the sound of a key in the downstairs door ten minutes later. He glanced across to the CCTV monitoring screens, Thomas looked up at the camera and waved from where he was standing outside unlocking the door. Colton sighed with relief. Thomas came into the room and nodded at Colton. Thomas lifted Aubrey's wrist and checked his pulse. Thomas picked up Aubrey's glass and sniffed it. He looked at the glass decanter holding the brandy.

"He's not touched anything else all night?" were his first words to Colton.

Colton shook his head, "It's not the same as when he's drunk, his face changed colour, and he's drunk the same amount as me, he can usually drink me under the table."

Thomas pulled out a small strip of paper from his wallet, and dipped this in Aubrey's decanter. It changed colour.

"You're going to have to call your mum." Thomas said, "His brandy might have been spiked, she's going to need to come here and sort him out."

"Can't we just phone for an ambulance? She's really not going to want to come here."

"Pick up your phone, and call your mother. Aubrey is not to leave this building tonight under any circumstances in ambulance."

"What?"

"Colton, just shut up and phone your mother." Thomas snapped.

Colton pulled his phone back out and phoned his mum, after six rings she answered, her voice was croaky, evidently just having been woken up by the phone, "Colton, what's wrong?"

"Aubrey's in trouble mum, can you to come to the club with your medical stuff." Colton said in a childish boys voice, "It's about six o'clock I think? Maybe seven? We don't know, we think his drinks been spiked. Thomas doesn't want to call an ambulance for him. I know you hate him, but for me, can you come over for me? Thank you."

"Well?" Thomas asked.

"She said she's going to come over but just to make sure the jobs done properly." Colton grimaced.

Thomas smiled, "She will never let anyone kill Aubrey except herself, it is a strange love they have."

"Mum said we are to put him in the recovery position."

Colton and Thomas worked together to move Aubrey's slumped body onto the floor, bending his knee upwards, and his hand underneath his chin they rolled him onto his side.

"I really don't think my mum feels anything close to love for Aubrey, Thomas. On the phone there she really sounded like she wants to kill him. And why aren't we phoning an ambulance for him?"

Thomas walked over to the window staring out, "Because Aubrey made me swear if anything happens to him, we do not phone the ambulance, that it would be God's way of telling him it was his time to go. But he did not make me promise I could not phone the nurse we know to try to save him."

"But that's stupid, the hospital would save his life!"

"It's his choice Colton."

"None of this makes any sense, why would someone want to kill him?"

"Check the CCTV footage, someone must have been in here."

Colton walked round to the cabinet that housed the CCTV monitor screens, clicking buttons till it began to rewind the footage outside the main doors. He stopped the screen, checked the time on the lower right and rewound some more. He stopped it again, he thought he saw a movement, a change on the flickering image. He clicked the screen forwards again, slower this time, and back as a shadow appeared on the screen. He paused the image which clearly showed a female figure entering the building.

"That's Vivienne on the screen. But why would she come in here and spike Aubrey's drink? And she just walks straight in like she's got a key?" Colton exclaimed.

"Maybe her fiance sent her." Thomas suggested.

"That would make sense, wouldn't it? Maybe they knew I liked her from that night in the club?"

Thomas shook his head, "I doubt it, more like they would send someone dispensable round, someone who isn't a threat to us, isn't about to get their ass kicked by coming here after what they did to you."

"Oh."

With the time taken to find the piece of footage with Vivienne on the CCTV, and before there was time to look for other potential suspects, there was a knock at the door downstairs which came echoing up to the office. Colton flicked the monitors back to the live view and saw that it was his mum at the doors. She was wearing a large coat and was carrying a light coloured holdall.

Colton walked over to the desk and pressed a button, which opened the door downstairs, and he walked down the stairs to meet her, this was the first time she had ever set foot inside the Abattoir.

She stood at the bottom of the staircase, clutching the handles of the holdall nervously.

"Thanks for coming mum." Colton said, his feet stopping halfway down the stairs.

"Is he up there?" June asked nervously, looking up at the stairs. Her hair was tied in a loose, messy ponytail, her coat was only tied with the belt rather than buttoned up, and she was still in her slippers.

"Yes, he is." Colton said.

June stepped up the stairs, looking at her feet realising she was wearing her slippers when she did so. It seemed that she gained her confidence back as she walked up the staircase. She went into nurse mode the closer she was to the top, messy hair and slippers and all.

Colton showed her into the office, where she nodded at Thomas and attended straight away to the patient. She pulled various implements out of the holdall, the only ones of which Colton recognised were a stethoscope and a syringe.

"He'll be alright." June said after a time, "In about twelve hours or so he'll wake up with a headache from hell, but mostly he'll be fine, not a high enough dosage to kill him, unfortunately."

"Do you know what was in the drink?" Colton asked.

"No." June replied, "Not without sending his blood for testing, which, given that you've not sent him to hospital in an ambulance and called me instead, I reckon isn't going to happen."

"Thank you June." Thomas said, "Aubrey will know that you saved his life tonight."

June began packing her things back into her holdall. She looked at Thomas, then at her son, still seeing her young vulnerable child standing in front of her. She didn't reply to Thomas.

"He needs to rest, and you need to keep yourself out of danger Colton. But you'll tell me you know that already and you're not in danger, won't you?" she sighed, standing up. brushing strands away from her face, looking intently into Colton's face.

Colton couldn't face his mum's gaze and looked away.

"Okay, Colton, have it your way." June said sadly, and walked away.

Thomas went after her, to escort her down the stairs, "June, thank you so much for doing this tonight." Thomas started saying as he jogged to catch her up.

She stopped on the top of the staircase, a tear slipping down her face which she caught with the sleeve of her coat, "That's my son up there, Thomas." she said.

"I know."

"If that means anything to you, please, don't let any harm come to him. I can see my own way out."

Chapter Nine

That was the last time anyone saw Colton's mother alive. She left the Abattoir, a movement which was registered by the CCTV cameras, but neighbours advised she never returned home, her car never returned to her driveway, the lights never came on in the house, and she didn't turn up for work the next day.

It was her boss who reported her missing, the only one with any wariness of her not turning up for work, after June advised him an 'abusive ex' had returned and she decided to remain living where she was. He knew it wasn't like June not to turn up, she'd never missed a shift. One of the indestructible sort of people who never fell ill except maybe during their holidays.

Colton didn't know any of this until the police appeared on the CCTV monitors the day after Aubrey's suspected spiking incident. There were two of them, one a light-set male with neatly combed blonde hair, the other a small framed female with bobbed mousy brown hair.

"God would you look at that, how did she make it into the force, there's nothing of her?" Thomas said as he stood looking at the CCTV monitor in his underpants, scratching his stubble, then his balls intermittently, "I'd best go put some clothes on, let them in Colton."

Thomas slept on the sofa overnight to keep an eye on Aubrey.

"Are they real police?" Colton yawned, "Do we let them in? What if they're sent by the Alessi's? Aubrey's still not up yet."

Thomas shrugged, "I am too tired to even think right now."

The police knocked at the door again.

"Fucksake let them in Colton it'll stop them knocking at the fucking door." Thomas swore.

Colton pushed the buzzer door allowing the Police to enter the building. Colton was wearing a pair of jogging bottoms, with no top on, his chest was increasingly svelte, toned and he looked strong now, and he was barefoot. The stairs were cold on his feet as he walked down to meet the two police.

They stood on the doormat, waiting for someone to attend to them and both looked up suspiciously at the sound of someone walking about upstairs. Colton smiled at them, "Can I help you officers?"

"We're looking for Colton Cooper?" The female asked him.

"That's me." Colton replied.

The man stepped forward, "Is there somewhere we can speak to you?"

"Up here." Colton held out his hand in a guiding gesture.

The female police officer stepped up first, followed by the man.

Colton led them into Aubrey's office. Surprisingly Aubrey was seated at the desk, with a fully clothed Thomas leaning over the CCTV unit.

"To what do we owe this pleasure?" Aubrey greeted the officer warmly, "Can we get you a drink? Tea or coffee perhaps?"

Colton was unaware of the speed in which Thomas managed to wake Aubrey up, and they both got dressed to look fresh enough to welcome police officers, rather than leave Colton to deal with them on his own.

"No thank you." the female said politely.

She may have also introduced who they were, but no one remembered their names.

"We are just here to ask a couple of questions to Colton." she turned to address Colton, "Your mother didn't show up for work this morning, and we are trying to trace her most recent whereabouts."

Colton raised his eyebrows, "Have you been round to her house?"

"Yes, there is no sign of her there." the male responded.

"When was the last time you saw her Colton?" the female asked gently.

Aubrey cleared his throat, Colton shot the most fleeting of glances his way to see that Aubrey was shaking his head behind the policemen's backs.

"I haven't seen her for a while." Colton replied, "We had a bit of a fall out, we've not been getting on and I've been living here."

"I see. And she hasn't been in touch recently, on the phone maybe? Or email?" the female asked.

The tone in her voice put Colton on the defensive, he shook his head, "We haven't really been speaking."

The female clenched her mouth, "Well, it's hopefully nothing to worry about, Colton, I'm sure your mum will turn up, we haven't opened up a missing persons case yet." the woman reached into a pocket and pulled out a business card, "Here's our number, if you could let us know if your mum gets in touch then we can close our file."

"Thanks." Colton stepped over and took the card.

"We can see ourselves out gentlemen." the female smiled.

The man stood up from where he was leaning against the arm of the oxblood sofa and they left the office, Colton opened his mouth to speak but Aubrey raised his hand motioning Colton not to speak, and pointed at the monitor, indicating that the police hadn't left the building yet. There came the noise of the door closing, the two police officers walked into view of the CCTV monitor, and they stood for a moment or two outside the building.

"Well handled." Aubrey smiled grimly, rubbing his pounding temples.

Colton whipped out his mobile and tried calling his mum's mobile number, which rang out, and then the house phone, which did the same.

"Don't panic Colton, when you panic, mistakes happen." Aubrey said, "You did okay there kid, you let the cops in but you had nothing to hide. They got a good sniff about the place, got to scope it out and see we're not filling the place with dope plants or prostitutes, your mum's probably fine and not missing at all, nothing to worry about."

"Don't you think it's a bit odd though, your drink was spiked just last night and now the police are round saying my mum's missing." Colton asked.

Aubrey rubbed his temples again, "Only time will tell, and we aren't the ones playing their hand right now so all we can do is sit back and watch the game play on."

"What if my mum is missing Aubrey, if she's went missing it can only have been from leaving here last night?"

"I'm thinking kid, I'm thinking. Thomas can you go fix up a batch of fresh coffee? My heads pounding."

"Yes boss. June said you would come round in twelve hours, that was six hours ago. You should go back to bed to rest."

"I need to be up and thinking about things, Thomas."

Thomas nodded and left the room. Colton sat down on the leather sofa, putting his feet up on the arm.

"Colton you need to wash those stinking feet of yours, get them away from my face." Aubrey grimaced.

"Sorry." Colton moved his feet and sat up into a sitting position on the sofa, "We checked the CCTV footage last night, while you were out cold. It showed Vivienne coming to the door and entering the building. That was it, no one else."

"It wouldn't have been her Colton." Aubrey said quietly, "There's no way that girl would do that, Marius wouldn't put his future wife in danger by sending her round to do his dirty work."

"But nobody else came into the building." Colton frowned.

"Who let her in?" Aubrey asked.

"I don't know, I wasn't here." Colton said, "I was with you, out at lunch. When we left yesterday, Thomas was cleaning up."

"And now that we have eliminated all other possibilities…" Aubrey broke off sadly.

"Why would Thomas spike you? That makes no sense?"

"Vivienne will have relayed a message, no doubt made him an offer he couldn't refuse." Aubrey said, "I expected more of him though."

"He should have told you!"

"Keep your voice down Colton. Do me a favour, go through there and make sure he's not adding something extra to the coffee, I could do without going through that all again. And do not tell him anything, he doesn't need to know that we know yet."

Colton stood up and strode through to the kitchen, Thomas was looking at his phone, with a slightly concerned expression on his face.

"Alright?" Colton asked nonchalantly, his hands in the pockets of his jeans, "How's the coffee coming along?"

"Just waiting for the kettle to boil." Thomas said, putting his phone away.

Colton looked around, relieved to see the coffee hadn't even begun to be prepared yet.

"Had to take a call." Thomas said.

"Okay. Wasn't my mum by any chance?" Colton smiled with vague hopefulness

Thomas's face pulled back a fraction, "No, it was not." he replied.

They busied themselves with preparing the coffee and took it through to the office. Aubrey looked at Colton as the coffee cup was set down in front of him, Colton nodded.

"Well someone out there is going to be wishing they'd done a better job at trying to kill me last night." Aubrey said, taking a sip of his coffee.

Colton glanced over at Thomas, he was looking into his coffee cup.

"Have you checked the CCTV cameras from last night?" Aubrey asked, knowing the answer already.

Thomas nodded, shaking himself a little with it, "Yes, it showed Vivienne coming to the door."

"And did she come into the building?" Aubrey asked.

Thomas shrugged, "Yes, but we don't know how she got in. Might be worth changing the locks boss."

"Well let's have a look at the footage, shall we?" Aubrey said, "Colton, do the honours."

Colton got up and went over to the CCTV monitor, where he tried to rewind the footage, as he had done last night. It didn't work. He frowned, taking a slurp of his coffee he tried again.

"It's not working." Colton said.

"Interesting." Aubrey said, "You two both checked it last night and saw Vivienne outside the Abattoir?"

"Yes, but the CCTV's not rewinding now, it's like, it's just not there." Colton said.

"Would you suggest that the footage has been erased?" Aubrey asked him.

"Maybe." Colton replied, "I don't really know though."

"Has someone been in here?" Thomas asked.

"Possibly." Aubrey said, and laughed one solitary laugh, "But we'll never know now will we? As they've erased the evidence."

At that moment, Thomas' phone rang, he answered the call then said, "Excuse me boss, I have to go out."

Aubrey turned on him, "Nobody leaves here! No one is leaving the Abattoir until we figure out what the fuck is going on. Who let Vivienne into the Abattoir? Who spiked my fucking drink? And where the fuck is June? No one is leaving and no one gets in until we have some fucking answers. I will reign hell upon them all and they will rue the day they ever thought they could mess with Aubrey Delaney."

Thomas gulped, hanging up his phone. But in that moment, something left Aubrey, he had no strength left, he still needed to rest and his head was pounding.

"Piss off Thomas, go on, run to them as they've come calling you." Aubrey shooed at Thomas wearily with his hand, "Of all the people I ever thought I could trust, it was you. They better have your family in chains for you to be doing this to me."

Thomas said nothing, he placed his phone away into his pocket and he walked away. Colton heard the door close behind Thomas downstairs, he pressed the CCTV monitor onto current mode and watched Thomas walk away with his head bowed.

"It's just you and me left now kid, you're going to have to trust me." Aubrey sighed.

"My own mother said you couldn't be trusted. Now she's missing." Colton replied.

Aubrey rubbed his temples again, "Colton, your mother has her secrets too. Sit down."

Aubrey's his head was pounding, he was struggling to think straight, "Colton please, I need you to sit down."

Aubrey stood up and gestured at the usual place on the sofa where Colton normally sat.

"Can you sit down please?" Aubrey sighed.

Colton finally heard him properly, and walked over to the oxblood chair and sat down on the edge of it, tense.

"This is not how I wanted you to find out, but you are going to have to know why she hated me so much and know that you can trust me throughout all of this." Aubrey paused, partly through his sore head and partly due to what he was about to say, "Colton, I'm your father."

Colton didn't move or change expression.

"Did you hear me?" Aubrey asked.

Colton slowly nodded once, looking away from Aubrey, out of the window.

"That is why I would never hurt you, or your mother. I love her and I love you."

Colton's world was crashing down on him all on one day, his mother was apparently missing, Vivienne had been here with some sort of intention of killing Aubrey, Thomas had betrayed them to the Alessi brothers somehow. No one was left except for Aubrey who had just dealt a massive blow to him which was possibly bullshit too, after all he was someone his mum swore couldn't be trusted. Why was everyone in the world so against Aubrey if he was a good guy? Everyone except Colton. Maybe everyone else was right and Colton was wrong to like him. Colton put his blind faith in Aubrey and now his mum had vanished, potentially as a result of Colton associating with Aubrey.

"Colton, speak to me?" Aubrey said.

"I don't know what you expect me to say." Colton mumbled, "I think I need some air." as he stood up and walked to the doorway.

"Colton, don't leave me." Aubrey said, sounding so vulnerable.

Colton walked out of the office. His head felt like it was going to explode. He walked into his room, pulling on a top and a pair of trainers, popped his wallet and phone in his pocket and went downstairs. He shut the door behind him and broke into a run, jogging through the cobbled alleyway, he ran down to the roundabout, onto the main A7 road and headed to the outskirts of town. He passed the college buildings, the entrance to the rugby ground and then under the hardwood trees he reached the town speed limit signs, pausing to catch his breath, and aimed for the park across the footbridge. Just over the bridge, there was a blue bandstand where he stopped to stretch his leg muscles.

He saw another runner jogging towards the bandstand, who stopped to stretch there as well.

"Alright?" The runner asked him. He was older than Colton, with red hair that was beginning to grey.

"Aye." Colton replied.

"Thought I'd get the run over with before the storm hits later on today." The man said to him.

"What storm?" Colton asked.

"I dunno, they've given it a name though. Meant to be the storm of the century, this whole place will be under water the way they're talking." The man lifted his right leg to stretch it, placing his trainer on the edge of the bandstand bench, "Can you believe that?"

"Wouldn't have thought it could hit that bad." Colton said.

The man lowered his leg and pulled the other one onto the bench, "Naw, me neither, but if it does, the town will pull together and look after each other." the man spoke with some sort of aged wisdom, "The Teri blood will stand strong in any storm."

Colton felt goosebumps prickle his arms, the wind was picking up.

"Cheerio." The man said, jogging away.

"Nothing fucking cheery about today." Colton muttered.

Chapter Ten

When Colton returned from his run, he went upstairs for a shower, went through to his room to change, then decided to face Aubrey. He found Aubrey lying face down on the floor by the side of his desk, he was pale and barely breathing. Colton yanked his mobile out from his back jeans pocket and struggled to swipe the screen to unlock it. Then he couldn't focus on the App icons on the screen, they blurred in front of his eyes, he couldn't remember which one held the dial out function. He finally focussed on the green telephone symbol and pressed it, but once he was in the menu he couldn't find the number keypad function. Panic began to set in, this was taking too long, all he wanted to do was dial 999 to summon an ambulance, time slowed down as he stared at the screen.

He leaped up to the desk to use the office phone, feeling like an idiot for not using it in the first place. It was an old fashioned looking phone, with an imitation rotary dial and mouth and earpiece. Only it was off the hook. He placed the handset back on the base and picked it up to dial 999. As it rang he noticed a slip of paper on the desk, with the words, "June, body found." hastily scribbled on it in Aubrey's hand writing. Colton realised a voice was speaking to him from the other end of the line.

"Ambulance please. Yes, my ... father's collapsed. He's barely breathing I don't know what's wrong with him. The Abattoir. It's a training club in Hawick. Hawick's in the Scottish Borders. H.A.W.I.C.K. It's in the Scottish Borders? The Borders General Hospital is the nearest hospital that's where the ambulances come from I think? Would it be quicker if I got him in a taxi if you don't actually know where he is? Please, he's barely breathing can you please tell me you know where we are?"

The centralisation of the emergency call centres meant that Colton was speaking to someone in Aberdeen who didn't have a clue where Hawick was and thought the Borders was a place in Wales.

The ambulance ended up double parked on the High Street, the driver running into a local pub with motorbikes and a Smart Car parked outside to ask for directions. Malcolm, the owner, knowing where the club was, ran round with the ambulance men to the alley way and pressed the call buzzer. Colton let them in and the paramedics set to work straight away on Aubrey, whose breathing was now barely audible.

They loaded him onto the stretcher, and rather than going to the BGH, he was blue lighted to Edinburgh. Colton went with them, the world beginning to haze and blur around him.

He was in a hospital waiting room for what seemed like hours. He tried calling his mum but the phone kept ringing out.

Then a female Doctor came in the room to speak to him.

"We've stabilised him but … Colton, he's not going to recover. He can't breathe on his own he's suffered a massive trauma to the heart, which has caused excessive tissue damage and his brain has been starved of oxygen. You need to prepare to say goodbye to him. Is there anyone else we can call to be here?"

"No." Colton mumbled, his heart lurching at remembering the note on Aubrey's desk.

"Are you his only relative?"

"Yes."

"Okay, Colton, this is up to you, you can wait until the end, but, I need to warn you, it's not pleasant. You can say your goodbyes now, and choose to leave without putting yourself through that."

"But he'll die alone." Colton replied.

"He's not there any more honey. It's the machines keeping his body alive. Your dad's gone. It's a whole lot less traumatic for you if you leave before the end"

It was one of those moments in life where Colton was given a choice. He was given the warnings, from a Doctor who witnessed the last moments of patients on a regular basis, but until someone experienced it themselves, they had no idea what they were about to put themselves through. Or that the memories would stay with them for life, to sit next to death as it strode through the door and claimed someone they loved.

Colton didn't think he knew better than the Doctor who was trying to spare him witnessing a damaged body, still trying to hold on when the machines were turned off, when it was just too late for the person to recover. The Doctor didn't want the young boy in front of her carrying that memory for the rest of his life.

But Colton stayed, so that Aubrey wasn't alone, and he was haunted by the sight of his father's last moments for many years to come. It would change him and affect him in many ways that he was not to know in that moment when he decided to stay.

At two minutes past eight Aubrey Delaney was declared dead. There was to be a post mortem, but Colton didn't stay to hear further details.

Colton left the hospital in a daze, waited at the bus stop in the howling wind and rain in a dreary dark night. He carried no memory of the bus journey back to Hawick later in life, other than the torrential rain slowing the journey. He returned to the Abattoir, packed a bag of belongings, packed his passport into his side pocket, bolted the shutters of the windows, set the alarm, closed the Abattoir doors and walked to the bus stop. He caught the last bus back to Edinburgh, found his way to the Airport and at midnight asked the girl at the only check-in desk when the next flight was with a spare seat. He paid for the ticket in cash and boarded a plane out of the country. He had no idea where he was headed as he hadn't even registered what the girl said his destination was when he bought the ticket.

<u>Chapter Eleven</u>

It was a three hour flight, Colton stared out of the window into nothingness for most of it. He didn't hear the man praying in the seat behind him, nor the young child crying intermittently two rows down. He landed in Alicante airport, he finally registered some information in his numb brain. He was in Spain. The air was warm as he walked down the metal steps and stepped off the plane.

He picked up his bag, and began walking. It was the middle of the night, but it was warm. He walked out of the airport, along a motorway for hours until his legs could barely carry him. He stepped off the motorway and slept fitfully under a bush for a few hours, then woke up and began walking again. It was still dark. At some point he turned off the motorway, he found himself walking through a small town and up another road. He wandered up smaller and smaller roads. It was some time since he'd seen the small town when he came across a gated entranceway, with a cluster of flats and houses up a driveway, cast all in darkness. None of the street lights were on, not a single car was parked on the street.

The first rays of the morning sun were beginning to hit off the rooftops. Empty windows stared down at him, gardens and border hedges completely overgrown.

He climbed over the gateway and made his way up the drive, it opened out into a square with a large central building made of light stone. He tried the door, found it unlocked, and walked in. Inside the lights came on at the flick of the switch, revealing a reception desk and through a doorway behind the desk, a back room with rows of keys hanging on the wall. He was in a hotel of a holiday complex that was built but never used, a victim of the recession.

He lifted the key for room twenty three from the hook, walked up to the room, opened it, and, despite a veil of dust, everything was in its rightful place. A dusty sheet lay on the bed, a dust covered kettle and cups sat on a counter at the side near to a dusty television. The window looked out over a kidney shaped pool which was empty and had foliage growing intermittently through the tilework.

Colton tried the bathroom taps, realising he hadn't had a drink for over twelve hours. Miraculously they worked, he ran them for a little while, and he took a drink. Pain reached his dulled senses as the water poured over his chapped lips. He splashed his face, shook the dust off the bed and collapsed onto it. He was somewhere the world would never find him, and that was the only comfort he took to sleep with him.

It wasn't a restful sleep, there was no hiding from his own nightmares. Colton was to find that sleep would not be a comfort to him in the months ahead. It was filled with memories, events as well as fabrications. He would wake up sweating throughout the early hours and never fell into the sort of deep sleep that restored the soul. He fought with himself, wrestling with the sheets, kicking out at the memories, fighting the past, but he could never win.

Colton wasn't sure how long he stayed in the bed in the hotel room for, it may have been one day or two. He woke up in the early hours of one morning with crippling hunger pangs. He hadn't eaten for days now. He hadn't even registered that he had been hungry, his appetite just wasn't there. Now it was unconsolable. And he didn't have anything to eat with him. He got up from the bed, still wearing the clothes he had arrived in.

He rubbed his hair, feeling greasy, put on his trainers and wandered back through the hotel to the grounds outside. He looked about him, sun rays were just forming on the horizon allowing enough light to hit off the trees all around him in the courtyard. The light bounced off fruit. He ran over to the trees, they were covered in ripe oranges. He pulled the nearest one from the tree and dug his thumb into the thick orange peel, tearing it off in pieces which scattered on the ground around him. The first segment dampened his dry mouth, and he hastily ate the entire orange, the sticky sweet juice dripping down his chin and all over his hands. He reached for another, then a third.

He plucked more from the tree, using the bottom of his t-shirt as a way of carrying them into the hotel. He walked around the ground floor, finding the dining room which led through a set of swing doors into a kitchen. He put the oranges on a countertop and opened the cupboards looking for a glass to drink from, he found tumblers, and miraculously the tap poured fresh cold water into it. He drank glass after glass until he finally felt full.

Then, he remembered again, and he felt sick. He leaned over the sink waiting, but nothing happened. Leaning there, he realised he wanted to be drunk so he wouldn't feel the pain anymore, and he needed to eat. He resolved to walk into the small town to buy food and much needed alcohol.

Chapter Twelve

Colton walked from his ghost town and back down the rough roads, with a vague memory of the route he used to arrive there. He saw signs for Fuente Alamo and realised that was probably the name of the town he was heading to.

It wasn't a place of remarkable artworks or architecture, a small town with little cosmetic beauty. But it carried character in the arid dusty air. The houses were made of concrete and white washed or painted yellow. Occasional window boxes lent a little colour to the buildings.

The pavements were smooth underneath his worn out trainers, pattern of criss-crossing mosaics. The sun radiated in blinding light off the tops of the buildings, but it was shadowy and cool where Colton walked. When he walked past alleyways and streetways he was hit with gusts of chilling wind. It was as if the wind itself was blocking Colton's way down these streets, pushing him to the centre of town, where the life was, where the town hall was, where redemption waited.

The only outstanding feature in the whole town, the only detail thought about with any care and with any time taken on it, was in the carved archway above the entrance of the original townhall. There were statues standing over the arch, bathing in the sunlight hitting them, they were carved in what he took to be some sort of sandstone, they were holding items in their hands that Colton couldn't make out from where he stood. Part of him thought it would be too much effort to gaze any longer and try to figure the statues out, so he stopped looking at them.

Colton didn't trouble himself to walk through the doors and look inside the building, he didn't want a priest speaking another language at him, trying to tell him about faith and believing in the goodness of mankind. He thought maybe it was the town hall and not a church, that there wouldn't be a priest inside, but he still felt suspicious about the place.

He decided he needed a drink before he needed to eat, looking at the statues calling him to believe in God was enough for that. He walked away from the centre of town, up an alleyway where the wind wasn't blowing.

There was one bar at the end of the street of low-rise buildings. After the bar the town ended abruptly. The sign hanging outside was still, it was a rich orange background, with the silhouette of a man in a flat-brimmed hat riding a rearing white horse. The bar was square shaped with a flat roof, quite basic to look at with peeling flakes of paint revealing cement underneath.

Colton guessed it wouldn't be busy which suited him, and he went inside. It took a moment for his eyes to adjust. The room was dimly lit, with a blue hue coming from the fridges and mirrored bottle display behind the bar on his right. Wooden stools sat underneath the bar counter, with sawdust around them on the ground. An assortment of tables and chairs were in the room. Posters adorned the walls, vintage almost abstract scenes of conquistadors on horseback or in the ring. It was rough and ready, Colton liked it, he didn't feel underdressed in his unwashed clothes.

The bartender came out from through the back to greet him holding a glass and tea-towel in his hand. He greeted Colton in Spanish, then looked closely at him and broke into rough English with a thick accent. He was about the same age as Colton, who was relieved that the bartender understood him. He ordered a pint and since there was no one else in the bar, he sat on one of the stools and chatted to the barman, who was in no hurry to continue working through the back and introduced himself as Paulio, pouring himself a pint as well.

Colton kept responses about his personal life brief, mentioning only that he was recently arrived and wanted to stay in Spain for a little while longer, but needed a job. Paulio looked at him intently, and smiled a little smile that played at the edges of his eyes as well as his mouth. He liked the strange shit-looking Scotsman who chose to walk into his bar that morning, carrying his heavy heart laden with secrets into a bar that usually only accepted certain clientele and was not really open to visitors or regular residents of the town. He offered Colton a part time job in the bar, starting that afternoon. His only condition was that Colton knew how to keep his mouth shut about what he saw there, or he might well never leave Spain unless it was in a body bag.

Colton liked the terms. He agreed, he needed the money if he was going to stay, and didn't care particularly what went on in the bar, nor if he ended up in a body bag himself. It sounded like there was just going to be another round of fucked up individuals frequenting the place and these were ones he didn't care about. He told Paulio that he'd done a little bar work back home and it was just a case of learning the Spanish equivalents of names for drinks, which he could get away with initially by pointing at them all. He added that he couldn't understand a word of Spanish so wouldn't understand any of the conversations that were held there anyway. Paulio laughed, held out his hand and the deal was struck. Colton forgot to ask what his wage was, but even that he was something he didn't really care about.

Paulio seemed nonplussed that Colton drank three pints before his first shift started, and was in fact drinking with him. It wasn't a thing to make an issue out of in this bar. Paulio showed Colton the ropes, gave him some food, and that afternoon their first customers, four men, arrived at two o'clock. Paulio advised he would see to them, if Colton would continue with the cleaning behind the bar. They were wearing suits, the sort of suits that silently spoke 'we mean business, mean business' to anyone paying attention. With slicked black hair and neat collars, slightly distended stomachs and guns at their sides. Yes, guns. Colton could make them out, glinting in the dim light of the bar.

The business men sat down and shook hands with each other, some sort of introduction, Colton guessed a deal was being struck.

One of the men, a heavy set man, did a double take at Colton as he noticed him behind the bar, but was then taken up with the conversation by the other men and paid him no further attention.

Colton served the men drinks and plates of tapas, anchovies and tomatoes on round bread toasted, drizzled with olive oil, plates of olives, chicken legs coated in spicy barbecue sauce, potatoes in red sauce. All of which Paulio prepared himself and told Colton he would show him how to make it all in due course, but not when these customers were in.

At about three o'clock, two of the gentlemen left, leaving the man that had looked at Colton and another thinner man with long wavy dark hair and a thin moustache sitting at the table. The bar manager indicated to Colton to clear their table of glasses and dirty plates at this point, asking him not to talk to the men.

Colton walked over to the table, but the larger man who had watched him earlier looked up as he came over and asked him what his name was in English.

"Colton Cooper." Colton replied, continuing to clear the table.

"Where are you from Mr Cooper?" The man said to him, a statement made in a flat tone, not a question.

"Hawick." Colton replied.

"And do you happen to know my old friend Aubrey Delaney, he is from there?" Again, flat, expressionless.

The moustached man next to the larger man shifted forward in his seat a little, staring intently at Colton.

Colton couldn't tell the meaning behind the questions, "Yes sir, I did." Colton replied.

"You did?" This one was a question, this one the man did not understand.

"He passed away recently sir." Colton said, his voice breaking with emotion

The man leaned up and back a little, inhaling with surprise, "This I did not know." he said, "This I did not know. Are you working here now boy?" another question.

"Yes, I just started today."

"Good, then we will speak of this again another time. Today is not the day to talk of such things."

"Yes sir." Colton said and took this as a cue to walk away with the balanced dishes and glasses in his hands.

"What did he say to you?" Paulio asked him.

"He asked me if I knew someone back home who was his friend."

"Ah." Paulio replied.

"Would he actually be 'a friend' to that guy out there, or would there be trouble behind the question?" Colton indicated to the man who was standing up at the table, dabbing round his mouth a final time before placing a napkin on the table.

"That is the Baron, he does not lie. If he says your friend is his friend, it will be so."

Once the lunch glasses and plates were cleaned and put away, Paulio told Colton he was free to go for the day, as they would not be opening that evening. He pulled a note out of the till and gave it to Colton, saying "I trust I will see you back here tomorrow?"

Colton nodded, "Yes, thank you. What time?"

"Oh after lunch some time, tomorrow is no customers at lunch time so no rushing, we have people at five o'clock, so you will help me prepare the food."

"Okay. Thank you. And where can I buy food in town is there a supermarket?"

Paulio smiled, "Down the street, take a left at the town square you will see it, the Mercadona. They will be having the horse sales further in town it will be very busy try to walk another way home unless you want to go home with a horse."

Colton walked into the supermarket, picked up a basket and placed some much needed food into it. He was surprised to see a large fully iced up fish display as well as row upon row of pigs legs descended in the air, he read the words 'jamon serrano' on the label. He decided to give them a miss. A huge weight of tiredness was descending upon him now that he was away from Paulio's company and his memories were beginning to haunt him. He found the aisle stocking liquor and topped up his basket with bottles.

He paid with his bank card, grateful that it worked overseas and filled a couple of heavy duty carrier bags with his items.

Chapter Thirteen

Completely forgetting Paulio's advice about the town being busy, Colton walked the only route he knew to get back to the ghost town, and walked right into the middle of the horse sales.

The horses were situated in makeshift pens at the bottom of a dried up riverbed, utilising the steep sides to help keep the animals in one area, while the pavements that ran alongside the river were heaving with crowds of people, deals being struck, and horses being led this way and that. There were clouds of dust in the air as the horses stamped up the dried up bottom of the riverbed, and the noise of neighing and whinnying on top of human voices shouting above the din.

Colton could barely get through the crowds. His hands were beginning to ache from the weight of his shopping, and his mood plummeted quickly into wondering why he would even bother to walk back to the ghost town, it wasn't home or anything, so he stopped to distract himself by watching with a couple of men beneath him on the riverbed, discussing horses that were nearby, putting his bags between his feet so no one would grab them, losing himself in watching them.

He looked at the horse they were pointing at, a skinny grey, made almost solely of skeleton, under a layer of caked mud, with limp mane and its head lowered in complete dismal defeat. It looked about as sorry for itself as he felt. One of them was making a slitting motion across his throat, Colton gathered the horse was no use except as meat and something stirred, a sense of pity and understanding of the horses predicament.

"Hey Gringo, you want a horse or you stand looking at it any longer I will have to charge you rent."

Colton realised the men had stopped talking and one of them was shouting up at him.

"I can't ride." he shouted down at them.

"Well we will teach you right now! Come down here!"

Both men smiled at that point and the first man nudged the second with a knowing glance. Colton shrugged, picked up his shopping and the men helped him clamber down.

"You like the grey?" The first one said, "Franco wants her for meat, but she is very pretty no? Just look at her eyes, and her nose. Very pretty."

The horse dealer pulled at the horse's headcollar. She barely reacted. Colton knew the men both thought they were going to be able to sell him a horse at death's door. And he didn't care. He would take her back to the ghost town where she could live out her last days in peace.

"Jump on her back Gringo." The Dealer said.

"I don't think she looks strong enough to take me." Colton replied.

"This horse will take three men! We can all sit on her with you to show you!" The Dealer exclaimed.

"No, it's okay, I'll try myself."

Colton received a leg-up onto the horse from Franco. The horse shifted its weight, but did not raise its head.

"Do not kick this horse, she is very sensitive, like a woman, you stroke her and whisper sweet nothings. Do not kick her. Comprende?"

Colton sat on the horse's back, the world was swaying around him as his eyes adapted to the change in perspective and height.

"How do you get her to move then?" Colton asked.

"Don't you know any Spanish?"

Colton shook his head.

"Well you are going to need a translator! Extra charge for a translator! Thees horse, she only know Spanish, you say to her 'andale' and she will walk, si."

Colton tested the word in his mouth. The horse pricked its ears round towards him.

"Louder she say she can't hear you!"

Colton tried the word again. Alien to his mouth, he knew he wasn't pronouncing the command with the same lilts as the Dealer's Spanish tongue.

The horse broke from a standstill and in a single leap, bounded straight into a canter. Colton fell straight out of the saddle and fell ungraciously to the ground. The men around him were in hysterics, as were many people up above them standing on the walls above the dried up riverbed. The horse plodded back to him, peered down her big long nose at him, and snorted.

"I think she like you!" The Dealer laughed.

"I don't really have a need for a horse." Colton said, rubbing at his arse where he landed.

"Every man needs a horse." As if that was an answer.

"Why are you selling her if she's so good? She looks a bit thin to me."

"She is a moody horse and I have many happy horses, she is no good to me. I say, if she no happy with me, she can go live someplaceelse."

"I only have this much in cash." Colton said, pulling out the note Paulio paid him with.

"Ah it is so little!" The Dealer said.

"It's more than I was going to give you!" Franco said.

"I tell you what, I will sell you her, for that note, and I will throw in the saddle for that bottle there in your bag." The Dealer pointed to the bottle of brandy visible in the shopping bag.

Colton grimaced, now the Dealer was hitting him where it hurt.

"Okay." Colton said.

The Dealer smiled, took the note and the bottle, and handed the reins to Colton.

"Does she have a name?" Colton asked.

"Esta yegua tan dificil" Franco laughed.

Colton looked at him, puzzled.

"No, she have no name." The Dealer said.

So Colton found himself the owner of a horse. He had no idea what to do with a horse, how to ride her or look after her apart from the basic tips the horse dealer gave him before he left the hustle and bustle of the riverbed for the dusty roads leading to the ghost town.

Colton rode at a slow pace, grateful that the shopping bags were balanced on the horse's shoulders in front of him, rather than breaking his wrists. The horse plodded along, unenthusiastically, with what he took to be her similar melancholy to his, of being just plain tired of living.

Colton pulled out a bottle of brandy from his shopping bags, untwisted the lid and took a drink. The horse twisted her ears back to listen to what he was doing.

"There is no way you're getting any of this." he said.

As the brandy took effect Colton began to laugh at his situation, "I rode through the desert on a horse with no name, it felt good to get out of the rain." He sung in time to the horse's hoof beats.

Then he felt guilty for the moment of happiness, the darkness clouded over him again and he fell silent, listening to only the sound of the horse treading her way up the dusty road while he supped on his brandy.

Colton dismounted at the ghost town gates and opened them to allow the horse to pass through. Once he'd closed them behind him, he removed her reins and saddle to allow her to go free, placing them in the small security shack a the entrance gateway. She followed him the whole way to the hotel.

"Don't you want to go and eat something? There's fruit on the trees." Colton pointed to the oranges on the trees.

The horse stopped walking and looked earnestly at his face. He placed his shopping on the ground, plucked one of the oranges and held it out to the horse. She sniffed it and it rolled off his hand onto the road. He picked it up, "What do I have to peel it for you? Are you kidding me?"

Colton peeled the orange, throwing the skin across the road into the brush beyond it. He held out a slice to the horse. She looked blankly at him. "You eat it, here like this." He put a slice in his mouth and took a bite from it, then offered the other half to the horse. She gingerly picked the chunk of orange from his hand with her big hairy clumsy mouth and started chewing on it. Saliva ran in globlets down out of her mouth and onto the ground.

"You're pretty gross." Colton said, handing her the rest of the orange, which she accepted.

He felt good that the horse had eaten something, maybe it would learn to eat oranges off the trees itself rather than relying on him. He didn't want her relying on him, she'd wind up quicker in her grave.

He left her standing at the front door peering curiously inside the hallway, and closed the door behind him. He could hear her sniffing and snorting at the door, he imagined indignant at being abandoned outside.

He went round into the lounge and peered out of the window at her. She finally moved away from the door and lowered her head, sniffing the ground. She found her way to an orange tree in the lawn-like circular turning area and began nibbling on an orange on the ground. She turned her head towards the hotel and pulled faces as she chewed.

Colton wandered away to the kitchen to dump his shopping and find a glass for his brandy, planning to spend the rest of the afternoon sitting in the sunshine on a balcony or by the pool, getting drunk.

Which was exactly what he did.

Chapter Fourteen

Colton took the horse to work with him the next day, though not by choice. She started following him down from the hotel to the gate and whinnied when he shut the gate on her, she trotted away from the closed gate, bucking about and ran at it, snorting and skidding to a stop when she reached it. She was angry that Colton had left her there. Colton walked back to the gate and reached into the security office, the horse stood patiently while he fumbled about with the saddle and bridle. He didn't dare get on her without the aid of other people, he just walked her to work behind him.

Paulio saw Colton arriving, as he was cleaning out the ashtrays on the outside tables, "What is that behind you?"

Colton turned and looked down the road behind him.

"That!" Paulio said, pointing at the horse.

"It's my horse." Colton replied.

The barman burst out laughing, "I heard the men had sold the angriest horse at the market to a stupid white boy, and it was you!"

"I tried leaving her at home and she was going to do herself an injury following me, she would have been running loose on the road."

"Hah." Paulio was still laughing, "Well put her out the back, it's fenced off, you can see if she will stay there. If not you will have to get rid of her or find another job."

"Thank you. I'd get rid of her but I feel a bit responsible for her now."

"Well make use of her. What's wrong with riding her?"

"I don't know how to ride, and she's a bit thin."

"I will teach you to ride, and you will feed the horse."

The dirty grey horse was set loose in the back area, it was a dusty overflow car park that was fenced off and gated, never needing to be used, it was mainly a storage area now. She paced it out, walked around the yard sniffing the gaps in the fence. Then she broke into a bucking canter, snorting and bucking about the yard.

"That horse is crazy." Paulio said.

Colton banged on the window, "Stop that!" he shouted.

The horse pricked her ears and trotted over to the window, she peered in and spotted Colton doing the dishes in the sink in the back kitchen and snorted at him, leaving splatters of snort on the window.

"She has found you." Paulio laughed.

They watched her watching them, then continued to prepare the bar and food for the afternoon. The horse moved around the windows, looking in and watching them.

"She will not run away if she knows you are in here I think." Paulio laughed, "Crazy horse."

After preparing the bar, Paulio went out into the back yard with Colton, they had a couple of hours till their late afternoon reservation arrived. Colton put the horse's bridle back on and Paulio helped him with the saddle, showing him how to tie it correctly and where to position it on her back.

"Right, foot in, then up, you must be able to get on her yourself from the ground."

Colton couldn't stretch his leg that far.

"Okay, small steps to start with." Paulio went inside and came back out with a chair for Colton to stand on.

Colton stood on the chair and got slowly into the saddle, and began his first riding lesson. He was terrified the horse was going to start its bucking again.

"You need to relax, no tension on your legs, or the horse feels it too, you stop her breathing properly if your legs are like this, tight on her sides. Breath in and out, in and out, steady."

Colton breathed in and out slowly, he found himself relaxing, and to his surprise noticed that the horse was copying his breathing.

"Now tonight you can ride her home. And in the morning she can get you to work on time." Paulio laughed, "What are you going to call her?"

Colton got off and unbuckled the saddle,"Becky." he replied.

"Bucking Becky hah, I like this name for this horse." Paulio patted Becky's bum and she flicked her back hoof towards him. He took a quick step backwards.

"She is a crazy horse, very angry at the world. Just like you!" he laughed, "You would be wise not to kick me senorita, I am paying your boss's wages so he can look after you." Paulio wagged his finger at the horse.

Becky snorted at him and turned to Colton, chewing on her lip thoughtfully. Colton pulled out an orange from his pocket and peeled it for Becky, giving her the slices from his hand.

Paulio laughed, "You peel the orange for the horse! Hah. You spoil her! I advise you, do not feed her from your hands it makes her bite you. Feed her from the ground or a bucket and not from your hands. And you need to give her a bath. Ah, I am glad I hired you, you are proving to be entertainment."

While the Baron made an appearance at the bar that afternoon, and many times afterwards, he did not speak to Colton again.

Becky the horse became a permanent fixture in Colton's life. She lived in the grounds of the ghost town as Colton's only companion. He had grown to appreciate his quiet reclusive time in the ghost town, listening to Becky grazing the dry grass or chewing on oranges, while he drank to forget the rest of the world.

Colton had no real routine, he rose when he woke up, unless Paulio needed him at the bar early, he did a few half-hearted push-ups or the occasional jog around the ghost town, followed by Becky, but he let his overall fitness slide.

Colton would go into the bar at the start of his shifts, put on a British radio station playing the same old hits that Aubrey used to blast in the Abattoir, and he would begin his routine of cleaning the bar from the night before, clearing the empty glasses and bottles, putting the rubbish out, doing the dishes, mopping the floors, cleaning the tables and countertops, preparing the tapas dishes for the day, restocking the shelves. He prided himself on the transformation of the bar in the routine.

At eleven he would put the oven on to warm up, venture out of the bar, picking up fresh loaves of bread from the supermarket. He would return and heat up a dish of olive oil and warm a couple of the loaves up in the oven the way Paulio had shown him to do and chop up tomatoes into fine pieces and place those in another dish.

He would cut the loaves up and have them sitting on a plate next to the dish of oil and tomatoes whereby Paulio would arrive at midday to enjoy the meal with him over strong coffee, or a pint, depending on how their moods were.

Colton started picking up some of the language, helped by body language and the gestures people made at him. One of the passing tourists who accidently stumbled into the bar one day, left their tattered phrasebook with him as they didn't need it anymore, they had no intention of returning to a part of Spain where hardly anyone spoke any English.

Chapter Fifteen

Over time Becky the horse grew better about being left on her own in the grounds or in the yard at the back of the bar. Colton could leave her in the yard and venture onto other bars after finishing his shift, then at the end of the night, she would carry him home. Becky always saw to it that she got them both home, she knew the route well enough.

Colton's hair grew long, he saw no point in cutting it, and he was frequently unshaven, as shaving was mostly pointless too. He still served drinks in the bar whether he was shaven or not. His clothes, which he acquired from the second hand stalls on the markets, grew a little looser as he barely ate when he wasn't at the bar.

Some nights the sadness would take hold of him completely, he would see the faces of the past, maybe someone had been in the bar that afternoon who reminded him of Aubrey, or of his mum, or a voice on the radio would sound like them. It would hit him from behind, across the back of the knees like some cheap low life fighting dirty, knocking all the remaining life out from under him leaving him just an empty void needing to be filled with drink until he reached oblivion.

At that point he had a routine too, he would pour a brandy down his throat and wash it down with a line of cocaine, which he and Paulio occasionally indulged in, then pour himself another brandy and head into town till the light rose in the sky again.

This was one of those evenings. Colton was thrown out of the bar he had been in, though he no longer remembered why, and found himself wandering the streets in the early hours of the morning.

His formerly toned lithe body was failing him, he had lost most of his muscle definition and tonight his body was much use as a newborn baby's, he could only stumble around the streets, leaning on the walls when his legs refused to carry him. He managed to command a walk that navigated him into another bar. He sat at the nearest vacant bar stool and the man next to him offered to buy him a drink. They were the only two customers in the bar.

Colton looked at the other man through milky eyes, he looked to be one of the workers from Ecuador, though he would be the same age as Colton he was very much shorter in stature with a weather beaten face which aged him considerably. He smiled a weak worn out smile at Colton.

Colton took an instant liking to him. They conversed for a time well enough with a mixture of broken English and Spanish, until three men roughly entered the bar, local Spanish men in dark clothing, and without any word of warning, they grabbed Colton's new friend by the shoulders, and hauled him up from the bar stool. The man's eyes rolled upwards in his eye sockets with panic, his drink fell from his grasp, the glass shattering on the ground. Then the men were laying into him on the bar floor, punch followed kick followed kick after punch.

Panting, one of the men looked up at Colton, "This is not your business." he said.

"Leave me out of this." Colton said, holding his hands up.

"He owes us money, and a lot more than that." The man replied.

"My business is my business, yours is yours." Colton replied.

"This is not your business." The man repeated, straightening himself up and looking at Colton threateningly.

"You really don't need to tell me twice." Colton said, knowing that at this moment, he could end up bleeding next to the man on the floor unless he chose his words very carefully, "Do you think I'd be sitting here drinking on my own unless I wasn't well connected?"

"Who do you know?"

"I can't say who I know, but they're bigger than this small town. I'm on my last drop of the night for them and just wanted to enjoy a quiet drink before I clock off."

"Thats your business."

"And that's your business." Colton indicated to the man on the floor.

Colton finished his drink, stood up and stepped over the Ecuadorian on the floor, and left the bar.

He still wasn't in the mood to return to the hotel at the ghost town, so he wandered along the streets and found himself being beckoned into a familiar entrance way.

Chapter Sixteen

He was stopped just in the entranceway, at a counter where a woman demanded his credit card details.

"I just want a drink." he told her, "And for that I'll be paying in cash."

"If you want more, you pay with credit card." she insisted.

A burly man standing next to her in a dark suit crossed his arms and frowned at Colton.

"Look, lady, you are not getting my bank details, I want a drink. I've been here before. If you won't let me just come in and have a drink I will go someplace else."

A man walked through from the main room into the foyer.

"Carmella what is the problem here, if the man wants to come in for a drink, let him." He smiled a greasy smile at Colton and held the door open for him.

Colton thanked him and stepped through into a dimly lit room. Once his eyes adjusted, he went straight to the bar to the right of the door and ordered a drink. With a glass in his hand, he was content again, and turned to take in his surroundings.

A handful of men were in the room, seated at tables round a stage area with poles and glitter balls hanging from the ceiling. Music began to play and a scantily clad young woman in red lingerie walked along the stage, grabbed the pole and began dancing seductively. She had long dark hair which hung down the pole in waves, touching the ground as she danced.

Colton leaned against the bar and watched the girl.

The barman leaned over, "You can have a private session with her if you like, just a small charge. A little extra, and she will go all the way, comprende?"

Colton nodded. He knew how far the girls went already. He felt something stirring in his loins, the result of the lines of cocaine from earlier in the night, he felt desire beginning to course through him.

"I'll pay cash." Colton said, reaching for his wallet.

"How much?" The barman smiled.

"All the way." Colton replied.

He paid his money and was guided through to the back rooms to the left of the bar. He was told to wait, that 'Romina' would be through once she finished her dance.

Romina walked in a moment later. She was a little breathless, which he liked.

"They have sent me a Scottish man." she smiled, reaching over to the counter by the dressing table and putting on a little more lipgloss, ensuring the curves of her back were arched and accentuated her toned derriere.

Colton watched her, feeling aroused, but his drunken melancholy decided to wash over him like the inevitability of the waves on the shore.

"Can we talk a little first?" he asked her.

She placed her lip gloss down and pouted into the mirror.

"What do you want to talk about white boy?" she asked him.

"Are you happy?" he said. He could hear himself say it, and wished he could stop himself and just grab her ass and take her from behind.

"Hah." she said. "What is happiness? I am free to do what I want. I say my price and no one owns me. Not one. I walk away to my own house after work, there are no dishes, there is no fat-bellied man with his feet up shouting at me for being lazy and for not cooking his favourite meal, while he screws the woman next door while I'm at work. My home is mine, my money is mine."

She turned and looked at Colton, leaning against the dressing table counter. She crossed her legs at her ankles. Colton wanted to run his tongue up her toned muscular legs.

"Sometimes though, these men, they throw money at you. They are so drunk they will pay any amount to me for a dance. Sometimes, they are so drunk they just think you have danced for them, they come in their pants already, and you just take their money off them. Money machines, thats all men are good for, cheating on their wives, hiding their ugly truth from their children. I am free here."

"Freedom, hmm, I never thought of stripping like that before." Colton slurred.

"And you ones that just want to talk, chuh, you bore me to death. Go see a counsellor for God's sake, I'm not here to listen to you whine on and on about your awful life. If I was I would have trained to be a doctor. I like my men silent, for them to stay for their short stipulated time period, pay me my money and then go away."

"You seem to do quite a bit of talking yourself." Colton said.

"That's the coke." she sniffed, then laughed, "You know what, you of all men, bore me so much I think this is going to be my last call here, my last night. Tomorrow, I'm going to go someplace else where the men keep their mouths shut. I don't want to know your problems, I'm sick of all your problems."

The stripper walked around the room, packing a small bag of her belongings, "Santiago?" she yelled, banging on a side door, "Santiago, get this guy outta here and call me a cab, I quit."

Romina flounced out of the room in her heels to wait for her cab.

The man called Santiago walked in, he was the giant hulk of a man who was at the entrance when Colton first arrived. His massive arms were outstretched waiting to grab the man who upset one of their star attractions.

Colton wasn't sure what to say, "We didn't do anything, I asked her how she was and she went on this big rant, packed her bags and walked out."

Santiago lowered his arms and sighed, "I'll get you your money back, Romina does this about once a month, it's her hormones. She'll be back tomorrow night if you want to see her, she'll behave, good as gold, for you then."

Chapter Seventeen

The next evening found Colton back at the strip bar. He hadn't sobered up since the night before, perhaps he had snatched an hour of sleep in the very early hours of the morning, he couldn't tell. He wasn't needed at Paulio's bar, so he'd worked his way steadily through another bottle of brandy, then went on a familiar pub crawl which wound him up at the same strip bar asking Santiago if Romina was there.

Romina stirred Colton's drunken curiosity, how someone so passionate, determined and defiant could also be so undertermindly weak and fall like a kitten back into her work routine the next night. Someone like that wasn't really free at all. And he wanted to challenge her on that, for her one night encounters where she ranted at confused lost men about freedom. Men who might be looking for a small chat before they laid her. Was Romina just another hypocrite?

Santiago smiled with bemusement when Colton asked him if Romina had come back, "Of course she has."

"But she told me she was going to break free from it all." Colton slurred.

"Romina says these things, like I told you last night, about once a month, for about two years now. Did you not notice how well rehearsed the whole thing was?

Colton shook his head, "I thought she meant every word."

Santiago frowned slightly, "Now, if you still wanna see her, I gotta ask if you're gonna be nice to her or if you're gonna go in there and cross words with her. Coz I'm telling you, you not gonna do that."

"I wasn't going to."

"You were. That's why you back. We've seen every type in here before. None of you any different. If you wanted a dance tonight, you'd have asked for a dance, but you asked for Romina which means you want to talk to her again. Didn't she make it clear enough to you last night that she don't like talking?"

"I swear I won't talk. I wanted my dance last night so as you suggested, I'm back tonight for my dance."

Santiago shrugged and laughed, "Very well, you go in there and prove me wrong. You go in there for your dance it will be me throwing you straight back out again. I know your type a mile off."

"Well what type are you Santiago?" Colton asked as he handed a few scrunched up notes to the big man, who said nothing in reply and just opened the door.

Colton walked through the back rooms, found Romina's door, knocked and went in.

"Well, the Scottish man is back." Romina said immediately.

"So are you." Colton said.

"I told you last night I don't like men who talk."

"Why did you tell me all that, about freedom, and it was untrue if you're straight back here the next night?" Colton struggled to get the entire day's frustrations out in one brief sentence, hoping Romina would reveal something to him before she flipped out at him.

"Santiago! Santiago!" Romina opened her door, "Get this kid out of here!" she yelled, "and don't let him back in here again!"

Santiago walked in and crossed his arms at Colton, "You couldn't resist could you." he grizzled, "I told you, I know your type."

"I'm not a type!" Colton said.

"Oh yes you fucking are." Romina walked up to him and pointed at his chest, "You're a time wasting piece of shit, wanting me to talk about my feelings, I'm a fucking stripper, not your goddamn mother and god help her for raising a son like you. I have not got time to sit and listen to your problems and I sure as hell ain't here to answer them. Get him the hell outta here Santiago."

"And you not getting your money back either." Santiago said as he grabbed Colton by his shoulders.

As Colton lay there on the dusty ground outside the back door of the club, with his blood beginning to soak into the thirsty arid earth, he realised that Romina was right, he missed talking to his mother. He was a type. A predictable, stereotypical punter. A drunken bum. He was a money machine that wasn't agreeing to pay. And his balls ached at another night of not getting laid.

He stood up, dusted himself off and walked straight back into the strip bar.

Santiago raised almost up off the ground in incredulation when he saw him.

"I want a dance." Colton said through his crusting lip, "Doesn't matter which girl."

"You got some balls kid." Santiago said.

"I'm a paying customer."

Santiago grimaced.

"Just let him through." Carmella sighed, "He has cash to spend, so take his money and let him through!"

Santiago shrugged.

Colton was shown through to the back rooms, where Romina was just coming out of her room.

"Why is the Scottish man back?" she asked Santiago.

"He wants a dance, said it doesn't matter with who." Santiago replied.

"I will dance for him." she said, appearing annoyed at Colton's rejection of her.

Santiago sighed resignedly and walked away.

Romina took Colton's hand and guided him into her room. She encouraged him to sit on the chair at the dressing table, while she laid out two lines of cocaine on her dressing table and offered one to him, which he took readily.

Then, she crouched down on her knees and began unbuttoning his jeans. Colton sighed and closed his eyes.

Chapter Eighteen

The dawn was just beginning to break when Colton exited the strip club.

A man was standing against the wall opposite the entrance, one black booted foot leaning against the wall. His head was bowed under a flat brimmed dark hat. Colton could make out the tan colour of native Spanish skin, and a black moustache. And a grey and white poncho draped the man's shoulders while he puffed on a cigarette. He looked vaguely familiar.

"You take your time." The man said to Colton, "Been waiting for you and you take yourself a long time."

"Who the fuck are you?" Colton said aggressively.

"I been sent to watch over you. I can see now it is for good reason. The Baron has sent one of his best, the Dark Angel, to watch over you. You will come with me now."

"I ain't going anywhere with you, I've already been kidnapped twice this week thanks." Colton replied sarcastically.

"I am not here to kidnap you, but you will be coming with me."

"I've got to get home I have a horse that needs feeding."

The man raised his head and the effect was quite striking. He had black hair but glittering bright blue eyes, "The Baron wants to speak with you." the man sneered, "but this is not the man he wants to speak with, a man who visits the whore house."

"I am a weak man." Colton shrugged bitterly.

"And the Baron needs you strong. You will come with me now."

The man lowered his foot which was resting against the wall slowly to the floor to stub out his spent cigarette. There were three other cigarette butts at his feet. He had evidently been waiting for a while. He emitted a whistle and three large men appeared from around a corner. Colton looking the other way for a route to run. The man shook his head.

"Mm-mm" the man said, "Not to run. You do as I say now."

"No. I don't follow any man's orders." Colton said defiantly.

"Do not say 'no' to me." The man warned, "Well, you can try, but struggling makes it worse. You struggle, you fight, or you come of your own accord, but the outcome will be the same."

Colton lunged forward to attack the man. Had he been sober and his body clean of chemicals, he may have chosen just to walk alongside the man as the wiser option. Colton stumbled and fell over into the dirt, a used cigarette stub sticking to his lips.

"No, you do not fight the Dark Angel that has been sent to look after you. I do not think you are worth looking after, but I do not make the rules. Get up out of the dirt you good for nothing waste of space. You are annoying me already with the waste of my time. Stupid drunk white boy. Get up." The man kicked his black boot out at Colton, making contact with Colton's rib cage,

"Get up now you piece of shit. Why you couldn't stay with doing dishes at the bar like a good boy hmm?" The man kicked Colton again.

"Stop kicking me!" Colton said.

"Well get up then you stupid shit."

Colton moved to get up, "Stop calling me stupid."

"I stop insulting you when you do as I say.   Walk." The man commanded.

Colton stood staring at the man with cold contempt in his eyes. His rib cage was burning with pain from the kicks the man made at him. He grimaced with a stab of pain, which the man in front of him noticed.

"You got to toughen up white boy, that was not pain. I hate you white men, snivelling stupid pricks they are so weak and useless. Words are sent to sting you and you let them in like punches. Well here are the punches too in your ugly little face. I despise you, wasting my time." The man took a swing at Colton which impacted on his jaw line.

Colton went down onto the dusty ground again, his outstretched hands aching with the impact of landing on them.

"You bite every time like a hungry stupid little fish biting a hook, isn't your mouth full of holes yet, baited boy? Bite, bite, snap, snap each time someone says cold cruel words to you. You take each punch like a girl, like a weak little girl, get up off the dirt! I've seen braver donkeys than you, I've kidnapped braver donkeys than you, snivelling stupid little white boy."

Colton stayed on the ground. his dust covered hands reaching to his jawline which was pounding with pain.

"You are not going to make this easy for me. Stupid boy. I will make it easy for myself"

Colton was hit on the back of his head and his world went dark.

The man Colton only knew as the Dark Angel was not a kind man to Colton that day. He was tetchy at being made to wait outside a whore house in the early hours of the day, for a weak broken boy that the Baron seemed to think was worth something.

Chapter Nineteen

Colton came round lying face down on a hard black leather sofa. For a moment he thought he was back in the office of The Abattoir, then his memory returned to him of the time between then and now.

He reached for his face, grimacing with pain at his jaw and the back of his head. His eyes stung with the bright light in the room. His head was pounding.

"He is awake." a voice said nearby.

Colton looked over at the voice, it was the Dark Angel. The room was empty apart from the two of them, it was small, with two sofas, a flat screen television on the wall. One of the sides of the room was fully glazed, which was why it was so bright. There was a coffee table in front of him with a plate of food, scrambled eggs, toasted bread and tomatoes, and hot steaming coffee.

"You will eat something, then you will have a shower and get changed into new clothes, and then you will meet the Baron." The Dark Angel ordered.

"Fine." Colton said.

Colton's mood was black, he didn't want to face another beating either. He supped painfully at the coffee and ate readily, chewing through pain, but he ate every last mouthful.

The Dark Angel said nothing the whole time, just stared blankly out of the window at the street below them, looking bored. When Colton stood up after eating, The Dark Angel raised a gloved hand and pointed at a doorway, which Colton took to be the location of the bathroom.

It was tiled from floor to ceiling, containing a toilet, sink and shower, and a set of clothes were sitting on a small stool next to the shower cubicle.

Colton showered, the water was too hot and burned the cuts on his skin. He turned the water shades of brown from the blood and dust caked on his hair and body. He left his dirty clothes in a bundle on the floor next to the stool and changed into the jeans, which were a little loose, and the white long sleeved shirt left out for him.

"Better." The Dark Angel said when Colton exited the bathroom, "Now, you come this way, to talk to the Baron."

The Dark Angel stood up from the sofa, exiting the room by another door, leading into a hallway. Colton surmised they were in the corridor of some sort of hotel or office building, judging by the numerous doors on either side of them.

The Dark Angel led him to a set of stairs, ascended two flights to the top floor, and walked along the hallway to a set of double doors, he opened these into a secretary's office, which housed a secretary at a desk and two burly men guarding another set of doors behind her desk.

The Dark Angel nodded at the secretary, walking on he knocked and opened the main doors, and ushered Colton in, not entering the room himself he closed the door behind Colton. Colton found himself in a slightly larger room than the one downstairs, with the same panels of glass looking out onto the streets below them.

This room contained two black sofas, and a desk which faced the door. The Baron was sitting at the desk, with the fingertips of his hands placed together. A chair on the opposite side of the desk was empty. The Baron raised one hand and motioned at the chair, "Sit." he said.

Colton walked over and sat at the chair.

"You are quite a mess." The Baron said to him in accented English.

"No thanks to that man out there." Colton said.

"No. You have made yourself a mess." The Baron said, "A mess of a man."

The Baron shook his head solemnly.

Colton scowled, "What is it to you how I am anyway?" he asked.

"Your father would not want to see you like this." The Baron said.

"You said you knew my father, but then you have never spoken to me since."

Colton realised he'd never told the Baron that he was related to Aubrey.

"I am a busy man Colton. Very busy. My men were sent to find out what happened to Aubrey Delaney. Only recently do I know everything, and when I come to find you, you are nothing. When you first arrive at my bar, I think to myself, this boy is the son of Aubrey Delaney. And I am not mistaken. After you leave Hawick, they tried to frame you for your parents' murders, and when that did not work, they have put this onto Rose Armstrong, who has been sent to jail."

Rose Armstrong was June's best friend. Colton and her son Calvin grew up together.

"Calvin's mum? There's no way she did that! Hold on, you say "They" who do you mean exactly?" though Colton thought he already knew who the Baron was talking about.

"The Alessi brothers. They take over your town like it is their own. They kill Aubrey Delaney like he is nothing. I tell you this, Aubrey Delaney, he was more than nothing to me. He was like a brother to me."

"How's that even possible?" Colton asked.

"Que?" The Baron asked.

"How is it that you know Aubrey, my dad? I came here, to this town, at random I had no idea where I was going."

The Baron shrugged his shoulders, "Perhaps not so random. Perhaps Aubrey brought you here. Who knows. Aubrey wandered into this town the same way you did, only he was sent from men in Las Vegas to kill me when this town belonged to my padre. A misunderstanding between business associates. Once we got such … formalities … out of the way, we became good friends, and he stayed here many years."

The Baron reached into a drawer and pulled out a cigar, beginning the lighting process.

"Learning of his death made me very sad, more so when I learn he was murdered."

"I thought he died of a broken heart." Colton said miserably.

"No. June was killed first by them, and then Aubrey."

Colton gritted his teeth in anger, "I want the assholes that did this to them dead." Colton said grimly.

The Baron watched this change wash over Colton, leaning back in his chair he took a puff on his cigar.

Chapter Twenty

The Baron allowed a moment of thought filled silence to drift around the room like his cigar smoke before speaking again, "I am in the business of revenge Colton. Day after day, I see death walk in that door. I see death every day. It is my business. Your business, what you want to see happen, it is very small to me. The Alessi brothers, to me, they are nothing, small fish." The Baron leaned forward, "but it consumes you. You cannot eat properly, you are wasting away, these big strong muscles of yours that I saw the first day at the bar, they are not there anymore. You are not sleeping, your brain, it is rotting. You cannot think about anything except where your next drink is coming from. You do not leave any room in your heart for love. I could bring you one hundred thousand women and you would not delight in a single one of them. Do you think revenge will make you happy?"

Colton shook his head, "Don't think anything will."

"But it will consume you. What do you think you would do, after these men are dead?"

Colton shrugged.

The Baron leaned back in his chair and lit up his cigar again, then exhaled, tapping the box of matches on his black desk top. The air was thick and still. "I tell you what," he breathed cigar smoke into the already stifling room, "I will help you with your revenge but to do this, you will owe me a debt. Which I want paid off first, before I help."

Colton raised his eyes to meet the Baron's, "You would help me?"

"As I said, the Alessi's are very small for me, and Aubrey, he was my brother. It is you who thinks they are big men and are letting their actions kill you from the inside. They have no power here Colton, this is my town."

"I worry that there is some sort of catch to all this."

"No catch. This is a business deal and once we shake hands we will not break our promise on either side. We are men of honour, we are both in the same business. I will assist you in honouring the death of your father and mother. It will put a stop to their ridiculous notions that they are powerful in this underground world we live in. But first, you must do something for me."

"What?"

"I need you fit and strong again Colton. No more drinking, no more drugs and no more whoring. You are not in a fit state to face these men. When you are ready, I will claim your debt to me."

Colton's face went blank.

"Do not worry about this Colton, the debt, it will serve you It is no coincidence that you wander into my town, I am exactly who you need to help you.

"I have nothing left to lose." Colton said, "You have me at my last grain of trust, my last thread of hope. If I shake your hand, that is what I give you, my very last grain of trust. It may seem like nothing to you, but to me, that is everything that holds me together now. I give you all that is left of me."

"I know what this means. I have seen the look you are wearing on other men before you. I am very angry for your father. I think if you were not taking revenge yourself, I would probably get these men my own way. To me, Colton, these men are small, small fish. But I leave it to you. I wait to see a look in your eye which is not there yet."

"What do you mean?"

"Right now, I cannot see death in your eyes except for your own self. You will get the chance to kill them, perhaps at a point where you no longer think they deserve to die, or want to do so, can you do that?"

The question lingered in the cigar smoke, filling air like they were caught in a slow poisonous trap. It made it real, it made it a possibility instead of just a dark thought in his own mind. It was exposed, out in the open, and by doing that, by shining a searchlight on Colton's darkest thought, the Baron was finding out what sort of man was sitting in front of him.

Even by the length of time it took Colton to reply, by the swallow in his throat, by the rightwards glance of his eyes, to his final stare, right into the Baron's soul, which told the Baron what sort of a man Colton could become, without any words being spoken at all. Yes, it was buried very deep, beneath the drink addled mixed up kid sitting in front of him, but it was there.

"Yes I can. Though I haven't before." Colton said slowly, "An eye for an eye. Two lives for the two people they stole from me."

"You are not ready for this yet." The Baron quickly replied, "They would capture you, torture you and kill you and it would all be for nothing. You are not ready, but in time, I think, perhaps." The Baron drifted off, taking a slow inhalation of his cigar, murmuring, "Aubrey Delaney what have you brought to my door, my friend. Unfinished business, unfinished business."

The Baron turned in his chair and gazed out of the window, then looked back at Colton, "Men of honour Colton, stay to their word. Shake my hand now, and we have a deal. Or you can walk away. This is your last chance to walk away, there is no walking after this.

However it plays out, you put the wheels in motion for it here and now, and it does not stop when you think things are hard, or when things get too much for you or when you get scared, it keeps playing out till the end. If you do not want this, I understand."

When a man shakes his hand into such deals, while he says he understands what's on offer completely, more often than not, with all the actual living still to come later on, the deal usually far suprasses anything in his mind that he thought he was going to go through. But Colton, being an optimist despite himself, didn't know the worst that could possibly happen in these situations, and found himself about to place his last grain of trust straight into the Baron's outstretched hand.

The chance for revenge was a chance worth taking. The path of his life had led him to the Baron's door, on his knees, and here the Baron was, holding out his hand not only to help Colton get back on his feet, but to help him rise up and return stronger than anyone back home ever thought he could be.

Colton rose up from his chair, already feeling a stronger man, holding out his hand to the Baron. The Baron clasped it, and Colton felt a rush of anxiety pass over him. There was no going back now.

The Baron was a ruler in a criminal underworld, but he was fair in his code. There was good as well as bad in him. He chose when to tip the balance in either direction, his position in life gave him that choice. Aubrey should have been able to pass this knowledge onto his son, that was his legacy, and the Baron would have made sure the boy standing before him with tremors coursing through his body would know that. It was just up to the boy to adhere to his side of the deal and the Baron would make him the man his father would have done.

The boy was belittled by lesser demons, transient matters that consumed his thoughts. The Baron needed the boy's mind to be retrained as well as his weakened body, so that the boy was calm, focussed on his tasks, able to think straight and able to plan. Able to think on his feet when it was required of him. With this boy, the Baron was going to have to be in it for the long haul, he was not a quick fixer upper.

The Baron unclasped Colton's hand and sat heavily down in his chair, taking another inhalation of his cigar, "Go home Colton, go back to your work at the bar. I will send a man for you at the end of the week. This week you do not drink, you eat well and you go home at night to sleep. You feed your poor skinny horse, she is too thin, and you clean and wash properly. At the end of the week, I will come for you."

"Okay." Colton said, running his hand absentmindedly through his damp hair.

"Get a haircut. It does not suit you. You are free to go now."

The Baron placed his cigar in the clear glass ashtray and indicated Colton to leave with a motion of his hand.

Colton nodded at the Baron, "Thank you sir."

He got up and left the room, stepping into the brighter hallway, feeling as if the pressure of a momentous weight had lifted slightly from his shoulders.

It was not going to be easy, it wasn't going to be quick, whatever the Baron had in store for him, Colton guessed that he was going to have to prove himself. He nodded at the two burly men standing to attention outside the door and at the secretary as he walked passed her. He looked at her in more detail than he had on the way in, she was his age but he found nothing attractive or remarkable about her despite the fact she was incredibly beautiful. The Baron's words echoed in his mind, "You will never love as there is no room for it in your heart."

Colton had no desire to make room for it either. He put his hands in his jeans as he walked out of the set of double doors.

The Dark Angel was loitering in the hallway, pacing up and down smoking a cigarette.

"Your horse is tied up outside, waiting for you." he snarled at Colton, "And give her a bath you lazy son of a bitch, she stink like the whorehouse."

Colton waved acknowledgement at him and kept walking.

Chapter Twenty-One

Becky raised her head and pricked her ears forwards when she heard his familiar footsteps coming towards her. Colton took her in for the first time with an outsider's eye, and noted that she did seem to still be quite thin. And she was absolutely filthy. He'd never washed her since he got her. A wave of guilt coursed through him, one of the rare times he had felt anything at all recently.

"No room for anyone in my heart except maybe for a horse and even then I can't look after you properly." Colton said to her as he untied her reins from the lamppost she was tethered to.

He glanced up at the building he had just left, a four storey modern building, at odds with some of the older buildings nearby. He noted the street it was on and walked Becky by his side to the supermarket, where he tethered her while he went in and bought, among other items, a sack of carrots, a large bag of porridge oats, three bags of bargain basement green leaves as well as a large papaya, meat steaks and fifteen eggs. He loaded these into heavy duty bags and tied them onto Becky's saddle, while he walked by her side the long road back to the ghost town.

Once there he topped up Becky's water trough, chopped up five carrots and put these and some of the greens into a cold mix with the porridge oats into the largest bowl from the kitchen. He placed the bowl down in front of her and she snorted at the mixture, testing it tentatively with her top lip. When she raised her head to look at him questioningly, there were porridge oats stuck to her nose and chin whiskers.

"It'll build you up. It's either that or the steaks and I bought those for me." he said, "And once you've eaten that you're having a bath."

Becky pawed at the ground with her front hoof twice, then lowered her nose back into the bucket and began chomping noisily.

Colton wandered back into the kitchen. He rummaged about and found a fruit juicer tool, he squashed up two oranges plucked fresh from the yard outside, and drunk the liquid content greedily. Zingy, zesty and ultimately refreshing. He was probably lacking in every single vitamin going at that moment. His body screamed for more orange juice, then asked for a brandy instead. A half full brandy bottle stood glistening and beckoning to him further along the kitchen counter. He could taste it already, the fiery liquid that would course down his throat, warming it, the gratifying burin in his stomach and then the sweet haze of oblivion that would begin with that first satisfying sip.

Surely the Baron didn't intend for him to be completely sober the whole week. Surely he meant just for Colton not to overdo things. Not to take it to excess like he was prone to do of late. If he just toned it down a notch, that would do, surely. Colton eyed the bottle. It was going to seduce him. And who was he to resist? Who was the Baron to offer false promises and false hope to him?

Here, in the hotel, away from the Baron and his strength inducing words, Colton faced the painful truth. He was all alone and that bottle would soothe it all away. Just one for the morning, one drink to chase it all away, to put dark thoughts back into their cages where their outstretched talons would be unable to tear at him, leaving shreds of tattered memories in their wake.

The brandy bottle called again. One drink really wouldn't hurt. It would help with the shakes, he'd heard with alcohol you weren't supposed to go cold turkey as it would lead to spasms, fits and strokes. He was risking killing himself if he didn't have a drink.

A crow cawed loudly from outside, its warning cry, "caw, caw, caw, caw, caw". It was enough for Colton to break himself free from the hypnotising pull of the bottle. He went to use the bathroom instead.

Colton stood in front of the long mirror. He scrutinised himself. Unshaven, tattered hair, saggy beer belly to be ashamed of. He realised his belly had been hanging over his jeans for a while but he hid it under his loose t-shirts. He hadn't trained for a long time. There was no muscle definition in his arms. His hair was a dishevelled mess. There were long shadows under his eyes and lines on his forehead and down his cheeks where his cheeky smile used to be. His skin was pale and sallow despite the Spanish sunshine.

But the Baron thought he was worth saving?

He decided to take another shower, he set the temperature of the water up as high as he could stand it. Within moments his skin began to turn red with the heat. He relished it, feeling like the water was cleaning him inside and out. He picked up a scrubbing brush, lathering the bar of soap and cleaned as hard as he could.

Sweat, alcohol and chemicals seeped out of his every pore. He was scrubbing it all away, taking at least one layer of tired skin away with the dirty water.

His hair received the same vigourous treatment, lathered and pulled about, lots of strands washed away down the water rivulets. He guessed that was because he hadn't washed it properly in so long the dead hair was clinging to the living.

He stood, resting, leaning his hands against the tiles with his head bowed, letting the steaming water wash over him. It was a moment of calm, where he felt his problems washing away, down the drain, taking all the troubles away. He ran his hand over his flaccid cock, thinking briefly of the strip bar, but nothing stirred, it rarely did unless it was fuelled with cocaine these days. He washed there too, washing the memory of Romina away.

He brushed his teeth, ignoring his body's pleas for alcohol. He didn't drink in the shower anyway. He leaned against the tiles with his hands again. The heat of the water was finally saturating through to his cold bones. He stood there for perhaps another minute, then reluctantly stopped the shower. He grabbed the embroidered gold coloured hotel towel that was draped over the shower panel and pressed it to his skin. A clean towel against clean skin, it felt good.

He stepped out of the cubicle and walked through to his bedroom. A single solitary pair of clean trousers greeted him from his wardrobe. The rest were in a heap on the floor. Various heaps in fact. He wasn't particular about where he threw his filthy clothes.

He grimaced as he realised today was finally going to have to be wash day. Such a long neglected day that it might turn into two days. It would keep him busy, he thought as he donned the last pair of clean trousers. He struggled to button them up round his belly, that would be why they were the only clean pair, as they'd been too small for him when he bought them and he'd never thrown them away. He gave up and decided not to bother with clothes, it was a warm enough temperature that day. It wasn't like there were neighbours to embarrass with the sight of his nakedness.

He realised then that his bedroom was reeking. His bed linen was stained and desperate to be washed. He opened a window to let the air in. It felt strangely exhilarating, standing there with the warm air lapping about his skin. He hadn't noticed what a disgusting pig he'd become, it just crept up on him.

Aubrey would have been ashamed at the way his son was living, and his mum would have been… she would have been disappointed in him. It's all he ever seemed to do, was disappoint her.

Before the memory of his mum had a chance to form fully in his memory with a face filled with disappointment, Colton turned back to the room, back to the present day, and piled some of the dirty laundry onto the middle of the bed, and lifted the dirty sheet from the four corners of the bed, into a bundle. Laundry lifted successfully, he wound his way through the hotel and down into the laundry rooms. Six heavy duty washing machines gleamed back at him. He had no excuse. He had six washing machines at his disposal. Just as he always had since the day he arrived. He also had market stalls that sold clothes for one euro and a habit of wearing dirty clothes again as fuck it, what did it matter.

Colton dumped the bundle on the floor and put armfuls of clothes in each machine. Throwing some liquid detergent in, of a debatable age and switching them on to what he hoped was the right setting for his clothes. Six loads of washing, there was more on the floor in front of him and more in the bedroom. He realised it had been too easy to buy one euro clothes at the market rather than wash the ones he owned.

He walked up one flight of stairs, taking in the different temperature of the stonework in his bare feet and made his way along the hall into the main kitchen. Where his dishes lay in wait for him. Dirty dish after dirty dish after dirty dish. Flies buzzed about the room groggily. It had been too easy to just pull clean plates out of the well stocked cupboards rather than clean anything. Initially he never thought ahead that he would be staying in the hotel any length of time, and then it was fuck it, what did it matter. Now there was a mountain of dirty dishes and an unbelievable stench he had never even noticed before now.

The dishes were set hard, a mixture of mould, food, grease and god knows what. He had flashbacks of using them as ashtrays but he stopped there. He ran hot water into the three sinks and stacked the worst dishes up in the water to soak. He stacked others into the dishwashers and set them running. He grabbed a waiter's trolley and wandered round the rooms he used, gathering up the other dishes, cutlery and glasses he'd dumped there. There were quite a few broken ones.

There was never a reason to tidy before, and there was equally no reason to clean now. It didn't matter to anyone in the world what state Colton kept the hotel in, it was a forgotten place that would never be used. He could move into a smaller house on the complex and leave all the dishes where they were. But he felt marginally better making the first steps to cleaning the place. It lent him its hospitality, provided him with free board and lodgings, and all he'd done was shit all over it.

The dishes in the sinks began to give way a little when he returned to the kitchen. And the clean plates began to stack up on the draining boards.

He cursed his previous lazy self now, that he decided to clean up his outer shell, his adopted home. Clean the outside first, then the inside body, and finally his mind would follow. He would have the inner peace needed to think about planning revenge if his home wasn't festering with mould and flies, stinking with dirty laundry and plates.

He had been careful the whole time he stayed at the hotel not to use too many appliances, he remembered now that was his excuse at the start, in case it drew attention to the abandoned complex suddenly using electricity, and it was found out. He realised if it was the Baron's town, then this complex probably belonged to him as well. They all knew where to find him after all, the Dark Angel knew where to find Becky.

Becky who needed a bath too. Colton sighed and filled a bucket with soapy water, grabbed a scouring brush and found Becky outside, licking the remnants of her porridge meal from her whiskers. He filled the bucket with more oats and carrots to keep her distracted and returned outside.

She did not enjoy being bathed, but tolerated it. By the end of it, he realised he had a completely white horse, not a grey mare at all, but a shining beauty, radiating in the sunlight. She looked magnificent. He watched her for a while, then returned to the dishes waiting for him in the sink.

An hour later Colton's hands were wrinkled to beyond tolerable levels. He dried them uncomfortably on a tea towel he found in a drawer. He walked back down to the laundry room, waving his hands in the air trying to waft the wrinkles out. He found the washing machines were finished, all but one. He gathered the bundle from the nearest machine and realised there was nowhere to dry them. He looked around the laundry room, and it dawned on him that the last two washing machines looked completely different to the others. He put the wet bundle down and walked over to them, feeling the heat emanating from them on his naked skin. He realised they were tumble driers. He pulled one of the doors open and was met with a blast of stinking hot air. He'd steamed his stinking clothes in the tumble driers thinking they were washing machines. He doubled over, his lungs taking too much of that putrid stinking air into his body. He grabbed the clothes and put them hastily into the vacant washing machine, fighting a wave of nausea. Why was he putting himself through this?

Colton was desperate for another shower now. And a drink. It would make this day more tolerable. He'd never had to say no to it before. He tried to think back to a time when he'd actually said no to anything, and realised he couldn't remember any. He'd never said no. Except to his mum. That was the only time he could remember really saying no in his adult life. Over here, he'd said yes to everyone and everything that crossed his path. The liquor was just a part of that. A habit he'd never tried to break as there was no reason to.

He wondered if he enjoyed any of it at all, everything he said yes to. Of if he was trying to fill a void, but it was a black abyss that swallowed everything he fed it and asked for more, none of it made him happy. But that wasn't to say he didn't enjoy it, he loved drinking and drugs and fucking.

He sighed and went back to his washing up. There was way too much free thinking time today. What did any of it matter anyway? Did it really matter if what he did made him happy or not? It was done, it was in the past. He was putting his first step forward to meeting his fate, the very thing he had run away from for so long. It felt like a disappointed angel watching over him, showing him this great place and an opportunity, and he messed it all up. But he couldn't have faced anything else then, and he didn't know if he could face it now. Actually he knew he couldn't face anything just now, his life was a complete shambles.

It was going to take time, time to get strong again. Time to prepare. Maybe he'd wasted the last few months, or maybe it was just exactly what he needed to do to work things out and reach the point he was at now. Ready to be the Baron's bitch. He pushed that thought around, scrubbing furiously at the worn out food on the plate. He loved what he did, he loved his shambles of a life. Why did he have to stop? As some dick of a Baron said so?

Self loathing coursed through him in waves. Filthy house for a dogsbody waste of space, world's biggest loser, no one loved him, no one knew him. He hated all of them. All the people who didn't know him. Or what he'd been through. He wondered if anyone even remembered who he was. He'd only met the Alessi brothers a handful of times, would they recognise him now? What would they do if they saw him again?

The Baron's conversation resounded round his mind - "Do you think revenge will make you happy?"

Small steps. Small easy steps. Like doing the dishes, one plate at a time and the whole place would eventually be void of dirty dishes. One dish at a time. One life step at a time. He hated comparing his life to dirty dishes all of a sudden. But he was drowning in murky soap suds. His hands were wrinkled up again. The walls were closing in on him. One more plate, just one more plate. He'd be doing dishes in his sleep.

Air, he needed air. He really didn't need a drink he just needed some fresh air. Just one more plate, keep those hands busy, those wrinkly shaking hands.

Shaking hands, it could stop, it could all stop. He really didn't have to do the dishes, he really didn't have to do anything. It was his day off work for god's sake why was he wasting a beautiful day of sunshine stuck in the kitchen doing dishes. Get out of here. He could be out there on the sun terrace with a brandy in his hand right now. Someone else could do the Baron's dirty work for him, that's all it was really it wasn't about revenge it was the Baron just wanting someone else to do his work. Didn't the Baron say he could deal with the Alessi's himself anyway? Maybe he just needed Colton as a scapegoat.

Colton placed the plate on the drainer and methodically dried his hands, patting the cloth to each trembling finger individually, trying to draw the wrinkles out as well as the moisture.

He put the tea towel down and calmly walked out of the kitchen, up the flight of stairs and onto the sun terrace where a bottle of brandy stood glistening in the heat on the table top.

He lifted his shaking hands to the bottle and raised it to him, cradling it to his naked chest like a baby. It was his. It belonged to him. He turned round with it in his arms, moving in slow motion like a lover. It was his love. Turning the bottle to face the sunshine, away from the kitchen, away from the prying eyes of the vacant hotel windows.

He sat down at the table, placing the bottle down on the surface slowly, like a valuable priceless antique heirloom. It was his dream. Slowly he unscrewed the cap and carefully placed the cap on the table.

This was the greatest seduction of them all, the banished lover, the one he was supposed to say no to, but just could not resist one last, intimate time together. A shiver ran down his spine as he leaned closer to the bottle. He tilted it slightly towards him and inhaled the heady scent of his lover's perfume, running his nose up her neckline. One last time. It had to be the last time. His body ached for her, craved to taste her, just one taste upon his lips, her kisses would be so sweet. His and his alone. No one would ever know. They weren't hurting anyone. Oh sweet temptation.

He groaned with pleasure and ran the tip of his tongue around the rim of the bottle. It was too much to resist her, he belonged to her. He lifted the bottle to his mouth and took one small sip. But it wasn't enough. The sweet nectar ran down his throat and he ached for more. He took a large gulp, his thirst overwhelming him. It would never be enough. He put the bottle down and stood up quickly, slamming his chair back and strode away from the table. He was disgusted with himself, he was so weak. He ran away from the sun terrace, down the steps into the gardens, stopping by the pond. He knelt down and splashed water on his face.

It tasted so good, he could still feel the burn from her kisses all the way down his throat. He leaned over and peered at the ripples on the pond water, which calmed and formed his reflection, "You are a weak man." the reflection said to him. He moved his hand to brush it away and gazed at his hands, the tremors had stopped. His heart was no longer racing, he didn't ache and knawe at himself for the taste of the liquor. Maybe he did need to wean himself off it slowly.

"You are a weak man." The reflection settled and said back to him again.

Maybe he just needed to get laid, work some of his frustrations out on a hooker. Colton picked himself up and went back to the hotel. He showered quickly, squeezed into the tight jeans, threw on a t-shirt from the dirty piles on the floor, picked up his half bottle of brandy as he left and began the walk into town, to the dark side of the streets, which was always open to him. Romina was there.

After a double brandy and two lines of coke, he smacked his hand off her naked taut backside, over and over again, thrusting inside her until he was spent and done. He buttoned up his jeans, saying nothing to her on his way out, and left the room. He stood in the hallway for a moment, which led back to the main room, "Fuck it." he muttered, turning and walking back into the room he'd just left.

He threw more money on the dresser and Romina arched an eyebrow at him in surprise but said nothing. Colton moved his head and eyes to the bed. Romina got up and lay herself back down, while Colton unbuttoned his jeans and lowered them to the floor, not bothering to fight the denim tangle from his feet. He thrust as hard as he could, wanting to go deeper and deeper, his feet pawed at the base of the bed in the tangle of jeans as he strove to get grip good enough to go as deep as he desired. Romina held his ass, squeezing it in rhythm to his thrusts. He felt her orgasm around him, he groaned with pleasure as gasps of delight escaped her. Then it was over.

"You're one of the few men who can do that to me." Romina smiled as he got back up.

"You talk too much." he replied, smiling.

She probably said that to everyone but it made Colton feel like a king. He buttoned himself up and walked out, through the bar out into the light of day outside. He was who he was, the Baron could go fuck himself.

Chapter Twenty-Two

The next thing Colton was aware of was that he was in an enclosed space, curled up and bound. He was in complete darkness, and his face was wet. The liquid was warm on his face, it was his own blood, he realised as the taste reached his tongue, saturated through a foul tasting rag that was stuffed in his mouth.

He was in the boot of a car, he could tell because now that his senses were slowly returning to him, he could hear and feel the rumbling of a diesel car engine bumping along rough roads.

He remembered being told that if he ever found himself tied up and trapped in the boot of a car, which, coincidentally he seemed to be at this point in time, they recommended kicking the corner lights out and waving a hand or other free limb out of the hole so that some passer by or other driver would see him and get help. Colton's hands and legs were too tightly bound to even attempt it.

Panic began to set in when he realised he was completely trapped and powerless to do anything about where he was or where they were taking him. His breathing quickened till he was hyperventilating, all the while breathing in that foul tasting rag stuck in his mouth, which was simultaneously drying out his throat, and he began to sweat profusely.

A flashbacks hit him, four men had grabbed him on his walk home from town, after he left the strip bar.

The car lurched as they turned a corner, then it began to slow down, onto a rougher road, with more potholes. Colton bumped his already painful head each time the car drove over another hole.

Colton's head hurt so much that along with the leftover remnants of the cocaine, he grew just plain pissed off with it all. It had to be the

Baron, testing him, no one else would kidnap him, he hardly knew anyone and he didn't think he'd pissed anyone off enough to warrant a kidnapping and murder. Though a few people possibly could have wanted to murder him in the past. He didn't rule out the fact that just because he wasn't dead yet didn't mean the Alessi's weren't still planning on killing him.

The car slowed to a stop. Colton clearly made out the sound of the doors opening, crunching boots walking to the boot and opening the boot hatch. The sudden light hitting his eyes caused him to wince in pain. Two arms, thick burly arms hauled him out. He'd been hauled about by those arms before. They belonged to Santiago, the bouncer from the strip bar, what the hell was Santiago doing kidnapping him? The arms suddenly dropped him. Colton landed with a thud on the dusty desert ground.

Santiago pulled the gag out of Colton's mouth. His jaw ached, he couldn't scream even if he wanted to, pain was seeping into his jawline where the rag had been tied too tight and his throat was coarse with drying out. He looked around desperate to get a handle on his surroundings and any possible means of escape. He was sitting on his bum on dusty earth, in the middle of a rustic farm courtyard. There was a white farm house nearby, outbuildings, and the whole place was surrounded by a tall whitewashed wall. The gate behind the car was shut and guarded by two men. He couldn't see the land beyond the farm, just hills in the distance.

"A little bird tells me we are expecting trouble from a wriggly worm that really should know better by now." a voice behind Colton spoke, which he recognised as belonging to the man who called himself the Dark Angel.

Colton frowned and looked at Santiago for help, who at that moment was a blank expressionless tower of stupor.

"You should know better little wriggly worm." the Dark Angel said, wagging his finger at Colton.

Colton couldn't help himself, he laughed. Maybe the ominousness of the threat was lost in translation, but he suddenly found the whole situation hilarious. That was their threat, a little bird and a wriggly worm? It was kids stuff. What were they all, five years old?

"What's so funny Mr Cooper?" the Dark Angel asked, peering at him from under the shadow of his black brimmed hat.

The Dark Angel leaned forward and pulled the rag out of Colton's mouth.

"Is that the best you can do?" the hoarse words slipped out with a choke of laughter. Laughter derived from the hysteria of being kidnapped and locked in a car boot and potentially about to be killed.

"Mr Cooper this is a warning to you, I would not be finding the laughing so easily much. This time we are kidnapping you."

Colton laughed again, he really must take the little wriggly worm analogy seriously. Peck Peck Peck, Cheep Cheep Cheep.

"Cheep Cheep." Colton replied, "What are you doing wasting your time kidnapping me for?"

"As you are already know, you made a deal with the Baron."

"Never heard of him." Colton sniffed, "Next time he comes into the bar where I work he should make sure he introduces himself properly." Colton wasn't giving anything away to this madman.

"You should not mock me Mr Cooper." The Dark Angel shifted weight on his feet, he was becoming agitated.

"Well, you seem to think of me as some sort of dangerous mastermind or something, kidnapping me when I was just minding my own business. Santiago here will be able to tell you I'm a good for nothing loser that likes to drink, take drugs and screw hookers. Believe me I'm not worth all this effort you're going to."

Now that he was out of the cramped car boot space Colton was able to work on the ropes binding his wrists behind his back, they were beginning to cut into his skin, he felt them loosen a little, it gave him hope. He just had to keep them talking but not agitate them so much that they would kill him too quickly.

The Dark Angel looked at Santiago, who spoke his words of wisdom for the day, "This kid's a pain in the ass. World's biggest loser."

That stung Colton a little, being judged as a worthless nobody by Santiago the Bouncer of the strip club. Colton blinked briefly, then felt the force of the Dark Angels black boot in his chest. He coughed and fell forward, taking in a mouth full of the dusty ground. World's biggest loser's worst day ever. Except when his parents died. Yeah, he'd had worse than being kidnapped by Angels and Bouncers.

The Dark Angel cleared his throat, his men recognised that he was cranking up a gear. Colton had no idea what was about to happen but he sensed a change of atmosphere in the air. The Dark Angel wasn't given this task for nothing, he had years of experience under his belt for breaking an already broken spirit, his task was to snap Colton out of the spiral of destruction he'd started and right him again. His methods were not orthodox. But he was the best at what he did in his world, and he knew what he needed to do when he observed the comment from Santiago stinging the drunken cocky coked up boy sitting in the dirt in front of him.

He saw the flit of emotion dance briefly across Colton's features, and he knew then that he could save Colton, but he would have to break him first. He owed it to Aubrey Delaney to save his only son, and he needed the son of Aubrey Delaney on his feet, as it was the closest thing to having Aubrey Delaney himself there, who the Dark Angel knew as one of the best criminal masterminds he had ever come across. He also knew that Aubrey would approve of what was about to happen to his son and that gave him strength in his convictions. Redemption from the Dark Angel was a still however, a rather rough path to salvation.

Chapter Twenty-Three

"The sins of the father are repeated by the son. Didn't you learn from your padre's mistakes? No, you're sort never do. You just keep repeating the same mistakes over and over again. Yes, you are an exact replica of him. A snivelling, stupid little white boy." The Dark Angel snarled.

Colton smarted at the mention of Aubrey in such a derogatory way, tears forming immediately in his eyes at the mention of his father. The Dark Angel knew then, absolutely, that he was taking the right course of action with Colton.

"Here I am, hurting your feelings, breaking your spirit. Go home to cry but there's no one there, so cry, cry in a corner lost little boy. You are not a man. Don't you care who killed your father and mother? Don't you want to get strong enough to get revenge?"

"My father had a heart attack." Colton said from his knees on the ground.

"No, your father was murdered. He was poisoned. Have you pushed that out of your coked up little mind already? He suffered, he died in agony after finding out his woman was killed. And this is how his son becomes."

The Dark Angel pushed Colton back over into the ground, holding his face in the dirt.

"I cannot make a simple man of you let alone one borne of revenge. I am wasting my time. The Baron has placed a broken bet on you. I should feed you to my dogs and rid the world of one less snivelling white boy. You can't even help yourself, look at you! Hookers, cocaine, brandy and you care for nothing. You can't do anything except fuck and vomit and shit and drink. Get down in the dirt where you belong, and stay there stupid little white boy."

Colton groaned with pain.

"Your stupid skinny horse, also good for nothing, I will feed you both to my dogs. Santiago, get my pistol I will go shoot the useless horse. She takes up space in our stables and kicks the place to bits."

"No!" Colton said, leaning upwards, fighting the boot placed on his back, "Don't you touch her!"

The Dark Angel looked down at Colton, shadows flitting across his face from the brim of his hat, "I have no plans to touch the flea ridden animal, that is why I use my gun and leave my dogs to clean up the mess."

"No! You let me go. I didn't ask to come here, I didn't ask you to take me or my horse anywhere."

The man stared down at him, "You will not defend your own honour, or your father's honour but you defend the honour of a horse?"

"She doesn't deserve to die, she's done nothing wrong." Colton looked down at the Dark Angel's boots as looking at his face, silhouetted by the sun, hurt his eyes.

"But you deserve to die?"

"I have no reason to live." Colton replied.

"Then perhaps you need to live to stop me from killing your horse, huh?" The man laughed.

"Just let her go."

"My dogs need feeding. I will not let a good meal wander off to die in the desert. Santiago where is my gun? I ask you to bring me my gun like six minutes ago."

"It's here boss." Santiago walked over and presented a gun to the Dark Angel.

Colton noticed that Santiago held another in his hands, setting a cold chill running through his body.

"Gracias, Is it loaded now, yes?"

"Si."

The Dark Angel promptly opened up the barrel and dropped four bullets out of the six chambered gun, "One for your horse, and one for you." he clicked the barrel shut and spun it round, "Santiago bring me that flea ridden horse."

Colton cowered in a heap, he was going to die. He deserved to die, but Becky didn't. He saved her at the market and now he was bringing about her death. Colton recognised the steady hoof beat as it came within hearing range. His heart was racing. That asshole was about to shoot his horse. For no reason. If he was quick enough, maybe he could jump on Becky's back and ride them both out of there away to safety., he worked again at the ropes round his wrists.

"The Baron promised me a fearless man." The Dark Angel chided, "A man worth saving, a man worthy of being the son of Aubrey Delaney and I get a snivelling coked up little wretch. Your mother must have been very stupid, you must take after her, yah."

Colton clenched his fists. He heard the gun click, and from under his arms he saw the Dark Angel take aim at Becky's head. She looked down at Colton on the ground with her big brown eyes, pricking her ears forward with curiosity. With a final painful jolt, Colton freed his hands from the ropes, he grabbed a fist full of dirt and leaped up, throwing the dirt into the Dark Angels face, yelling with a guttural rage as he did so. He grabbed Becky's reins from the hands of Santiago who was still processing his boss shouting in pain, and with one movement had wrenched the gun from Santiago's hand. He aimed the gun at the Dark Angel who was smiting his eyes, rubbing them furiously, unable to see.

Colton turned and leaped onto Becky's bare back, kicking her urgently she broke into a gallop and they sped away from the entrance with the armed guards, heading towards the farmhouse, where Colton thought there had to be a back gate somewhere. Colton rounded the house and saw it, a small latch gate too high for Becky to jump. He jumped off Becky's back and strode forward to unlatch the gate.

A woman's voice caught his attention, "Take a step further and I shoot you."

Colton span round and saw looking down onto the gate from a top window, a middle aged woman with dark hair and blazing brown eyes glaring down at him through the sight of a double barrelled shot gun, "Don't think I no' know how to shoot, my husband he teach me."

Then The Dark Angel and Santiago were coming towards Colton and Becky, Colton narrowed his eyes, "I can take one of you out with me, so I'll take the woman at the window, you hit me and I hit you. I might be dead but you will lose your wife in the process."

"You are a piece of shit, white boy." The Dark Angel spat.

"You should have let me go."Colton cocked the pistol, the woman was moments away from pulling the trigger of the shotgun.

"Then we are at an impasse." The Dark Angel said.

"Don't shoot my horse and I won't shoot your wife."

"She is not my wife she is my sister." The Dark Angel snarled.

"My husband is dead." The woman said with anger and pain in her voice.

Colton turned his head to look at her, hell he'd managed to piss her off too, husband, brother, who knew. There was something there in her face though, it carried the same haunted shadows under her eyes as his did.

"Who killed him?" Colton asked, he didn't know why, in that moment of a life or death standoff, he attempted to communicate with the woman and exchange a dialogue about the pain of losing people you love.

"White men from Scotland."

Colton's eyes widened, "The Alessi's." he heard himself saying.

The woman looked suspiciously down at him from the window, "You know these men?"

"They killed my father." Colton said.

"And you do not seek revenge?"

"Six minutes ago he tells me his father died of a heart attack Marta, he is a stupid white boy." The Dark Angel snarled up at his sister.

"I do not want to live." Colton replied.

"And yet you are still alive." Marta muttered, "Esteban, you must let this boy live, I wish to speak with him." she ordered her brother.

"What? Marta no! Can I just kill his horse instead?"

"No!" she said, "Bring the white boy inside, and leave his horse alone."

"God damn Marta, the horse kick everything." The Dark Angel Esteban glowered.

"You never let the boy talk! All you did was talk talk talk at him you didn't let him tell his story. All your threats. Well maybe he will talk to me. Bring him inside. And put his horse in the stable, and for gods sake someone give it some food it is such a thin horse."

The Dark Angel looked like any other brow-beaten brother who had been told to stop playing his favourite game. Colton reluctantly handed Becky's reins to his outstretched hands.

"I am watching you white boy, we are not finished business with each other." Esteban said.

Chapter Twenty-Four

Colton followed Esteban to the front of the house and into the front door which had been opened for him. He turned to the left through an open door into a stone floored kitchen, where Marta was now sitting at the large chunky wooden table. She had a bottle of brandy and two glasses sitting in front of her.

"They said I had to stay sober." Colton said warily, eying the glass nervously and hungrily.

Marta shrugged, "They tell me this too. I tell them 'Fuck You, you never lost your husband, I drink the brandy and you shut the fuck up."

Marta handed Colton a glass. He felt the edge of a smile on his mouth, hungry for the taste of the liquor in the bottle. Marta unstopped the cork and poured the caramel coloured liquid into his glass, a generous measure.

"Stand in the light, let me look at you." Marta said.

Colton moved over to the window. Marta nodded, "Yes, you are the son of Aubrey Delaney." she said taking her first drink.

"Did you know him?"

Marta nodded, "Yes I knew him"

"Both my parents are dead." Colton said, knocking the brandy back in one gulp.

Marta did the same and poured them both another measure.

"The Baron says they were murdered by the Alessi brothers." Colton said, "Though I tell everyone it was a heart attack as I can't bear to think about what happened."

Marta nodded sympathetically, "The Alessi family, they kill my husband and they kidnap my little girl."

The brandy soothed Colton's jarred nerves. From a matter of hours ago when he'd taken his steps out of the whore house, his head had been pounding, now it found its solace with the brandy in front of him.

"The Baron wanted me sober." Colton said guiltily, looking at the drink.

"And you will be." she smiled, "Just not today."

Colton considered how attractive she was when she smiled. She held his gaze.

"He wanted me fit for revenge."

He felt brave around Marta, like he could confide in her all of his deep secrets as she bled from the same wound.

"My brother, he says you are a weak man, that he cannot train you, that you are good for nothing but fucking and drinking." Marta said, laughing a little.

Colton looked at his glass.

"Maybe my brother doesn't need a fucking white boy, but his sister sure does." Marta smiled and topped up Colton's glass.

He looked up at her in surprise. She picked up the bottle and stood up, saying, "Come." to him, in a command he could not disobey and she led him upstairs to her bedroom, "Let me see if drinking is the only thing you are good at."

Colton wholly didn't know what in God's name was going on in this crazy day. He wasn't even sure it was really happening to him at all. He followed the older Spanish woman up a wooden staircase and down a hall into a light airy bedroom.

Marta placed the bottle and her glass on the bedside table. She lowered her dress to the floor and lay naked on the covers. Colton closed the bedroom door behind him. He walked over and lay down next to her in bed, taking in her darker skinned body. He took a drink from his brandy glass, which she moved to the side table and straddled him, unbuttoning his jeans. She looked at him with hostility in her eyes, he knew it wasn't directed at him but at the world that had taken her family away from her, her purpose for existing. The same need was in both of them, the same empty void that they could never fill, tormented by frustrations, an endless hunger and bottomless anger. Marta cried and whispered another man's name when they were entwined together.

"My brother will teach you." she said when it was over and her head was resting on his shoulder, "Your revenge is buried deep in your heart but it is there, and he can draw it out of you. We will both make a man of you in our own way." she smiled, stroking his chest.

Her touch sent shivers down Colton's spine, he nodded and she turned his head towards her own and kissed him, "Again." she commanded.

When he woke up the bed was empty. He took the last measure from the brandy bottle and drank thirstily from the glass, then donned his clothes and went downstairs. Marta was preparing food at the kitchen table.

"You do not speak of this to my brother." she said, pointing her knife at him, "My brother, he taught Aubrey how to fight like us, he taught him what it was to be a brave and fearless man. But he will kill you if he knows you touched me. To us, we both know, what happened means nothing between us. But he will not see it that way." she began to scrape chopped meat into a pan on the hob.

"I understand." Colton said.

It was the same as fucking a whore, Colton understood that. Only Marta was incredibly beautiful while she was with him, she was a broken creature trying to fix herself with the same unholy medicines he used, while the whore's were blank faces who were counting down the minutes waiting for their payment. He could barely resist walking over to the stove where she had her back to him, bending her over the kitchen table and finding that moment of escape again with her. He barely registered that Marta had just told him Aubrey had learned to fight from the Dark Angel. He was jarred from his thoughts as the front door opened and male voices came into the kitchen from the hallway.

Esteban looked at him, "I do not want the white boy eating with us." he said to Marta who hadn't turned round.

"Well send him away then, I'm done speaking to him for now." she shrugged, turning to face them with a chopping board and knife in her hands.

"You will go and sleep next door in the guest quarters. Someone will bring you a meal when it is ready. There is a wash room in there." Esteban said, "You will rise early tomorrow and we will talk then."

Colton nodded and left the room, he made his way out of the farmhouse and into the guest quarters, a separate building set just apart from the farmhouse. Inside was a single room, containing a bed made with plain sheets, two soft backed chairs with a small table between them, a unit with a small television resting on it, and a bathroom to the rear. Colton walked through to the bathroom, threw his clothes off and stepped into the shower. As the hot water washed over him, stinging both old and new wounds at once, he realised he had absolutely no idea what tomorrow would bring, but he was experiencing an unfamiliar feeling of relief and even gratitude at being alive for the very first time in months. A kidnapping and potential shooting would do that to a man. He knew that Marta just somehow saved his life, he owed her big time. Two tears slid down his face and mingled with the shower water. It had been a long day.

While he was in the shower he heard a knock at the door, which he ignored. When he stepped out of the bathroom a tray of food was sitting at the small coffee table, some sort of meat paella, it smelled delicious. He ate it ravenously then went to bed, utterly exhausted.

Chapter Twenty-Five

Colton couldn't understand what he was watching on the news on the little buzzing television screen in the farmhouse kitchen. He was crushing oranges to make fresh juice for everyone, watching the Spanish news, and there were images of guns, knives, and bulletproof vests, and the scrolling text bar at the bottom of the screen definitely displayed the name of the neighbouring town of Cartagena.

Esteban came down the stairs in a white vest and jeans, rubbing the three day stubble gathering round his established moustache, yawning.

"Hey, Esteban, can you tell me what this is saying please?" Colton pointed at the screen, "There's images of guns and they're talking about Cartagena."

"Shut up then white boy and I will be able to hear it." Esteban snapped at him.

Esteban was not a cheerful early riser. Esteban took three cups of strong fresh coffee each morning before he would return to his usual insulting but more awake self.

"This is bad." Esteban said after the programme cut to a commercial of a woman jogging, which seemed to be an advert for incontinence pads.

"What's going on?" Colton asked.

"We will need to speak to the Baron about this. There has been a raid on a hotel in Cartagena, they have arrested six Scottish men from Galashiels."

"That's near where I'm from." Colton said surprised.

"Yes, they were sent to carry out a job, the Policia know from their intelligence."

"A job? You mean a killing?"

"Si."

"Do you have any idea who they were aiming for?"

"Si, with any luck they would be aiming for you." Esteban said only half jokingly, taking a sip of his coffee with visible relief, "The Baron will know for sure. If it is you, then we are all in danger. Maybe they are after him, but most dumb low life white men don't even know he exists. Come. No time for training today, we eat on the way, police will be making their moves too and we must be ahead of them."

Colton had been at the farm for a several weeks now, to his reckoning. Esteban took him out each morning for training, they and the four guards including Santiago jogged along tracks laid out around the farm, with training rings and jumps laid out along them. On returning to the farm, Marta would give them breakfast, after which they would go out into the yard and shoot guns at targets. Colton was allowed a brief respite for lunch then Esteban would continue with physical combat training. Colton realised this was where Aubrey's inspiration came from for the fight club. They didn't talk about Aubrey, Esteban wanted to keep Colton's mind focussed away from the pain of his past. Marta did not seduce him again, nor were there any visible alcohol bottles around the house after that first day. She mostly kept to herself, doing housework, tending to the garden or shopping for them all.

No one would tell Colton why they were training him, but this gun raid seemed to be a call to action for Esteban, cutting the training shorter than planned.

Colton found himself riding in the front of the car to return to visit the Baron.

Chapter Twenty-Six

"Mr Cooper." The Baron frowned at him, "The Dark Angel has taken care of you I see you have regained some of your muscle. Not much. But you are improved a little."

Esteban and Colton were standing in the Baron's office.

The Baron motioned both of them to take a seat.

"We saw gun raids on the television, people from near where I'm from were arrested by police, over here, to do a job on someone." Colton began.

The Baron held up his hand gently to stop him, "I am aware of this, it was a set-up to flush us out. I have more contacts in the Guarda over here than the Alessi brothers know." A wry smile flashed the corners of his mouth, "Those fools think they can come over here and start swinging their weight about. I was merely lying low and biding my time, watching the moves they make. Which brings me to the job I want you to do." The Baron crossed his hands on his desk, "Colton I expect you to bring back Marta's daughter from where the Alessi's men are holding her."

Esteban widened his eyes, "You know where she is?"

The Baron moved his eyes to look at Esteban, "I have only recently found out. Hence why the Alessi's send their men with guns, to scare us into acting. Their arrogance annoys me like an irritating fly, I have allowed them to buzz round my head for too long and now it is time to swat them, and crush them like the little flies they are. This is my town and the men that side with the Alessi's have forgotten their respect. Yes, I know where she is. She is being held in an apartment block on the West Side of Cartagena, Alessi's only outpost here. They want more and more, they are greedy. I do not like greedy men. This is how they behave, they take the children to turn them against their mothers, the husbands die, the brothers spirit dies and they give up, Alessi's own them, and then, they own the town."

Colton understood enough that the Baron was implying Esteban and Marta directly, but was also talking about his people and his towns.

The Baron continued, "Colton, you are to go to the apartment where they are holding Sofia, with the Dark Angel, and you are to take my guns, and you are to shoot them all dead."

"It's a suicide mission." Esteban said.

"The Dark Angel never speaks of suicide!" The Baron said sharply, "If there is no one here by that name, then it is only Colton Cooper, son of El Rey Blanco, who goes on this journey alone." The Baron challenged them both.

Esteban sat back in his chair and bit his lip.

"You tell me it can't be done?" challenged the Baron.

"Maybe once, I could do this, but now?" Esteban replied, "With only him?" indicating Colton.

"They will have her hooked to a drip feeding her drugs already, and you tell me you will not risk your life and his for hers? Whose life do you value more, Sofia's or yours?"

"I'll do it on my own." Colton heard himself saying, "If it's a suicide mission, I'll go in there myself, hopefully enough to shake things up for you, then you can make another move after that."

The Baron laughed, "He has his father's bravery as well as his foolishness."

"I will not let him go on his own to save her, what will her mother say if I am not the one holding the gun that rescues her, but the white boy?" Esteban said.

"You have talked each other into it I see." The Baron said, "That took considerably less time than I thought it would." The Baron switched on a television screen to his right, which displayed a Google Map street view of a small dusty street of white washed buildings.

"Okay, here is the plan, you are going to make your way to another apartment on the street by an underground tunnel, which begins inside this house here, which the Alessi brothers do not know about, and their men have not bothered to tell them about because none of them know this town as well as I do, I keep her secrets." he moved the street view, "The tunnel comes out here." he gestured, "Then you will move along to the front door, the back is heavily guarded, they expect an attack from the rear, you will not do this, it is the coward's way. You come in through the front door and you shoot your way through. You have the element of surprise until the first shot is fired, I would suggest you use the bullet wisely."

The Baron paused and sighed, "You will have perhaps ten minutes to find her before the guardia arrive. I cannot delay them any more than this as I do not want the Alessi brothers to know I have contacts in the force, any further delay will arouse suspicion. And you can only take her, not any others you may find there."

Colton swallowed air in his throat, "How many men are holding her?"

"Ten, maybe twelve at most." The Baron shrugged, "It changes."

"I've never killed anyone before." Colton said quietly.

"I know." The Baron said, "And if you want your revenge the first men you shoot at cannot be the Alessi's. You may no' succeed, you may get shot, you may be taken prisoner and tortured. This is why Esteban shows fear, he knows what he walks into. He want more men with him. He want any man with him, except you. He has no faith in you, now why could that be?"

Colton looked at Esteban, who was sitting slumped in his chair with his chin lowered, sucking his lower lip angrily.

"Have you no' taught him how to shoot, while he has stayed with you, Esteban?" The Baron asked.

"Si Seňor."

"And have you no' taught him how to take pain?"

"Si Seňor." Esteban replied.

"So is he fit for the job, or no'?"

"Si Seňor." Esteban acknowledged reluctantly.

"Colton?" The Baron turned, "Are you fit for the job?"

Colton raised his head and looked the Baron straight in the eye, and said, "I'm a Teri frae Hawick sir, and we don't go down till we're dead."

The Baron laughed, "I'm beginning to like you a bit more. No' so much when you first arrived but now, I think, I see a bit more of your padre in you. We are all involved in this job already, Colton, it is just you who pulls the trigger, I no' just sending you out there alone, there are other players. If any of us fail at any time this whole thing is ruined and Sofia is as good as dead."

"Why aren't we saving any of the other girls?" Colton asked.

"They are no' your concern and may well be plants. In the long run, the traffic operation will cease when we overthrow the Alessi's. Time is short now, I would suggest you gather your guns and get moving."

Esteban took his leave and stood up, "Si Seňor."

"The Dark Angel may remember where his silenced wings were left for him at such times as he was required to fly." The Baron added.

Esteban turned and looked at him, he nodded his understanding.

"They will not take my town." The Baron said, "It is time to fight back."

Chapter Twenty-Seven

Colton and Esteban stepped out of the office building, into the light of day, Colton feeling as if eyes from every window were suddenly watching him, aware of what had just been discussed in the Baron's office. Esteban was cool as a cucumber beside him.

This was grim. This was not what Colton wanted to be doing. But here he was, events taking their path, spiralling out of his control. He was just a pawn in a game. It needed more thought, it needed planned through, down to minute details, but Esteban was leading him intently through the streets, saying very little.

Stepping out of the cloud filled air in the Baron's office, into the heat of the day outside, reality began to seep into Colton's lungs. What the hell had he got himself into? He was just a pawn in the Baron's game, expendable, on this suicide mission. That's what Esteban had called it, and Colton trusted Esteban's call on it. God he needed a drink.

"Stop at this bar, and we have a drink." Esteban said, looking at Colton out of the corner of his eye, "You just licked your lips like you want wan."

"Did I?" Colton said, stopping outside the bar, which was a small open-windowed bar with only a few wooden stools inside, and fresh sawdust around the street area. He searched his pockets for change.

"God damn penniless white boy, he has no money." Esteban said.

"You took all my money off me so I couldn't bribe your guards to buy me drink." Colton replied.

"Well, even I want wan now." Esteban said, indicating to the barman for two shots and laying some coins on the counter.

They downed the liquid in the glasses in silence.

"Another." Colton said.

Esteban raised an eyebrow at him but ordered two more shots.

"Enough now." Esteban asked.

Colon nodded agreement, though no amount of alcohol was enough right then.

Esteban walked them through nameless alleys and down stairwells, only once did Colton notice Esteban glancing over his shoulder. Then Esteban was whisking the door of a basement open and motioning Colton quickly inside. Colton tripped downwards, reaching out and grabbing a wooden banister in the dark, "Mind the steps." Esteban chuckled.

Esteban pulled a cord which operated a single dim lightbulb, illuminating a set of steps leading down into a small basement room. Esteban and Colton walked down the steps, into the room, then Esteban opened a cupboard door at the back. The cupboard was filled with old blankets. Esteban reached behind these and flicked some sort of switch, the cupboard swung open as a whole, revealing a cave like area, hewn into the rock, with black cases resting on shelves inside it.

Esteban pulled a case out of the shelved area, placing it on a table and opened it. Inside were two handguns, "My wings" Esteban said, "I have no' seen these for a long time."

Colton looked at them.

"Tech Twenty-Two Scorpions." Esteban said, picking one up and testing the familiar weight in his hand.

"You should call them the sting in your tail then?" Colton suggested.

Esteban just glowered at him.

"Scorpions? Stinging?"

Colton went quiet. Part of him was already running up the stairs and out of the door into the light outside. But he was still standing down here in the dim semi-darkness with a crazed spaniard holding an automatic gun in his hands, "So, what, do we get one each?" he asked

"No, we have two each. Two guns, thirty rounds each, that gives us one hundred an' twenty bullets."

"Should be a piece of cake then. Twelve guys, one hundred and twenty bullets." Colton said.

"You are getting shot at, the whole time." Esteban explained.

"No bullet proof vests in your cupboard then?" Colton asked.

"No."

"Can't we sit down and plan this?" Colton asked.

"If the Baron says there is no time, then there is no time." Esteban put the gun down on the casing, reached into the cave and pulled out another case. He opened it, loading the guns inside with a round, he handed the guns to Colton.

He explained to Colton how they differed from the guns he'd been training with, then reached into the wardrobe of blankets and pulled one of the middle ones out, white with a red triangular shaped pattern, dusting it off, Colton realised they were Ponchos, "You will need to wear this to hide the guns on the street."

Colton figured out a way to tuck the heavy guns into his jeans and pulled the poncho over his head. Esteban took the hat from his head and placed it onto Colton's.

"I do not like you wearing my hat, it is not an honour. But you are standing out like a tourist with your white skin in a poncho." Esteban explained.

Esteban placed a yellow patterned poncho over his head, put the cases back onto the cave shelf and closed the wardrobe, it clicked, and he closed the door. He then scuffed the dirt on the cellar floor to hide where the wardrobe had slid open.

"Remember I value her life above mine. If I get shot, you leave me behind, you get her safe." Esteban said.

Colton nodded.

Esteban led them outside, opening the door carefully then stepping quickly out on the street into a quick walk, a pace that implied they had been walking along the street for a while, rather than just coming out of a basement. Colton had to quicken his own footing to keep up with him. The sun was just beginning to get high in the sky, beating down on Colton through the thick poncho.

They walked for about ten minutes, then Esteban took a sharp left turn and briskly walked into the gateway leading to a back yard. It was a short cut or a diversion to deter anyone possibly following them. He took another sharp left out onto a street, across the dusty road and straight into a ramshackle looking two storey building.

Once inside, Colton's eyes adjusted to the light, "This is where the tunnel begins." Esteban whispered, "From here, we do not talk to each other, only signals, like this." he indicated with his hands pointing to his face.

"I don't really know any sign language." Colton said.

Esteban frowned at him, "We will have to communicate with our eyes Colton, in our hands will be guns going off, like this, pap, pap pap." Esteban gestured with two fingers and his thumb pointed at invisible enemies.

"Right, okay." Colton replied warily.

"You are no' ready for this." Esteban shook his head, "You are going to get us both killed with your ignorance."

"I am not ignorant." Colton hissed.

"Yes you are stupid white trash. You are no help to me here. I will have to watch your back as well as my own."

"If you spend all your time looking at my back you won't find your niece will you?" Colton replied angrily, "I'd suggest you use your eyes to look for her instead of using them to scowl at me, especially if there are people firing at us."

The corner of Esteban's moustache twitched, "Take my hand Colton Cooper, son of El Rey Blanco, and when you take it, know you are going to dance with the Dark Angel today. If we get out of this alive, then you will have my respect for the rest of your ugly little life."

Esteban clenched Colton's hand in his, then embraced him very briefly, giving him a meaningful slap on the back. Colton found himself doing the same in return.

"But I will still hate you until then."

"That's fine."

"Especially if you get me killed."

"I swear I won't get you killed Esteban."

"Then you shoot to kill every fucker in there Colton, do not hesitate, do not look them in the eye and question yourself. Your pull that trigger fast."

Colton nodded.

"Are you ready?" Esteban said, he pulled out one of his guns and drew back the bolt action, readying the Scorpion for firing.

Colton did the same, he was scared shitless but nodded in response.

Esteban pulled open a door in the hallway, led Colton down to a dimly lit basement, turned to the right and pulled aside a curtain underneath the staircase, which revealed a tunnel, only wide enough for one man at a time. Colton had to crouch slightly to walk behind Esteban. He tried to keep his breathing under control, adrenalin coursing through him.

Colton figured that they must be walking back on themselves, under the road, then the tunnel curved to the right, it straightened out, with doors leading off either side. After what was perhaps five minutes, Esteban chose one of the doors to walk through. Another tunnel, another door at the end, and they were in another basement. Up the steps, into the apartment. They entered a living room, where Esteban peered through the window to the street outside..

He looked at Colton and raised his eyebrows signalling Colton to follow straight behind him, and he left the living room and opened the front door. They turned quickly to the left out of the house, and were then at the front door of what Colton took to be the actual house containing Sofia. There was no one in sight.

Esteban tried the front door, it was open. It swung open as Esteban raised his gun. Either a stroke of luck or carelessness meant that no one was guarding the door as they were fixing themselves a hearty lunch giving Colton and Esteban the upper hand they needed.

One man appeared in the hallway walking from one room to another carrying a bowl of food, with a spoon in his mouth, he looked vacantly at the front door and the two figures standing there, just as Esteban fired a single bullet straight into the man's head. Colton watched the spoon clatter to the floor as if in slow motion.

Esteban and Colton stepped quickly through a door on the left which led into a furnished room that was empty of people. There Esteban indicated Colton to step behind the open door, to hide behind it with him. Esteban aimed his gun through the crack of the open door, pointing it towards the hallway where they had just come from.

A man stepped over his colleague's body, striding to the front door, opening it to check outside, Esteban pulled his trigger and the man went down, the weight of his body closing the door as he fell, however he was just wounded in the shoulder, Esteban closed one eye to focus down the sight of the gun and fired a bullet into the man's head.

As Esteban was doing this, Colton looked around the room and noticed a door leading off into another room on the wall opposite the window. Sure enough, it began to open, Colton raised his gun and waited, a shadow appeared on the wall and a black gun pointed round the doorway into the room. Colton aimed for the actual door, and pulled the trigger, blasting a hole in the door, but his bullet hit its mark as he heard a male voice cry out in pain from the other side.

Esteban pulled round in surprise, then indicated that they must move out into the hallway. Just as they moved around the door, someone opened fire into the room beyond the other door, firing bullets through the thin dividing wall.

Esteban and Colton stepped quickly into the hall and strode forward, Esteban crouched down at the end of the hall and peered round the doorway at the end, leading to the kitchen, to see the man firing at the wall of the room they had just left. Esteban aimed and shot the man in the leg. He went down, and Esteban shot him again. Colton realised this was not the man who he had shot in the shoulder through the doorway and turned his focus to the door they had just come through. A man was stepping into the hallway aiming for him, with his arm bleeding. Colton raised his gun and fired, the man went down. That made four men down.

Colton's heart was beating so hard he thought it was going to hammer through his chest. Sweat was dripping down his face. Esteban pulled the gun to his lips and kissed it. Each time was so close, Colton needed to think quicker, to see each room and where people could appear from, he felt blind, and looked all around them in the hallway, waiting for other men to appear.

Esteban led them forward, turning to the left, opening a thick padded door to go down a set of basement steps. Colton was getting sick of basements, each one seemed to be leading him to another room in hell.

They crouched down at the top of the stairway, to look into the room before their whole bodies were lowered into the space. The small hall room was empty. Two doors led off to either side. Esteban shrugged at Colton, not knowing which door to take. They listened, but could hear nothing, which was worrying, no shouting, no raising of the alarm.

Colton looked around and realised that the padding on the rooms were sound proofing insulation. Who ever lay beyond the doors had no idea what had just transpired above them, as no one had sounded the alarm.

Esteban reached for the left hand door, and something in Colton made him reach out and stop him. Esteban shrugged and opened the right hand door instead. The room beyond it was dimly lit with blue lighting, it was segmented by waist height walls, as they walked along they realised they were booths, with girls lying on rough blankets in each one. Most of them were sleeping or passed out, some had syringes lying next to them. One looked dead with sick all over her face. Esteban paced over them anxiously, and at the sixth booth, found the girl he was looking for. She was passed out, emaciated and had a syringe lying next to her. Esteban struggled to lift her up into a sitting position. Colton motioned the older man away, gave him the gun to hold, and lifted Sofia easily over his shoulder. She hung like a limp rag, arms dangling. Colton used one hand to steady her and Esteban handed Colton his gun back.

They made eye contact, took a deep breath each and turned to leave. They saw a girl standing up, swaying slightly, in the first booth, looking at them with hatred on her face from under limp hanging hair. She slowly raised her hand and pushed a button on the wall, sounding a silent alarm.

"Mierda." Esteban said out loud and drew his second gun from his side so that he held one in each hand, "Now, we fly."

Three men appeared from nowhere and filled the doorway. Colton and Esteban raised their guns and fired, walking forward at the same time, Esteban firing from two guns and Colton from his.

Esteban stumbled backwards as a bullet made contact with his arm, he dropped his gun in pain and surprise. Colton grimaced, still firing, and the three men were down. The woman who sounded the alarm screamed rage at him, and began running towards him, he aimed and shot her in the stomach, she slumped to the ground.

Colton turned to look at Esteban who was clutching at his arm, which was seeping with blood through his clothing and dripping through his clenched fingertips.

"Get behind me." Colton said, he adjusted the body of Sofia on his shoulders so she was better balanced, and pulled out the second gun from his side. Esteban looked at him and stepped behind him, picking up his gun from the ground and putting it back into his holster, clutching his other gun as best he could while stopping the blood oozing from his arm.

Colton stepped forward, walking out of the room of girls and into the hallway, where the door on the left was swinging open from where the three men had ran through. Two men were beginning to clatter down the staircase towards him, big heavy machine guns in their arms. He raised both guns and fired, and then two bodies were falling down the stairs towards him.

He struggled but walked up the stairs with Sofia balanced on his shoulders. They made it to the top of the stairs when Esteban yelled a warning, turned and fired back down into the basement, where two men were aiming for him. Colton burst through into the hall with Esteban behind him, where Esteban slammed the basement door shut and they ran for the front door.

Colton counted nine men, that left three men still unaccounted for if the Baron's calculations of twelve guards was right. They didn't stop to check, just ran out of the house and back to the apartment hiding the tunnel.

Down into the basement they went, along the tunnel passing the doorways and round the curve, Colton stopped, turned and cocked his head, Esteban realised he had heard something, and turned. Colton dropped Sofia to the ground as gently as he could and both men crouched low down. Shadows were flickering on the wall, men were advancing towards them, possibly having trailed them from Esteban's drips of fresh blood from his arm.

Shots were fired, drawing up clouds of dust, and when the dust cleared, the bodies of the three men lay on the ground. Colton dipped his head as he exhaled, resting it on Esteban's shoulder, he didn't realise he had been holding his breath. He turned to pick up Sofia again, who seemed to be regaining some consciousness, her eyes half opened to gaze up at him.

Then they were out of the basement and making their way up the steps into the little house and out into the daylight beyond. But there was someone standing in the doorway blocking their exit with a gun pointed at them.

Colton's eyes adjusted to the room and realised it was a man in a Garda uniform. He raised his firearm at Colton, then Esteban stepped in front of him.

"The Dark Angel?" The man said incredulously, lowering his weapon. He glanced over his shoulder towards the street outside, then back at them, "Correr!" He urged them, stepping away from the doorway.

"Gracias mi hombre!" Esteban said to him as they stepped past him and broke into a run.

Sirens were ringing in the air as they ran around the street, through the shortcut in the back gardens, and there was a beaten up silver car car waiting for them. The door opened as they ran closer, Colton carefully placed Sofia along the backseat, climbing in next to her while Esteban took the front seat next to the driver, which Colton saw to be Santiago.

The engine was already running, and they drove away, slowly so as not to arouse suspicion. Police cars were flying past them with their sirens blaring.

"Are you okay?" Colton said to Esteban.

Esteban shook his head in response, "It's pretty bad. I have been shot before but not like this." he clutched at his arm, trying to stem the blood.

"Marta will work her magic." Santiago said.

"We'll be there soon, just hold on." Colton said.

Colton leaned back in his seat and looked down at Sofia. She was looking up at him through those heavily drugged eyes of emerald green, she was beautiful, even in that dim light with shadows around her face, she was beautiful. Colton looked out of the window, raising his hand to rest on, he noticed his hands were trembling, he bit his thumb and held onto it. It was an excruciating amount of time before they drove through the gates of the farm. Santiago already phoned ahead, the other three men were standing waiting with a stretcher waiting for Esteban, who was pale and weak in the front seat. They gently eased him out of the seat, onto the stretcher and into one of the side sheds, where Marta was waiting to tend to him with her nursing skills. The black gates were sealed shut behind them and two guards returned to stand by them, keeping watch.

Colton stood up out of the car and eased the body of Sofia to the edge of the car seat then hoisted her into his arms, slinging her limp arm round his neck. He was beginning to feel exhausted, he hadn't even noticed carrying her through the tunnel earlier, but now that the adrenaline was wearing off, he realised how tired he was. He wasn't as strong as he used to be back in Hawick, his muscles were running out of steam. He carried Sofia into the main house, up the wooden staircase and into the room he knew to be hers. He laid her gently down on the mattress, her arm trapping him somehow. He gave up, exhaustion taking over, lying down next to her he passed out, sleep claiming him.

Chapter Twenty-Eight

Colton woke with a start into complete darkness, the pain emanating from a gun digging into his hip woke him, he didn't know where he was, his heart was beating fast, so fast. He wasn't anywhere familiar, his mouth was coarse and dry, desperate for water he stood up in the dark room, fumbled his way round a bed, found a wall, and then, miraculously a light switch.

As soon as the room was illuminated, the memories of the evening came flooding back to him. But where Sofia should be lying, where he left her, the bed was empty. He pulled the gun from his side and found himself creeping along the hallway and down the stairs, trying to duck his body down to take in the view to the kitchen, he tripped and fell down the stairs, the gun going off twice before he lost his grip and both he and the gun went clattering all the way to the bottom of the staircase. Once again, he hit his head.

He heard light-hearted laughter, an alien noise, not from anyone he knew, coming from the kitchen, which was in the wrong place as he was upside down tangled in himself in a heap at the bottom of the stairs. The front door burst open and shot guns pointed into the house, guards staring into the room with panicked expressions on their faces.

"It's okay! It's just Colton falling down the stairs!" Marta's voice laughed, "He wants to keep Esteban company in the injury room he tried to shoot himself on the way down!"

Colton untangled himself and stood up, the room span a little, and there was that light-hearted laughter again, mingling with Marta's laugh. He looked across, there was Sofia, sitting at the kitchen table with her hands clasped round a mug, smiling across at him. Her face was still pale, her hair was now tied up in a loose bun, but the smile lit up her face like an angel's, setting off her green eyes so that they looked at him with an electrifying intensity. Colton felt himself blushing.

"Come and sit down Colton, I pour you a drink." Marta commanded, reaching for the brandy bottle.

"Thanks Marta." he stumbled over his words.

"Yes, the gun fights take it all out of you. My poor brother, we thought he was a goner, but he is alive, and resting now, and will be okay. Thank you for bringing them both home to me." Marta said, pouring liquid into a clear glass and passing it to Colton, "Perhaps now the Baron will let you go home and get your revenge on the men who kill your father and mother."

Sofia turned to look at Marta questioningly.

"This is the son of Aubrey Cooper." Marta explained, "He lost his father just like you lost yours, to the Alessi family, poor boy." Marta touched Colton's shoulder affectionately as she walked past him to get another glass, and Colton felt a shiver run through him.

He looked at the brandy in the glass, his medicine, and took a drink.

"Thank you." a delicate, lilting Spanish voice said next to him.

He realised the angel next to him was talking to him. He felt cumbersome and awkward next to her. Colton looked into her eyes, at a level with them now he was sitting down. Inwardly, something in him felt like dying, he was an unworthy creature, haunted by demons, sitting next to this delicate beautiful thing. He felt himself falling into her eyes, unable to look away, she held him there, on his knees, he would do anything for her, this angel in front of him. And he knew that she felt the same, electricity charged the air between them, Colton could swear Marta would see the sparks flying between them.

Tears filled his eyes as he realised so quickly that he loved her, and he reached for the brandy bottle to break away from the guilt-dredged pain already filling his loathsome being. They could never be together. Marta had seen fit to that already. Did she know? Had she known that Colton was going to be put to task to save her daughter? Did she know that Colton would fall in love at first sight with her, how attractive her daughter was would not have gone unnoticed by her own mother. He gripped the glass and took another drink, refusing to look at the angel radiating the love he craved next to him. Never had anything pulled him so strongly before. He wanted to protect her, hold her in his arms, let the rest of the world disappear. He hated himself, he felt unclean, carrying the secret that he and Marta shared between them.

He realised no time had passed at all, the revelation had arrived in a mere moment and Marta was speaking to him, "You may go and speak to Esteban now Colton, I would like time alone with my Sofia."

Sofia's eyes widened fractionally, a movement Colton caught but Marta didn't see. Colton refilled his glass with some more brandy, taking his leave, he picked up his gun and tucked it into his jeans. He was still on edge and convinced things were about to come down around them, that the Alessi's men were going to come pounding into the yard. He left the farmhouse to enter the building that Esteban was recovering in.

Esteban was awake, and looking at him as he walked through the door. The room was whitewashed, with basic medical equipment around a bed that Esteban lay on with a drip in his arm.

"Colton!" Esteban said, a tone of relief and joy at seeing him.

"Looks like we both made it Esteban." Colton replied.

"Thank you." Esteban said, "We did. Sofia is home, safe. She is not on the drugs. They were keeping her unconscious that was all. Marta examined her while she was out cold. Marta says Sofia has been … touched … by these men." Esteban grimaced with anger, "We do not know how much she remembers, but her spirit is broken now."

He laid his head back on the pillow as a wave of pain ran over him, "I worry about this later. Now, I am glad to be alive. Tomorrow, we will visit the Baron, though he will already know what has happened."

"Don't you need to rest? I could go alone?" Colton suggested.

"No, we do this together."

Colton sat with Esteban a while longer, then retired to his guest quarters. He found a meal there waiting for him, and a half bottle of brandy. He ate the meal, took two shots from the brandy, then lay back on his bed. His brain replayed the events of the day, over and over again. One more shot of brandy, and his thoughts turned to the beauty of Sofia, and he fell asleep.

He awoke as a body was creeping into his bed next to him. As he stirred, a female voice whispered, "I cannot sleep alone. Please, hold me?"

It was Sofia, she had snuck into his room. Colton hesitated, then leaned round, embracing her in his arms. She sighed contentedly, and was sleeping soundly shortly afterwards.

Chapter Twenty-Nine

Colton felt sick, Everything he'd done was for her. There she was, the love of his life, lying next to him. He knew Sofia was who he was supposed to be with. He screwed his face up in agony with a thousand frustrations and filled with hatred of himself. Had he said no to Marta he wouldn't be here now, the men would have killed him, and here he was, head over heels in love with her daughter. He fought with himself and knew how truly fucked up he'd made his life. That was all there was to it, he'd fucked his life up, he couldn't taint such beauty with his touch, he'd curse her too. But he couldn't stop gazing at her as she slept. He had to have her, desire coursed through him and he pained with it, pushing it away. Maybe he could see a priest and confess his sins, they could cleanse him. No chance. His scars were in his head. His memories of Marta pressed up against him in the farmhouse bedroom jarred him every time he looked at Sofia.

Marta picked up on it the very next morning as she fed them all breakfast. Sofia came down the stairs, having snuck back into the house in the early hours, she gazed at Colton as she came into the kitchen, which Marta saw straight away.

Marta bid Colton help her with the dishes, once the men returned outside and Sofia went upstairs for a bath.

"She is in love with you Colton." Marta said.

"There's nothing I can really do about that." Colton said.

Marta shook her head in disagreement, "She must never know. She has suffered greatly too, she saw the Alessi's kill her father, she was kidnapped by them, and what ensued afterwards, she will not tell me much. She needs someone who will love her and protect her. We take what little scraps of happiness this world offers the likes of us, Colton, make my daughter happy."

"I would sooner be a hundred miles away from her than be with her, I'll only hurt her Marta. How can you suggest that after what we did?"

"The past doesn't exist anymore Colton. It's done, forgotten. You will be with her and you will make her the happiest she can ever be."

"She'll be alot happier with someone else, believe me."

"Sofia has chosen you."

"If she knew who I was … all that I was … then she'd change her mind."

"You'd break her heart. She has never loved before. Let you be her first, last and only love, do you hear me?"

Colton's heart lurched, he felt sick, Marta was binding him to her daughter.

"You are not breaking my heart," Marta laughed, "If that's what you think, you young fool. I thought you knew that. What happened between us was of the moment, in the past and emotionless. Some secrets you have to carry with you your whole life, take them to the grave. You want to be happy? Her happiness comes first. So you never tell. You bury it fast and you bury it so deep she'll never find it."

Colton left the kitchen to take breakfast to Esteban. Esteban was sitting up, colour returning to his face. Colton asked him about Aubrey.

Esteban revealed Colton's mum had always been in love with Aubrey, she had dedicated her life to him, had a child to him and he fucked it all up with a night of debauchery, coked up, screwed someone else, someone he shouldn't have, and when he returned home he laughed in June's face, telling her all about it, as he was still on a high from the night before.

It was enough to wreck his mum, and he knew his life now mirrored his mum and dad's completely, like fate replaying the same set up over and over, hoping perhaps for a different outcome this time. He was hopelessly in love with Sofia, it hurt in every fibre of his being that she wasn't able to be his, he couldn't just reach over, take her delicate face in his and kiss her, telling her how he felt about her and that they could both smile and everything would be set right.

Colton finally learned what made a couple who were truly in love tear completely apart. It was themselves. It would be him, carrying the haunting memories of the past. It may not have been the same reason his mum couldn't be with Aubrey, but it was of the same nature, ultimate betrayal.

Colton remembered the advice Aubrey and Thomas had tried to instil on him years ago now, "Women bring nothing but trouble to your door."

"When we go to the Baron today," Esteban said, "I do not think you are coming back. I see it on you. I think he will send you home now."

Colton nodded.

"We leave after I finish breakfast." Esteban said.

"I want to say goodbye to Sofia." Colton said.

Esteban nodded, "I will send a man with your horse to the Baron's. You ride in the car with me."

Colton made his way up the stairs of the farmhouse and knocked at Sofia's door. Fresh out of the bath, she was sitting at a dressing table brushing her hair, wearing a light white dress.

She turned and smiled at him, "My mother has given her blessing, she say we can be together. You can kiss me now."

Colton lowered his head sadly, "You're the deepest arrow that has sunk into my heart. But I bleed from every wound that is inflicted upon me."

Sofia frowned a little, not understanding.

"We cannot be together Sofia. I am not capable of giving you the love you need."

"I know that you love me Colton! I know it! I know that we love each other, we can be together!"

He shook his head, "I have to go home Sofia, I do not belong here."

"You take me with you!" she pleaded.

"You know that wouldn't work. You need to be here, with your mother."

He took her hand, Sofia pulled away from him and sat down on her bed.

"You go then." she said miserably.

He made to walk over to the bed.

"Just go." she waved him away.

"I'm sorry." he said as he walked out of the room.

He descended the stairs and Marta was standing drying her hands on her apron, looking at him.

"I'm leaving today." Colton said firmly.

Marta bit her lip and nodded.

They looked at each other a moment, then Colton left the house, closing the door behind him.

Chapter Thirty

Colton left on Becky, along the dusty beaten tracks he knew he would never see again. He trotted her to town, tethering her outside the Baron's office, where The Dark Angel was waiting for him, having Santiago drive him in the car. The Baron hugged both of them when they entered his office. He looked at Colton.

"Now, you are ready to return home." he said.

"I know." Colton said, "I can feel its time."

"Revenge will be yours." the Baron said, "When the time is right, I will come through for you. Together, we will defeat the Alessi's and they will trouble no more towns, take no more lives from us."

"How will you get to Scotland?" Esteban asked Colton.

"I will ride there." Colton said, "I have my horse."

The Baron and Esteban looked at each other.

"Very well. However, I will make a suggestion that you leave on a truck that is heading out of town in twenty minutes. There is room for your horse in the back. It is heading to Calais and will save you some time." The Baron said.

Colton looked at him surprised, "Bit of a coincidence."

"Or just the right time for you to be leaving, perhaps. Adios, Colton." The Baron embraced him again.

Colton left the office, to find Becky waiting patiently at her lamppost for him. Esteban remained at the office to speak further with the

Baron. Colton had instructions where to meet the lorry. He jumped onto Becky's back and guided her along the streets.

Sure enough, he found a grey lorry with its back doors open, and a wooden ramp leading up to the storage area. Colton encouraged Becky up the ramp, then jumped down from her back once he was inside with her. He removed her saddle and bridle, and closed the door behind her. He jumped into the passenger seat and waited. Five minutes later, the driver door opened and a British man stepped into the cab. He had mousy blonde hair in a rough cut, and a tanned face, having spent a lot of time in the Spanish sunshine. He had a friendly smile.

"Colton?" the man said.

"Yes. Dave?" Colton asked.

"Pleased to meet you." Dave said, "Just have to wait for this beaut to charge up fully, otherwise she'll not make it to the stopping point."

Colton realised Dave was actually Australian by his accent.

"Charge up?" Colton asked.

"Electric lorry."

"What?" Colton asked, confused.

"Where've you been living, under a rock? Well maybe you have if you get around by horse all the time, they cant track them yet. The boss just phones me and tells me I've got to get this kid and his horse to Calais, I thought he was joking. The UK has gone electric crazy, banned all diesel and petrol engines."

"When did that happen?" Colton asked.

"Just the last few months, they took all the gas guzzlers off the road, just like that. People were up in arms, they were having to return brand new cars to the forecourts they got 'em from the previous week. Government didn't care. Just like that, the world's changed. Harder to move in and out the country now too, they keep tabs on everything."

"Are you being serious?"

"Haven't you seen, it's all over the news back in England? They closed the vehicle tunnel right up from Dover to Calais, Hardly anyone gets through. The country's in lock down mate."

"Aren't you going to the UK?"

"Naw mate, I stop at Calais to fill up with delivery and come back here."

"Then how am I going to get across the channel?" Colton asked.

Dave smiled knowingly, "You would need to sneak through the service tunnel or the closed off vehicle tunnel on foot, but be quick enough to not get caught by the motion sensors. Laser beams - shoot your legs clean out from under you. You can't walk for a week afterwards. Stopped the immigrants pushing through. Or you could steal a lift in the night freight train, you'll have a bit of bother doing that with the horse though."

"Christ." Colton said.

"Want some brekkie? I'm just going to nip to the shop while I'm waiting, it's a long journey you'll need some grub in your belly."

"Erm, yes, just get me the same as what you usually get?" Colton said, his head in a daze.

Dave chattered for the first hour or so of the journey.

"They've put a speed limiter on my truck I can't go over fifty miles an hour, twenty-five in built up areas." Dave said.

"Isn't there a way around it?"

"Oh, I wouldn't know about that." Dave laughed like he knew how to do it, "Too many people are readily prepared to delight in another man's misery and I'd get reported before I'd even blinked if anyone knew my truck could do a hundred miles an hour as and when required."

Colton smiled and bit into a sandwich, Dave was light relief from what he'd just left behind.

"The vehicles that are manually driven have trackers on them. The ones that are left in the cities drive themselves. It's all about control, Colton, it's scary stuff. I know thats what its about. Once you go back to England, you'll wish you stayed well away."

"Dave that sounds like a set of crazy conspiracy theories."

"Yeah, it does, doesn't it?"

"Its nuts. How did anyone even let that happen?"

"They all seemed like surprisingly good ideas at the time, but in practice we're finding it a whole other ball game." Dave said.

"What price is freedom?" Colton agreed.

Dave grinned, "They cannot track horses, yet. They will no doubt try very soon. Put a chip in us all soon enough. What price is freedom? We have been free men for years in a way, we just didn't see it that way, and now the next generation will think this is all the norm and won't question it. They won't even question the things that are happening to them! Brainwashed and dumbed down by the media."

"There'll always be those who question it, surely?" Colton interjected.

"Where? Where are they? In the places where people can actually make a difference? They've closed ranks Colton, no one can get in. People disappear or get framed and thrown in jail trying to change things!"

"Isn't that a risk some people are willing to take - look at Martin Luther King Jr, or JFK?"

"Have you known anyone stand up in the UK like that? Ever? Stood out, started making a difference? Not just the same wolf in different clothing? Those times are gone, no one wants to take risks anymore, they just want to be left alone. They've bred a culture of apathy, fear, laziness and denial. It suits them, they can do what they want, go where they want, have houses all over the world living off our broken backs."

"What do you think would change things?" Colton asked.

"Eradicate money. Get rid of it completely."

"Thats crazy."

"Is it Colton? Has anyone ever tried it?" Dave looked at him, then took a bite of his own sandwich.

"They could distribute the wealth more fairly, there's surely enough to go around everyone."

"Yes there is. It's been proven as F.A.C.T. there's enough money in the world and wisdom to cure world poverty and disease but what do they do instead? Hoard the wealth and spread diseases to wipe poor folks like us out."

Dave was going to extremes now, but Colton didn't mind. It was passing the time on the long journey.

"It's difficult to tell which way this world is turning. But meanwhile we live on, while those above us change the world around us without us having any say in the matter."

"You can vote." Colton suggested.

"Votings rigged." Dave sniffed, "And like I said, you're just getting the same thing but in different suits, the same guys using the same broken system and telling us they can fix things, but they can't. They can't. As they're using the same broken system that's based on greed, superiority and taking advantage of folks like us."

Dave and Colton's discussions went on for some time, it was the longest Colton had conversed with a native English speaker since he left Scotland and it took a little adjusting to, trying not to break into Spanish to help convey his meaning. Politics was not something Colton ever thought about, but he realised things were going to be very different on his return.

They were able to check on Becky using Dave's internal monitors. Occasionally she paced about, or sniffed at the front panels to make sure Colton was still nearby, but mostly she stood balancing against the knocks on the road.

They stopped occasionally for rest breaks, whereby Colton would give Becky some water and let her graze the grass in the lay-by or car park they found themselves in.

Eventually Dave parked up at the Calais docks and walked round to the back of the lorry with Colton.

"I've an idea, Colton mate, that might get you a bit further. No one really makes it past this point on foot. I know I told you to run along the closed off tunnels, but I've never heard of anyone making it through. But, on horseback, you might stand a chance. Its one of the craziest things I've seen, so mad it just might work. But what I was thinking, is if you put on my high-vis jacket, and my hat here, and you're on a horse, you'll look more official, and you might stand a better chance of slipping through security."

Dave reached into a grey metal storage box just inside the main doors of the lorry, handing Colton a bright yellow long sleeved jacket and a flat-brimmed hat with the logo of his company on the front.

"Worth a try." Colton shrugged.

Dave described the location of the tunnel Colton was to try to take, and how to get through the security barriers, "No one really guards it as the lasers do a good job, so once you're in the tunnel, don't look back, just get that horse running as fast as she can. I've heard the lasers cut off so far along the tunnel as no one makes it that far without being detected."

"Okay. Dave, thanks for everything." Colton said, picking up the saddle and bridle to tack Becky up with.

"No worries mate." Dave said smiling.

Becky was restless and keen to move out of the lorry. Colton climbed onto her back, and guided her through the lorry loading bays. He talked to her the whole way, while staring straight ahead of them, it was a busy place and he wanted to keep her calm in case she kicked out at anyone with her temper.

They made it through without raising attention other than a few glances from lorry drivers, which Colton acknowledged each time with a nod of presumed authority, reaching the closed off tunnel. Sure enough, Colton could see how to get through the barriers. Dave advised there were security monitors, but these were only activated if the lasers went off as it was too busy a place to watch all the time, and that was top secret insider knowledge.

Colton guided Becky through the barriers, took a deep breath at the dimly lit tunnel ahead of them, lit only with the dull yellow of emergency lighting, then kicked Becky and uttered the command to make her break into a canter. She pulled faces at entering the tunnel, shaking her head, he urged her on. She lowered her head, and at his insistence, sped up to her flat out gallop.

The sweeping lasers missed them. Still they rode on, till Colton felt it was safe for Becky to slow down. It was miles to the UK shore line, and he would have to do the same risky manoeuvre on that side too, not to mention the long ride from Dover to Hawick. Colton patted Becky's neck, it was going to be the longest ride of their lives.

Chapter Thirty-One

The roads were surprisingly empty when Colton trotted along them on Becky, He was amazed at how quickly such dramatic change could take place. Grassy weeds had begun to show through the tarmac, forming cracks on the road.

The whole situation made him feel uneasy. He didn't know if horses were even allowed on the roads anymore if the government were tracking movement to the extent Dave seemed to think they were.

Colton removed the High-Vis jacket early on in the journey, feeling the chill of the cold damp British air right through to his skin, but he was worried about being overly visible.

He took Becky off the road if he saw or heard a car coming, which was difficult due to their quiet electric engines, but he managed. They travelled day and night, stopping only briefly for food or short bouts of sleep in hidden away lay-bys, as he wanted to keep moving. Sometimes he rode, sometimes he walked with Becky to stretch his legs and give them both a break. His legs were sore and tired, but he wouldn't stop, driven by a blind determination to see familiar road signs and be on his way home.

It took a long time, Colton lost track of the days. Dave's supplies ran out quite quickly and Colton was forced to make a detour to a post office to change his Spanish money into British to enable him to buy food and the odd bottle of brandy.

Eventually the road signs began to look more familiar, and the hundred miles or so to Carlisle didn't seem that far anymore, given the distance they had already travelled. They left the A7 to rest for a few hours after Carlisle for some sleep and food. Colton estimated that it could take them a day at a steady pace to travel to Hawick. He didn't want to push Becky on the last leg of the journey more than he had to, she had ridden so far already, so decided against this and to take more breaks instead.

He figured he would take a final break at Mosspaul, where there was a large pub situated in a small glen about thirteen miles out of Hawick. He couldn't believe his eyes when he rounded the final corner of the road to see hoards of people at the usually quiet pub, complete with marquees and horses, all around. He racked his brains, for the time of year it was, of course, it was the annual common riding celebrations. Where the townsfolk would mount their horses and ride the old boundary lines, with celebratory events half way round.

Everyone was in high spirits he could hear their laughter and merriment from where he was on the road. People welcomed him as he rode closer, someone shouted that he must have been pretty lost, coming from completely the wrong direction. He smiled and waved, as was the custom on the rideouts. He spotted the cornet, who was just getting back onto his horse, as he rode close by him.

The cornet shouted his name, "Colton Cooper! Well get a look at the state of you! Where've you appeared from?"

Colton recognised him as Sam Turnbull, one of his closest friends from High School. Sam's cheeks were rosy, and his eyes were glittering with good spirits.

"Down the road." Colton replied.

"Yes, that completely explains everything." Sam laughed, "You know everyone thinks you're dead, right?"

"I've been away for a long time." Colton said.

"Aye, ye have that, alots changed, we think this is going to be the last common riding! They're going to ban it!" Sam exclaimed.

"What? Who?"

"The Alessi's of course, who else?" Sam smarted.

"Cornet! It's time to leave!" The Acting Father rode up and announced to him.

"Colton will you ride with me?" Sam asked, "Tuck in behind Ronnie there, we've got alot to catch up on."

Colton felt the hairs prickle up on the back of his neck when Sam the Cornet rode through to the front of the crowd of people on horseback, or just mounting their horses. Colton followed close behind Sam and the Acting Father Ronnie. Sam raised the blue flag emblazoned with the date 1514 in yellow into the sky, and the crowd behind them cheered. Though there would be a few followers on bikes and in cars, many of the people would stay for the afternoon at Mosspaul with their picnics. As the horses gathered behind Sam, the Saxhorn Band struck up a tune about Hawick, playing songs about returned heroes and ghosts of long ago.

Colton felt like the entire town had come out to see him return home. He knew that was not why they were there at all, but to him, it was a welcome he did not expect and it lifted his mood. Becky too, found a last lease of energy on the return journey home.

Through the hills and across the moors they rode, sometimes at a gallop, sometimes a trot. They stopped to let the horses and riders catch their breath and sup from their hip flasks, which was when Sam was able to speak to Colton.

Colton learned that the Alessi's effectively owned the town now, they were throwing innocent people in jail, most of the police were bribed to the hilt and in the Alessi's pockets, people were being framed for crimes they didn't commit if they went against the Alessi's in any way. Or disappearing. They were charging shopkeepers protection money, effectively to save the shopkeepers from the Alessi's own henchmen. Things were bad. The youngsters were getting addicted to the drugs the Alessi's were pumping into the town. They wanted to control the whole place, and hated that the common riding was something they weren't able to touch, Sam explained it gave the townsfolk hope. As well as encouraged free movement on horseback, which the Alessi's didn't want.

Colton grew grim as the ride continued. He had no idea how anyone could be in high spirits with that hanging over the whole town.

But in high spirits they were, if this was to be their last common riding, they were going to make it a good one. There were at least a hundred folk on horseback on the way back into town. The sound of the horse hooves reverberated up the High Street.

Chapter Thirty-Two

Marius Alessi stood smoking a cigarette on his balcony of the old Prudential building, overlooking the Horse Monument and up the High Street. He looked with deirsion at the people beneath him, nothing but low lifes, that he wanted to crush, crush and ruin them all so they were on their knees begging and crawling to him for help, and they would offer their money and their services to him.

Marius noted the man on the white horse at the front, he noted him only because something was amiss about him. The man wore no riding hat upon his head and was not clad in the usual smart attire. In fact he was rather under-dressed for the occasion. Where the other riders were in crisp white shirts, waistcoats, tweed jackets and long black boots, this man was in raggedy jeans and a rather dirty looking creased t-shirt. Who did he think he was? Marius was not a follower of the Hawick traditions, but this man was disrespecting Marius' town, Marius allowed the rideouts to continue only on a whim this year, and this man did not pay homage to them the way he was ought to.

Marius Alessi snubbed out his cigarette on the balcony railing, letting the stub fall into the street below, it was no odds to him where it landed. He turned and walked two paces to stand in the window frame to look into the room inside, it took a minute for his eyes to adjust from the dazzlingly brilliant sunshine outside. The man on the white horse bothered him. Marius liked control and order, the silly townsfolk with their ridiculous traditions, everyone who rode took pride in their appearance. So why was this man riding at the front like a figure of importance dressed like a tramp? He was a pretender, a charlatan.

Marius lifted the bell that was on a highly polished round table just inside the room, positioned to the left of the balcony doors, the white veil curtains wavered in the wind, brushing over the thicker grey velvet ones.

At the sound of the bell, being summoned, his man Craven entered the room. He was a tall man, with scar lines running along his cheekbones. His eyes were that of a reptile, green with no emotion behind them, with slicked back dark hair. He wore a grey suit.

"See to it that man is brought to me." Marius demanded.

"What man, Sir?" Craven asked.

"The man on the white horse out there. In amongst that lot. The shabbily dressed one, you can't miss him. I want to have a word with him about his lack of manners in my town."

"Do you mind if I take a look, Sir?" Craven said.

"Mm, well, stand at the side of the window so they don't see you. I will point him out." Marius said.

They stood hidden by the white veil of the curtains, by now the horses were much further up the street, still more horses rode and the crowds lined the streets on either side cheering them on.

"I can't see him, Sir." Craven said.

"He was at the front. See to it that you find him and bring him to me."

"I'll try my best, Sir, but it will be a hard job getting through that crowd and the horses to reach the front." Craven said.

"I didn't ask you how hard it would be, I asked you to find that man and bring him to me."

"Yes Sir." Craven said and left the room.

Craven knew it was a futile task to go out when the crowds were gathered for the welcoming return of the Cornet and his horsemen. Each and every person in the crowd would recognise him searching for that man and it was the rare time that the crowd openly showed their resentment of the Alessi's and did what they could to hinder them. Sure enough, when he stepped outside, he noticed the subtle glances out of the corners of their eyes, and the way the people just would not open up a space for him to manoeuvre through.

Craven pushed his way through to a side alley road to the right of the main street, jogged round to where it met another road that ran parallel to the river, ran along to the Medical Practice then cut back up the stairs there that ran back up to the High Street and emerged almost at the top of the street. A long way to take a short cut. But still, he could barely get through the crowd. He caught a glimpse of the stranger on the white horse. There was something familiar about him. The man frowned, it was just a local lad with a heavy tan, he didn't know what his boss was working himself up over. Craven would not to remember throwing a younger Colton out of the club with Thomas, having thrown many young lads out before and since.

Craven pulled out his phone, and took some photos of the boy, he zoomed it into the boy's face for a few close-ups. He couldn't reach the lad today, it would draw too much attention to him and the crowd might intervene, but he'd now be able to find out who he was, so he wasn't returning to the boss completely empty handed. Craven sniffed and spat on the ground, he didn't think the boy was even worth the effort.

Colton rode round to the left of the High Street, following the road round as it intersected with the one which led out of town. The streets were achingly familiar. As he was about to vanish from view round the corner towards the cinema, Sam called to him, "Where you off to Colton?"

"To see if The Abattoirs still standing." Colton replied.

"Ah right. Come round to meet us later on, aye?"

"Aye, alright." Colton agreed.

It was just after eight o'clock in the evening. Sam would put his horse away then return to the High Street for a few drinks.

Colton asked Becky to wander at a slow pace round the rest of the road and along to the little back lane, down the little vennel to the entrance. Sweat was pouring off her, she was exhausted from the excitement of the last gallop home with the other horses. He would need to see to her pretty quickly, and before his own weariness and exhaustion hit him fully.

The Abattoir double doors and windows were still shuttered up, the door was covered in cobwebs, looking like it hadn't been opened in years, which he found surprising, that the Alessi's or the Police hadn't broken into it. Nothing worth their time maybe after killing Aubrey and June.

Colton dismounted, and checked under the loose brick near the window ledge, he was surprised to find his old set of keys were still where he left them. Even Thomas hadn't known about that hiding place.

The smaller door swung open with a weary creak, a sound that Colton had forgotten, but now he felt comforted by in its familiar noise. The door pulled the cobwebs with it. The room was in darkness except where the light allowed in by the door touched the ground. He stepped into the dark room and flicked the lightswitch he knew to be on the left hand side of the doors, it didn't do anything, it was too much to hope for that there would be electricity on after all this time.

He was home.

Chapter Thirty-Three

A pile of mail lay strewn about the floor inside, Colton could make out the big angry red final warning letters amongst the envelopes. He suddenly missed the atmosphere of the crowd and the common riding celebrations taking place only a short distance away from him at the Tower Knowe, he could still hear cheers and hoof beats from where he stood.

Becky nudged his back, propelling him forward, "Yes, I'll have to get you a drink of water." he said to her.

He undid the bolts on the two large doors and swung them open, allowing the daylight to pour into the neglected forgotten room inside. The light hit the wall mirrors reflected onto the centre of the fight ring illuminating it in a softer light. A layer of dust covered everything, the fight ring, the training punch bags, the weights.

"Welcome back." Colton said to himself.

Becky wandered into the open doors sniffing and snorting at the layer of dust.

Then, Becky spun her head round to the doors, and Colton too heard the footsteps approaching. It was Vivienne! Colton was unaware of the interaction between Craven and Marius which took place in front of Vivienne, whereby Vivienne promptly left the Prudential building to come to find him, he was completely surprised, she was the last person he expected to see.

Vivienne was standing framed in the doorway, a perfect silhouette in the sunlight. Still tragically attractive, delicate and slender, her hair in the same twisted bun style knot as he remembered.

"It is you!"Vivienne said, her voice sending a cacophony of forgotten butterflies coursing through his chest. She held him in her power again immediately.

"Aye, I'm home." he said.

"I thought you were dead." she replied, her voice caressing the air, chasing away the shadows of the lonely forgotten Abattoir building.

"No." he replied, uncertain how to answer.

"May I come in?" she ducked her head to look at him where he was standing in the shadowy light, humbling her expression to seek permission.

"If you like." he replied, "But it's a bit dusty." he inferred to her choice of light clothing.

"I don't mind." she stepped across the threshold and walked towards him. Colton felt a lump in his throat, he could smell her perfume on the air now, it made his heart ache.

"How have you been?" she asked, choosing a place to stand less than half a metre from him.

Colton paused, wondering what to answer.

"Sorry, maybe that was a bad question, bet you've been really awful since your parents died. I never got a chance to speak to you, I didn't see you at the funerals."

"I wasn't there. I didn't need to be, I said my goodbyes in my own way." he said, painfully.

"I mean no disrespect." Vivienne said.

He barely heard what she said, he felt starved of looking at her and drank her in like the first drink of water after days in the desert. Only one other girl ever mastered this effect on him, and she wasn't here, nor would he ever be able to be with her.

"None taken." he said.

"What's the place like?" she asked, "Are you going to open it back up?"

Colton shrugged, "I don't know, I've only just arrived back." But the idea sunk home, to reopen the Abattoir …

"Oh, right, sorry I didn't realise, I saw you on the street on a horse and thought I was seeing a ghost. So I had to come round to see if it was true. That you are alive, and here." she smiled, looking around which was when she noticed the white horse sniffing one of the punch bags.

"Is that your horse?" she asked, indicating Becky.

"Yup, she's mine." he replied.

"Where did you get her? She's very pretty." Vivienne asked, looking across at Becky but not moving from where she stood.

"From a horse dealer in Appleby." Colton replied.

He decided right there in that moment that he would give nothing away to anyone, even to her, about where and who he'd been in his time away, it was a decision that was to protect him and the people around him. He knew now why Aubrey was a closed book and his mum too, to some extent. It was safer that way.

"Well," Vivienne said, "I'm glad you're back. Perhaps I can offer to take you for some food or something, hear about some of your adventures?"

"No, you're alright, thanks though. I have a lot to do here and I want to be getting on." he found himself saying, despite aching to spend more time with her, listen to her voice, forget everything except her, she was a dangerous drug. An old familiar addiction, difficult to grapple and contain at her unexpected arrival at his door, "But perhaps some other time soon?" he offered her a fleeting half smile.

Vivienne took that as an indication to leave, "Okay, well I know where to find you, cheerio." she smiled and left, leaving the lingering scent of perfume on the dusty air.

And so would everyone else know where to find him, Colton realised, the first thing he needed to do was to get the electricity back on, get the alarm and CCTV door system functioning again. And feed Becky. And himself.

He wandered round the back rooms, Becky could sleep in the back yard until he figured something else out. It was small, but could house her adequately enough. His thoughts returned to Vivienne, how twisted for fate to arrange his first visitor to be her, and have her invade his every waking thought again.

"Keep busy Colton. Keep your mind aff her." he said out loud.

He led Becky through to the back yard, removed her saddle and bridle and found an old towel to wipe over her sweated body. He found a bucket in the cleaning cupboard which he rinsed out to give her a drink of water.

He walked back through to the front, picking up some of the letters from the pile of mail and rifled through them, opening the final warnings from the electricity company. He jogged upstairs, what a familiar staircase, his feet remembered the depth of each step. He walked into Aubrey's - no, his - office and opened the shutters to allow light in to locate the telephone, the black old-fashioned looking thing with a round dial that Aubrey loved so much. The line was dead, or disconnected. That just made everything a little bit more tricky.

He decided to give up for the night, no where would be open anyway, and go and meet Sam for a few drinks before heading to bed and starting again tomorrow.

There was a knock at the double doors. Colton jogged downstairs, expecting to see Vivienne again. It was one of the lads, Chris, who used to train at the Abattoir.

"Are ee comin' oot the night Colton?" Chris asked, crossing his arms round his yellow waist-coated chest sternly, "Deh tell is yer no coming as yer too tired, all the lads are dying to see you again."

Colton stepped back a little in surprise at seeing him. Chris must have been in the ride out. Never mind pleasantries or hellos or anything with Chris, no, just straight to the point.

"Are they?" he found himself saying instead.

"Aye! They want to know when the club's opening up again."

That was it then, settled, the Abattoir was opening up again.

"But christ you'll need to take a shower first, ee stink."

Chris told him where to meet them all, and left Colton to get ready. He had a freezing cold shower downstairs then went upstairs into his old bedroom to look for a set of clean clothes. The first time he'd been back in the room since it was dusty but that didn't bother him.

He pulled out a blue shirt and a pair of jeans from his drawers. He checked himself in the mirror, tidied his hair a little, then left the building.

He met the lads, some of whom he remembered, some seemed to have grown up from young boys into men while he'd been away. Rum and milk was passed around at his arrival. Everyone was in high spirits after the celebrations and the success of the ride out.

Robbie was laughed at for falling off his horse and landing in a boggy stream meaning he looked like he'd shat his pants, and was still wearing the same trousers. They laughed and joked about the adventures on the ride out, the antics of their horses and the wonder of meeting up with Colton, a true Terie, so dedicated he apparently rode all the way from, where was it again? Just to join in on the last leg of the ride out. The lads were adamant that the Abattoir must open again. Sam was there, but milled around the various tables chatting to everyone.

The old boys at the other table were singing songs that everyone in the pub would join in with, "I like Auld Hawick the best" was one Colton could remember all the words to.

Hushed whispers were passed around about, people saying that they'd seen Marius Alessi on his balcony scowling at the crowds and how he'd sent one of his henchmen Craven into the crowd and no one knew why but they were damned sure they didn't help him get through. That was the only time it was discussed that night, everyone agreeing not to discuss the Alessi's any further and ruin their evening of celebration.

Colton had hoped to see Vivienne out, when he asked about her Robbie laughed, "She doesn't come out with the likes of us lesser people, she belongs to Marius Alessi."

"I'd heard they'd split up." Chris said.

"Oh aye, right enough, Stef did tell me that they'd broken off the engagement as he'd hit Vivienne yin night and that was that." Robbie said, "Christ, what a bastard, ye dinnae just gan roond hittin' lassies, if I had a lass I'd treat her like a princess the whole time." Robbie said.

"Ye'd be brow beaten Robbie!" Calvin laughed.

"I would no', I'd just love her and cook for her and take her nice places." Robbie replied.

"Aw look whit about yin o' these lassies over there then?" Chris laughed.

"No, there's only yin fir me," Robbie sighed, "And she'll no have me."

"Aw, Stef!" the others laughed.

"Can you not just tell her how you feel?" Colton asked.

"Och no, I cannae dae that." Robbie said.

"Why not?" Colton asked.

"Cause her brother already told him no' to go anywhere near her!" Calvin laughed, leaning over and punching Robbie on the arm, "ee cannae have my sister!"

"Aye." Robbie said rubbing his arm, "Aye, I ken."

Colton hadn't laughed so much in years, he felt like he belonged with the boys, like he was finally home.

Colton rocked back into the Abattoir at a little after twelve in the morning, having declined going into the nightclub owned by the Alessi's when the other boys thought it a was good idea. He quietly checked on Becky, by quietly, he tiptoed across the training floor through the back to the yard, where Becky was sniffing the door, having heard his 'quiet' approach from the cobbled street. He offered Becky some of his lamb kebab. She delicately took the proffered lettuce and the flat bread, while he munched the lamb slices next to her. Once they were finished, he sighed, patted her neck and went to sleep upstairs on his dusty bed.

Chapter Thirty-Four

In the late morning nursing his sore head Colton lay in bed and pondered over Vivienne, the boys said that she still belonged to Marius Alessi though she had broken off her engagement after he hit her. Maybe Marius just scared off any possible suitors laying some claim to her as his ex, he knew guys could be like that, especially guys like Marius.

He nudged himself out of bed to walk gingerly up the Howegate to buy a couple of bacon rolls and a takeaway cup of coffee for breakfast, returning to the Abattoir having munched through one of the rolls already en route.

Feeling marginally alive again he popped Becky's bridle on and walked her round to the outdoor and equine supply store, tied her up outside, and asked the shop worker what she had to feed a horse, and that he needed a blanket for her as she was used to a warmer climate. The girl asked what size the horse was and he pointed to Becky standing outside the window. He insisted that Becky try the blankets on rather than go by standard measurements, as she was an imported horse, so the girl lugged various blankets outside and tried them on Becky until they found one that fit He then said he would need food as well, the girl suggested sealed bags of haylage, nutrition licks for stabled horses, oats, and garlic granules, and he insisted that Becky get to taste test each product first as there was no point in buying something she didn't like. The girl opened factory sealed buckets of feed to offer to the curious Becky, all of which was much to the amusement of passers by who slowed down to watch what was happening. Colton was also advised to buy a hay net, a feed bucket, and several other items he'd never owned before. He grimaced at the total price as it was rung up, the girl agreed to deliver them all to the Abattoir in her four-by-four when she finished her shift at twelve thirty for an extra ten pounds. It was Sunday after all, she added, and she had places to be.

Colton used the rest of the morning to get his phone line and electricity back up and running. Dealing with it was enough to wear him out, having visited the library, the council offices which were shut, and several other places, explaining himself over and over, waited on hold for what seemed like forever on public use telephones, but finally he had electricity, on the promise of repayments, the threat of court action and insistence that he install solar panels as he was contravening some new Business Environment Act by having a business premises without them.

Colton grabbed a takeaway baguette for himself, he was too exhausted to think about serious food shopping for himself that day,

The girl from the supply store was as good as her word and turned up with the things Colton had bought. He grabbed them out the back of her car, then realised he didn't know how to set up the hay net, or even put the blanket on, so she went through to the back yard with him to help. She decided not to comment on the unusual location for a horse to be staying, but he decided to explain it was only temporary until he found somewhere more suitable, in case she went back and phoned the SSPCA on him and they took Becky away.

Becky contentedly chewed on her hay in her new hay net, warm and snuggled up in her new blanket. She nodded her head happily at him as he opened the door to the back yard after showing the girl out He rested his head against the doorframe and watched her for a moment, remembering the massive journey they had just accomplished together.

At two-thirty, a knock on the door brought Calvin to visit Colton, "Alright pal, I just want to sign up again, when can I start training?" he asked Colton.

"God, the place is barely close to being ready." Colton said, wiping his hands on his dusty jeans.

"No time like the present. We can train and clean it up at the same time, I can give you a hand. Did you hear about my mother? She was arrested for your parents' murders."

"What?" Colton acted surprised at Calvin's news.

"Aye." Calvin said solemnly, "She's sitting in the jail cells the now, she was framed Colton, and we all know who by. No time like the present to start getting well and truly fit. Fills my time, keeps my mind occupied. Ken what I mean?"

Colton knew enough to read between the lines, Calvin wasn't only the first recruit to training, he was the first in line for The Unmade Plan of Revenge.

"Looks like I'm the first one here?" Calvin said, "The rest will come, dinnae worry aboot that."

Calvin sauntered over to the lockers that ran the hall wall at the back of the main room, "Still got my key, left my trainers and that in my locker thanks to you doing a moonlight flit."

Calvin pulled out a set of keys and found his small key that fit the locker, opening the door he triumphantly pulled out his trainers and kit.

"I'll get changed shall I?" Calvin said.

"For what?" Colton asked.

"For oor run." Calvin smiled, "Deh tell is ee've forgotten your training schedule, it was you that made it."

"Just us two then." Colton said, "I'll get changed."

"The rest will come." Calvin said, pulling out his phone whistling a cheery tune.

Colton jogged up the stairs to his room, sure enough his training kit was waiting for him, where he'd left it in the drawer. He got changed into shorts and a vest top and donned his old running trainers. He still felt rough.

Chapter Thirty-Five

On the way downstairs Colton felt a little light headed, but there were three more lads standing in the entrance space waiting for him.

"You look like utter shite Colton." Robbie grinned.

Colton looked at them.

"We're here for our run, a few more o' us are going to meet us at the park. Then, you can sign us up." Dave said.

"Let's do this!" Calvin said.

"It takes a long time to get fit by training guys, it won't be a quick fix." Colton said.

"We've got time." Robbie said, "Sounds like you're trying to make excuses, get your airse oot this door and show us how it's done."

Colton felt a flame of heated pride well up inside his chest, he used to lead the boys round the park, he remembered the route, when he was at peak fitness no one could match him. But today he was rough as hell and his legs were still screaming from the ride from Dover.

"No excuses Colton." Robbie said, as if reading his thoughts.

Calvin jogged round the group and then stood next to Colton, jogging on the spot, "What are you waiting for Colton? Just get it done!"

"Okay boys!" Colton snapped to life, remembering what they were all waiting for, "Warm ups first, stretches, up down, up down, round the ring three times for luck then go, go, go!"

The boys cheered, running round the fight ring, tapping their hands off the top left support bar on their way out of the door. They ran out of the Abattoir, down to the Sandbed, left along past the High School, across the footbridge over the Teviot to the entrance gateway of Wilton Park.

Colton felt another surge of adrenalin when he counted six more lads standing at the gates to the park waiting for them in various stages of warm ups. Except for one lad who was standing leaning against one of the pillars smoking a cigarette, it was Jimmy, of all people, one of the farmer's sons from out of town.

"Alright lads." Colton said trying to sound fresh.

"Fucking hell Colton you're seriously going to make me run aren't you?" Jimmy growled at him. He was dressed in a pale blue shirt with a cashmere jumper with threadbare holes at the elbows, and a pair of rugby shorts.

"You want to be a member of The Abattoir Boys, you gotta run Jimmy." Colton smiled, flexing his legs.

"The Abattoir Boys, that has a nice ring to it." Robbie said, stretching down to touch his toes.

"The 'Notorious' Abattoir Boys." Jimmy said.

"We aren't exactly notorious." Dave piped up.

"Not yet." grinned Jimmy, "Imagine us on the front page of the Hawick Paper though, aih?."

"We'll be on the back pages boys, breaking records." Robbie said.

"Breaking skulls." Jimmy replied.

"Hei, we'll hae' nane o' that sort o' talk here. Eyes and ears boys, eyes and ears." Calvin said.

There was a naivety about the atmosphere that Colton wistfully lamented, he felt decades older than the group in front of him. They'd all been affected by the Alessi brothers' grip on the town in some way, they all carried a familiar bitter resentment at the back of their eyes, but none bled so deep as from the wounds which scarred him. Calvin sensed it, maybe Robbie too, but they kept quiet, biding their time, waiting to see what Colton would do now he had returned.

Colton kept it a relatively light afternoon of training, more like getting reacquainted with each other with some light running between. On arriving back at The Abattoir they showered, Colton relieved the water had heated up at all, as he'd forgot to check the settings on the boiler.

They went down to the Waverley bar for late liquid lunch or early dinner, this involved walking part way down the High Street, passing Blake's bar, where a line of retired motorcycles with their engines removed stood proud but celibate along the length of road, and a silver electric Smart car sat next to them.

They walked passed the Prudential Building, at which point they all lowered their voices to hushed murmurs to avoid drawing unwanted attention from any open windows.

The Green framed windows of the Waverley bar were decorated with blue and yellow bunting flags, and a silhouette of a man on a horse holding a flag triumphantly was embossed on the panes of glass. The door creaked open and the smell of stale beer greeted the boy's nostrils. A gruff looking man with a long white beard acknowledged them from behind the bar.

"What's your poison Colton?" Robbie asked him.

"Cider and black for me, ta." Colton replied.

They sat at a table opposite the bar and bowed their heads together. This was where plans would be made, within spitting distance of the Alessi residence, this would be where the beginnings of the plan for their downfall would be formed, Colton could feel it. Just not yet. Not on this day, this day was for catching up with old friends and familiar faces.

Colton returned to the Abattoir some time later in the evening, another kebab in hand. Tomorrow he would do a proper food shop, get some healthy food in. He'd grown so used to being able to pluck fresh fruit growing on trees all around him, he was missing the free food.

He checked on Becky, she was content in her back stable. He fed her some oats and noticed the piles of dung were going to need attention tomorrow.

"Manyana," he said to her, "Never do today what you could put off till tomorrow." he yawned sleepily.

His mother's scolding tone of voice came into his head, "Just get it done, Colton."

"I will, tomorrow." he said.

Tomorrow he would get organised, he wouldn't let day after day slip away from him, he'd end up settled in a routine and forget why he had even returned home, he promised his mum he would get it done.

Chapter Thirty-Six

Colton slept badly, his dreams filled with uncomfortable memories throughout the night, the ghosts of the past haunted his sleep. Thomas was there, then Aubrey, and his mum, all angry at him, always angry.

"My son," Aubrey said, "Get up, you have work to do."

When he woke up in the early hours of the day he was tangled up in his duvet, part of the cover had wrapped around his throat.

Becky was kicking at her door downstairs angrily, she must have heard him crying out. He untangled himself and went downstairs in his boxers to settle his horse, then went back up to the kitchenette to make a coffee. It was five in the morning. He decided to stay up and do some more work to the Abattoir.

He poured himself a coffee, wandered through to the office and put some music on through the overhead speakers. He dragged the hoover out of the cleaning cupboard, opening the upper windows to air the place out, and had to empty the hoover three times for the amount of dust it lifted. He opened the door to Aubrey's old bedroom, the air was stale but the smell of Aubrey's aftershave still lingered in the air. Colton looked around at it all, the closed wardrobe, the dressing table with everything in its right place, missing the watch and the rings that Aubrey had been wearing on that last day.

Colton sat on the bed, thinking back to his mother, her house would be the same, dusty, neglected, forgotten. Today would be a day for visiting solicitors. He would get that out of the way, sort out his affairs, get it all in order, then he could concentrate on formulating the plan.

"That's my boy." he heard Aubrey approve.

Colton showered, then he dressed in one of Aubrey's suits from the wardrobe, feeling the quality of the lining as he slid it over a white shirt, it fit him well. He brushed back his hair with water and borrowed a pair of Aubrey's polished black shoes.

"Got to look good for the legalities." he remembered Aubrey saying.

Colton pulled a tie from the wardrobe, tried to tie it then changed his mind, he put it on the dresser, checked himself and hung it back up in its correct place in the wardrobe.

Out onto the street, he glanced into a shop window and caught a reflection of himself along the way, he looked quite the part, and remarkably like Aubrey.

Vivienne was walking along the street, she saw him walking towards her and caught his attention, "Looking good Mr Cooper!" she smiled beneath her large sunglasses.

"Thank you." Colton replied, stopping to stand next to her.

"Where are you off to looking so smart and handsome?" she asked, adjusting her large black handbag and her cardigan, which dropped to expose her shoulder, Colton felt his eyes drawn to her tanned skin, how soft it looked, longing to touch it.

"Solomons solicitors." he replied.

"Christ, what do you want with them?" she asked.

Colton couldn't tell if she was fishing for information or if she was just making casual conversation.

"Sorting out my parent's affairs." he said.

Vivienne looked forlornly at him, "God has that never been sorted out?"

"I never got round to it." he replied.

"Do you want me to come in with you, it will be pretty tough on you, sometimes having someone else with you helps. Especially in there, you'll need a witness to everything Solomon says, he's so dodgy." she rolled her eyes and touched his arm tenderly.

Colton steadied himself, Vivienne wanted to be with him, to support him. He didn't know how to reply.

"Come on, I'll come with you and you can treat me to a coffee afterwards." she smiled, taking his arm in hers to walk by his side.

Colton didn't hear much of what the girl said to him when they went into the small office reception.

"You don't have an appointment." the girl said, checking through the diary on her desk and the one on the computer, dismissively, "What did you say it was about again, I can check with Mr Solomon to find out when he has time to see you."

The girl stood up and went through the back taking the desk diary with her. Vivienne squeezed his arm. He appreciated her being there, in that moment, as he felt about two feet tall, not welcome in the solicitors office.

The girl returned looking apologetic, sat down at her desk saying nothing and Carl Solomon himself came through from the back office.

"Mr Cooper, I am very pleased to see you. I have cleared my diary for the next hour or so in order to clear up your matters personally." Carl held out his hand.

Colton rose from the chair, removing himself from Vivienne's supportive arm, and shook Carl's hand, which was hot and sweaty. Carl's hair had turned a significant shade greyer since Colton last saw him.

"Please, come through to my office." Carl gestured, he eyed Vivienne uneasily.

"She's with me." Colton said, indicating that Vivienne was to go through with them.

"Very well." Carl said.

Carl adjusted the spectacles on his nose and saw them both into scratchy black material chairs in his small office. It was surprisingly tidy despite the first impression Carl gave Colton. Solomon excused himself while he located Colton's paperwork, then returned with two files in his hands.

Carl sat down, adjusting his glasses, and glanced again at Vivienne, "Shall we address your father first?" Carl asked formally.

Colton nodded.

Vivienne squeezed Colton's hand in a supportive way and held her hand on his. The movement of her thumb, a stroking gesture which was meant to soothe him irritated him in some way.

"Your father left a will, in which you are the sole benefactor. Everything has been left to you."

"What do you mean by 'everything'?" Colton asked.

"Well, everything he owned, The Abattoir Club, which he owned outright, his black Mercedes, which was last known to be in his garage at the property on Buccleuch Road, but bearing in mind the government cull on engines, this may no longer be the case, a four bedroom property on Buccleuch Road, a four bedroom house with swimming pool near Madrid, all contents of these, stocks and shares, which at the last check were worth approximately one million pounds, and a sum of two million pounds in his current account."

"Two million pounds?" Vivienne exclaimed.

"Yes, thats correct. You are a very wealthy man Mr Cooper." Mr Solomon said, looking up from the paperwork at Vivienne, and frowning slightly, "I knew Aubrey Delaney quite personally Miss Cowbridge." he said it as if it held unspoken details of some importance, but she did not acknowledge it.

Carl Solomon opened the other file, "With regards to your mother, Colton, she left you everything. Her two bedroom property in Denholm and contents, her Vauxhall Corsa which was unfortunately removed due to the changes in the law, though I have the hundred pound compensation fee in holding, and her savings of two thousand pounds."

"Sorry, I'm not really taking all of this in." Colton said, sitting back in his chair, running his hands through his hair.

"We were worried you were dead, we're so glad you have returned. We had to file a missing person's report as there was some pressure being put on us from other sources to wrap this estate up," He looked down his spectacles at Vivienne at this point, choosing his words carefully, "A challenge which would have seen the whole inheritance null and void had you not returned. However, here you are, just in time." he smiled.

Vivienne deflected Carl's gaze and smiled at Colton, "Colton, you're a millionaire!" she took his hands in hers and lifted them with glee.

"Aubrey never told me he was a millionaire." Colton mumbled.

"Would you have thought differently of him if he had?" Carl said, "On his return home to see his son, what would his son have done on finding his father a millionaire? He wanted a relationship with you Colton, not a price tag or a receipt slip."

They wrapped up the paperwork and formalities, after which the solicitor looked at Colton with sadness in his eyes, "Yes, I knew your father. So sad that you spent such a short space of time with him. I can see him reflected in you in so many ways. Do him proud, Colton."

"I will." Colton said, standing up to leave.

Colton stepped out into the broad light of day and exhaled, "Bloody hell." he said, bending to his knees as his legs weaken beneath him.

"Oh my god Colton, let's celebrate!" Vivienne exclaimed excitedly.

"I don't want people to know." Colton said, straightening up and tidying his suit, "I would appreciate it if you didn't tell anyone."

"Okay, no problem, this can be our little secret." Vivienne smiled coyly, "My lips are sealed, with a kiss!" she said, leaning forward to kiss Colton on the mouth, "Thats a promise not to tell." she smiled.

Colton felt like all his birthdays had come at once. His life had suddenly become a surreal dream. The boy who had lived in one set of clothes in a ghost town was actually a millionaire.

"We could always go back to your place and have ourselves our own private little celebration." Vivienne smiled.

Colton couldn't believe his ears, Vivienne, was propositioning him.

"Okay." he said, daring a cheeky smile to find its way to his face.

"Let's get some drinks in! Champagne, on the rocks!" Vivienne said triumphantly.

They walked together crossing the high street, going down an alley, across the iron Victorian footbridge to reach the supermarkets on Commercial Road. Vivienne filled a trolley with items which Colton paid for, including bottles of cava, luxurious snacks, bubble bath, candles. Colton remembered some of the things that he needed in the Abattoir, like toilet rolls, if there was a female coming round, but his mind was completely distracted at the thought of the night ahead Vivienne seemed to have lined up for them, judging by the contents of the trolley.

"This will make the place smell a bit fresher, less like testosterone." Vivienne said distractedly, concentrating on what she needed to buy.

Colton grimaced as the cashier read out the total to pay. They grabbed a taxi back along to the Abattoir, along past the Horse monument, up the High Street, pulling in at the back lane near the vennel. Vivienne got out lightly, lifting some of the bags out of the taxi to outside the Abattoir while Colton paid the driver. He'd almost run out of cash completely. Solomon told him it would take a while for the funds to transfer, he'd have to watch his budget till then, but a night on a promise with Vivienne was too much to resist.

Chapter Thirty-Seven

It was two months later. Colton was in a routine of running the Abattoir training club, and keeping Vivienne happy. Becky was rehomed in Sam's stables, happily sharing a field with his horses. For now, everything else could wait. Colton and Vivienne were having a disagreement upstairs in the Abattoir one evening. They'd grown very close, very quickly. It made the Abattoir Boys uncomfortable, but they said nothing, seeing how happy Colton was.

"Then stop trying to change me Vivienne, I am not a perfect guy, I don't feel comfortable in the clothes you want me to wear. If I go out, you gotta stop calling and trying to figure out where I am half the night. I come home to you no matter what the night brings."

Vivienne's hand trembled where she held the glass of half drunk white wine in the air, "I'm allowed to know where you are, who you've been with." she replied, staring at the glass, spinning the contents around slightly with a move of her hand.

"You're choking me! I'm trying to get stuff done, all hours of the day, for us, for our future. I can't set my mind on it for wondering if you're upset or mad at me for something I don't even know I've done wrong! You're going to have to try to relax."

"No, I'm not. You're going to have to learn you have a woman waiting for you back home worried sick about what you're getting up to."

"Why don't you go out and have fun?"Colton bent down and rested his hands lightly on Vivienne's knees.

Vivienne took a sip of her wine and looked down at him, "Because I haven't got anyone to go out with. I have to plan ahead to book time with my friends, they're all busy people. You go out on a whim and you don't even think of inviting me."

"It wasn't planned, Vivienne, it was just me and Calvin, and a couple of lads drinking at the bar, you wouldn't have enjoyed it."

"Wouldn't have been welcome no doubt, your friends all hate me, I've seen the way they look at me, I made a mistake by being with Marius Alessi it's not fair I be punished for it the rest of my life!"

"They don't all hate you." Colton said standing up and walking around the room.

"For all I know you hate me too!"

Vivienne threw her wine glass towards Colton, where it smashed off the wall into shards, which dripped down the wall along with the wine.

"I hate you!" she yelled at him, standing up.

She ran at him and hit her hands off his chest with tears streaming down her face.

Colton felt rage surge into him, "What's got into you?"

He grabbed her wrists and threw her backwards onto the chair, where she jarred with fright then burst into hysterical sobs. He knelt by the chair, "Vivienne, I'm sorry, I didn't mean it."

She wouldn't look at him.

"Vivienne, look at me." he touched her legs gently, then held one of her hands in his. He took her hand to his mouth and kissed it, "Vivienne I'm sorry, I'm so sorry. I didn't mean to get you so wound up."

"I can't stand it." she sobbed, "I know that you hate me, I can see it when you look at me."

"Vivienne, I don't hate you at all. I love you."

The words came out before he'd thought about them, he was so desperate to appease her. She lifted her head from her hands, brushing her hair back, she looked at him in wonder.

"You do?" she sniffed.

"Of course I do, I've loved you since the day I set eyes on you, you're sheer perfection, everything about you."

Vivienne smiled a little and Colton embraced her in his arms.

"Colton, that's so … touching." she whispered, "you're so wonderful." she sighed and he felt her go to sleep in his arms.

He lifted her and carried her through to his bedroom, which was drastically altered now that Vivienne was around. He walked back through to the office, glancing at the wine dripping down the wall. He walked through to the kitchen, grabbed a cloth and mopped it up. He put the shards into the bin and made himself some toast. Running his hands through his hair he thought about what just happened. He felt trapped by Vivienne, her constant scrutinising, but she was everything he ever wanted. He couldn't understand where all her anger and hatred was coming from, she should be as happy as he was, that they were together and she was safe with him. He bristled with anger about what Vivienne must have went through during her time with Marius Alessi, what she must have been subjected to, to make her behave this way now with him. He was nothing like Marius.

Colton sat on the sofa and put the television on at a low volume, and gradually dozed off into sleep. He awoke to the smell of bacon and the sound of it sizzling in the kitchen. Vivienne was standing in her white silk nightdress, flipping the bacon in the pan. She smiled when she saw him, and swung her arms round him, kissing his neck, then his mouth, "There you are my gorgeous hunk of a man. I am so sorry about last night, I drank far too much wine. I hope you had a nice night out." she stepped back to the pan, "I'm making you bacon rolls, but you'll need to go to the bakers for the rolls."

"I'll just have it on its own, thanks, with a couple of eggs or something." Colton replied.

"Oh. Right." she frowned as if this was affecting her plans for the entire day, "Okay then."

Colton leaned over to kiss her to cheer her up again, which she deftly side-stepped away from to reach for the eggs. Colton accepted that she did not know he was trying to kiss her, he turned and switched the kettle on for a coffee.

"I have a nail appointment at ten this morning do you have any cash, Zizi text to say her card machine isn't working." Vivienne turned to Colton and leaned back on the counter with her hands, and bent one of her knees, raising her leg in the air to lean against the cupboard. Colton ran his eyes up and down her lithe body.

"How much do you need?" he asked.

"Forty-five pounds." she said, popping her finger in her mouth coyly.

Colton reached into his back pocket for his wallet, pulling out three twenty pound notes.

"Thank you." she smiled, reaching for all three of them.

He put his wallet away and reached for her, aching with desire, but she had already turned away again, "Your bacon is ready." she smiled.

Colton held in a disappointed sigh and smiled as she presented the bacon and eggs to him.

Colton was in a crabbit mood on his run round the park that morning, he found himself snapping at the boys when they spoke to him.

"Jeesh what's up with you this morning?" Robbie asked him.

"Nothing." Colton simmered, then added, "Vivienne's just nabbed sixty quid off me to get her nails done, I don't know what's wrong or what more I can do for her."

"You're not getting laid, that's what's wrong." Jimmy stated. He was, as ever, donned in a shirt and holy cashmere jumper with his training shorts.

"How did you know that's what's wrong?" Colton growled.

"Oldest trick in the book, women withholding sex to get their own way. Drives a man crazy." Jimmy replied, "Are you sure she's not just using you for money?"

The other boys glanced at Jimmy warily.

"Naw. No way. Not Vivienne, she's not like that." Colton said with certainty.

The boys around him exchanged wary looks again.

"Okay, so how about taking her out for a meal or something?" Calvin suggested.

"Good idea." Colton said.

Colton pulled out his phone from its armband and dialled her number, "Hey babe!" he said cheerfully and his face fell immediately, "No, I'm still out running, sorry I didn't mean to call you when you are getting your nails done, I thought that was later on today. No it's not an emergency … Babe, don't be like that … sorry … I already said sorry for last night, but I thought we could go out for a meal tonight to make up for it?"

The boys jogged awkwardly in silence, waiting for the response on the other end of the phone.

"Oh, you have something on tonight? What are you doing? … Going to Libby's, that's great! … No, no I'm not glad that you're out of the house, I'm glad you're going to see your friend! … Of course you're allowed to go out without me knowing your every move … Okay, well, I'll not see you till … oh, you're staying over at her house? Okay, I'll see you tomorrow then … I love you." Colton hung up and put the phone back in the armband.

"Aw man, you've told her you love her?" Calvin said.

"Well, just since last night." Colton replied.

"Looks like you ain't getting any tonight either if she's staying at Libby's." Jimmy grunted.

"Aye, this staying loyal to one bird isn't all it's cracked up to be is it!" Calvin laughed.

"Argh!" Colton scuffed at the ground with his toes and kicked at a tree he was passing.

The other boys laughed, except Jimmy who chewed his lip and said nothing.

Chapter Thirty-Eight

Colton received an anonymous letter in the mail the next day. A plain white envelope with one folded piece of card inside it, it was stamp marked from Spain. When he opened the card it read,

"Hay dos clases de virtudes: las que hacen ganar el cielo y las que hacen ganar la tierra. B."

Colton knew it was from the Baron. Colton pulled out his phone to search for a translation as he didn't quite understand it, "There are two kinds of virtues: those that win us heaven and those that win us the earth." a quote by Noel Clarasó.

He stared at the card for a while, his brain running quickly over the message on the card. He held the card up to the light, nothing, he switched a lamp on and held it over the bulb and lo and behold further words appeared on the paper,

"The time has come. We are ready, we are waiting. B."

The Baron knew where he was, that he had returned home to the Abattoir without Colton getting in touch with him. Surely that meant someone else was in touch with the Baron. Suddenly reality distorted, memories of his time in Spain came flooding back to him, as well as memories of the beautiful Sofia.

Colton remembered talking to the Baron about the plan, jokingly, and yet here he was, back home and the Baron was asking him to make a move, when Colton just let it slip from his mind in favour of appeasing Vivienne. Colton chewed his lip thoughtfully, he was going to have to rally his army.

Chapter Thirty-Nine

Colton decided to visit Calvin at his home in Burnfoot Estate to discuss some things with him. He made his way up there on foot.

Calvin's next door neighbour was a little old woman of perhaps eighty six years old, or eighty four. She couldn't remember and she didn't care these days. She waved at Calvin through her living room window every time he walked up the path. She watched that boy grow up walking along that pathway from a toddler to the man he was now, and the same with his sister Stef. She'd taken his mother Rose in and called the police when his father Steve Armstrong got drunk and violent. She'd watched Marius Alessi's henchmen walk up in the dark and heard those hushed threatening tones of conversation. She'd watched Rose get dragged out of the house by the police. And Calvin's shoulders walk with a beaten slump every single day until two months ago. When the name Colton Cooper began drifting up the pathway and in through her window, and then, gradually, she noticed the slump was returning.

Violet had seen a lot of changes in her lifetime. When she saw Colton Cooper open the gate for the first time that year she knew something was going on, just by the way the boy carried his shoulders, he walked with purpose.

Violet rapped on her window when she saw Colton at Calvin's gate, rat-a-tat-tat with her walking stick and waved at the lad.

"Hello Mrs Lochhead." Colton smiled.

"Hello son." she called through her window, "Can you bring me my paper in from the garden? Would you mind?"

Colton turned back out of Calvin's gateway and walked up into Mrs Lochhead's path, he picked up her paper, "Just come in son, I cannae walk to the door to answer it," he heard her shout from the window.

Colton carefully opened the door to a wall of warmth, in an immaculate house filled with ornaments, crochet, knitting and pictures of family members.

"Thank you ... Colton isn't it?" Violet said from her chair by the window.

"Aye." he said, handing her the paper.

"Can you take the wrapping off it, my hands arnie what they used to be, ken."

Colton unwrapped the waterproof plastic from the paper.

"Thanks. Now ..." Violet sighed, spreading out her hands to straighten her gown, "Just what is it you think you're doing?"

Colton looked confusedly at her.

"I know you're up to something, you boys and your games, I saw the same look on your father when he came through that gateway all those years ago looking for Steve. I know when someone is concocting a plan. And I'm telling you, I want in."

Colton checked himself as to what he just heard, "Excuse me Mrs Lochhead?"

"You heard me. I'm seek o' seeing those Alessi brothers walking about like they own the town, and hearing that someone else has been arrested and got the jail for something they haven't done, or lost their hoose or been sent to the hospital or grave because of those men. I wasn't always this old ee ken. I used to hide your faither's guns for him back in the day and I'm telling you I'll do the same for you boys if I have to."

"Mrs Lochhead, I …"

"Dinnae try and lie to me, I'm no in with the Police. They won't suspect a poor old woman like me to be having any part o' your scheming, now will they?"

Colton laughed, "No, probably not."

Violet smiled at him, and leaned forward to whisper, "In fact, I think I've still got yin o' your faither's guns lying around here somewhere. Let me have a think." she leaned back into her chair, her eyes lighting up, "Aye, ye didnae ken that now did ye? Old Violet Lochhead has a gun stashed away in her hoose, waiting for your father to come back to claim it, but here you are instead."

Colton wondered if the old woman was losing it, he stood up to go, "I really can't stay Mrs Lochhead,"

"Go an' see fir yerself, go an, the cupboard under the stairs. Ye'll need tae pull out all my stuff, I cannae reach it these days of course. Go an!" she insisted.

"Okay, I'll do as I'm told!" Colton laughed.

"Aye, ye will!" Violet smiled.

Colton did as he was bid and pulled out the contents of the cupboard, dusty boxes of memories of the life of Mrs Lochhead filled the clean hallway.

"I've done that Mrs Lochhead." he said walking through to the living room.

"Right then, give me a hand onto my walking frame son I want to see this." Mrs Lochhead said.

Colton pulled the walking frame in front of the chair, Mrs Lochhead pushed a button on her chair and the chair raised her up higher to help her get up.

"Yes, you boys and your plans. Your fither brought a time of peace to this town, though only those in the know could credit him for it, and you'd better be dain' the same." she grunted as she edged herself out of the chair to lean on the walker.

"I'm going to try to bring peace to us all." Colton said, helping Violet rise slowly to her feet.

"Well, wid ye look at that, I'm up!" Violet exclaimed as she daintily walked through the hall with the aid of her walker, "Och pit the light on and shut the living room dair sae nae wan can look through the window and see whit we're dain'."

"Right." Colton said, doing as he was bid by the old woman, and returned to look at the hall cupboard.

Violet reached into her gown pocket and put her glasses on, peering into the cupboard, "Down there son, y'see underneath the stairs aye? Well its all fake, the real underneath o' the stairs is further back. If you push that nail there away and pull that bit of wood … "

Nothing happened, Colton knew this was too good to be true.

"Nevermind Mrs Lochhead, maybe once … " Colton began.

"Oh. Maybe it's the next one down, try the next one down."

Obliging the old lady one more time, Colton pushed and prodded at the next stair down, this time something went 'click' and the lower three steps swung open, he realised it was a well disguised door. There was a safe inside and space around it for further storage.

"Well, there. Didn't I tell you?" Mrs Lochhead said, "Now, the combination for that safe is well hidden too. It's on the handle of my walking stick, on the emblem, though dinnae expect me to remember what the number is. Thats why its on my old stick, so I don't have to remember it." she said, "It comes with age, I cannae rely on my memory. Hurry up and fetch my stick!"

Colton clambered out of the cupboard and went into the living room, he saw the stick resting against the chair where Violet sat. He picked it up, sure enough, there was a number etched onto the emblem of Mrs Lochhead's walking stick, "I always knew you were good boys who respected your elders." Violet said.

While Colton dialled the numbers into the safe he realised it was his date of birth. He heard a satisfying click and the door swung open. Inside were a few brown manilla envelopes, the top one rather bulky. Colton touched it and felt the heavy weight of the object inside it, sure enough when he pulled the envelope from the safe and looked inside, it was a hand gun.

"Wow, Mrs Lochhead …" Colton said, words evading him.

"I hope it still works son, if I could shoot straight I'd test it myself but my damn eyes have glaucoma now, and I need both hands to balance on my walker."

"Leave the shooting to me, Mrs Lochhead." Colton smiled.

Colton peered down the barrel of the gun. It was heavy, black cold metal between his fingertips, his father's gun, a legacy.

"He freed the town with that gun once before." Violet said knowingly, "Not many folks remember quite how bad things were afor. Why he took himself off to Las Vegas I'll never understand, he did good things here. Of course that was a few years before the police were in the back pocket of the money makers, before they all bowed down to the Alessi family." Violet gazed down at the gun, "Who knows if Aubrey would have been able to stop it all from happening, maybe they would have killed him sooner. Can you shoot?"

"A little." Colton replied, "But I've not used a gun like this before."

"Let me show you how it works." Violet smiled, "Here, give it to an expert."

The old woman's hands shook as she took the gun in her grasp.

Sitting in Mrs Lochhead's hallway with her, getting a sound bite in how to fire the gun was another stark realisation for Colton that anything was possible.

"I need to go next door and speak to Calvin, Mrs Lochhead." Colton said apologetically.

Colton tucked the gun into the back of his jeans, pulling his hoodie over it. The cold metal sent a chill up his spine and dazzling flashbacks of when he last held a gun in his hands.

"Yes, of course you do. The other envelopes are yours as well I expect, though I don't know what's in them."

"I don't know how to thank you." Colton said.

"Ach just come to my funeral when the time comes, there'll no be mony folk there, most of my friends are deed already and I've no family to speak of." Violet said, motioning back through to the living room with her slow shuffle.

Colton helped Violet over to her chair, already the light and excitement was fading from Violet's face.

"See yersel oot the door there son." she said.

Colton walked down Violet's path then round and up to Calvin's door.

"You're late." Calvin said, "Saw you coming up the road about half an hour ago."

Calvin was dressed in loose grey cotton jogging pants with white writing down the side, a white t-shirt and thick white socks.

"Aye, sorry, Violet wanted me to help her with something."

"Nosy old bat, last night she summoned me to move a bag of dirty woman's nappies out of her bathroom, hope she didn't get you to do that!" Calvin grumbled, then added, "Ach she's done a lot for us over the years, it's sad really watching her get old in front of us."

Calvin walked through to the kitchen, "Want a Resurgence?"

"A what?"

"Deh tell iz ee've never heard o' it?" Calvin said, "Resurgence? Its an energy drink, like Red Bull only ten times stronger."

"Nah, no thanks. I heard they make those drinks out of by-products from slaughterhouses, all the blood they drain off the cows, it's called Taurine in the ingredients." Colton said, sitting down at one of the two seats at the folded-down dining table. The table was covered with paperwork, mail mostly, takeaway menus, that sprawled almost to the middle of the table.

"Nah, no way, I deh believe that." Calvin said, twisting the metallic blue can in his hands, reading through the ingredients, "Taurine, god it's there. Fuck's sake Colton you've spoiled my drink now."

"Sorry." Colton said laughing.

"Right, anyway, I'm no stoppin' drinking it just coz ee said it's made o' blood." Calvin said, sitting at the opposite chair, "What's on today then?"

"I am going to bring down the corrupt cops, kill the Alessi brothers, and get our town back." Colton said starkly.

He reached round and pulled the gun out of where it was digging into his back, placing it on top of the paperwork on the table, as his statement of intent.

Calvin looked at it briefly then said, "What can I do to help?"

"I want to be able to send a message to Spain, by boat."

"Ach, Colton all the boats are gone, they got rid of those the same time as the cars for the diesel engines. My da' was left unemployed as they introduced these strict new fishing laws on top of everything else, they took his ship off him and gave him a grand. A grand. How's that supposed to keep him going?"

"If we can get a boat, somehow, would your dad drive it to Spain?" Colton asked.

"Dunno, I'd have to ask him. I don't know the ins and outs of it, if we'd get busted before leaving the port or what."

"We can't speak to him by phone, it's too risky." Colton said.

Calvin thought about it for a moment, supping a drink from his can, "Well, we could head over to see him tomorrow if you want, leave early doors?"

Calvin fished about amongst the pile of paperwork, "It's my filing system." Calvin explained, "Ma maw used to deal wi' all this crap. Here it is." Calvin pulled out a timetable.

"What's it for?" Colton asked.

"Train. To the city. Stef could take us in the company car to the rail station as it's on her route anyway, if we ask her nicely, and we can walk to the station when she drops us off. Then we get the train to Edinburgh, another train journey and we can go visit my Da' over in Eyemouth. If you need a boat driver, he's definitely your man. I deh really speak to him much, he was such a dick to my Ma' and us, I hate him actually, but apparently he was a legend back in his day."

"And he can drive boats?"

"He can drive boats."

"Is it worth me asking why you need to get a boat to Spain?" Calvin asked.

"I haven't fully figured that out yet. I have an idea, but it needs someone's help and that someone is in Spain, and he doesn't like using telephones."

Calvin burst out laughing, "So we sail a message to him instead, and risk the jail for it, ach, classic."

"Well, I expect a reply to come back too, a shipment, and that would definitely need to be by boat, and that would definitely involve a prison sentence if we get caught."

"Okay."

"Calvin?" Colton asked, "Would you mind if I crashed at yours tonight, I deh want Vivienne getting wind of any of this, and she's been a bit crazy nuts the now."

"Aye, no bother, let's get some beers in. We'll speak to Stef when she gets back from work."

Chapter Forty

Stef reluctantly agreed to help them through the bribery of a bottle of wine along with her swearing to secrecy. She only knew that Calvin and Colton were going to see her father the next day on matters of great importance. That was all she needed to know and she stopped them telling her anything further as she knew it would probably be a lie anyway.

The company car was parked outside her work offices, it was fitted with a tracking system and speed limiter on it, she had to programme in the route she was taking, to ensure she wasn't planning a journey that would drain the battery, and that her journey was fully accountable to her work. The only control she really had without causing undue suspicion was the ability to brake. The company were quite heavy handed with any attempt at deviating from the specified route without undue justification. However she was allowed to call into the shops at Commercial Road for a pee or coffee stop first thing, and on her lunch hour she was allowed a deviation to buy a sandwich as long as she kept her receipt to prove where she had been. Risky and awkward as it may be, it was the only car available to them to help them begin their journey to Eyemouth.

The next morning Stef pulled into Starbucks on Commercial Road in the car for a takeaway coffee, she parked at the back of the car park, leaving the car unlocked for Calvin and Colton to jump into the back seats while she was ordering. A moment or two later she opened the driver's door and the warm aroma of coffee filled the car.

"Dinnae expect me to buy you two onyhin' as ee's arnie supposed to be in the car and I'm no' taking any chances by someone telling my work they saw me buying three coffees this morning." Stef said to them in the mirror.

"Naw Stef it's 'cause you're just a steenge." Calvin said.

Stef leaned round and thumped her older brother on the arm, "Shut it or ee'll no be getting a lift onywhere."

"Gie is a sip of coffee at least then." Calvin moaned, "Colton's put is off my Resurgence I need a caffeine hit."

"Just a sip!" Stef said.

Calvin took a mouthful of the coffee.

"Calvin! I said a sip!" she squealed trying to snatch the hot coffee out of her brothers hands.

Colton grimaced and looked out of the window, it was a moment when he felt three times older than Calvin and his younger sister.

Stef clicked a button and the engine started.

Both boys ducked down low as the car pulled out of the car park, and didn't sit up until they were safely out of Hawick and any the risk of prying eyes that might get Stef into trouble were long past them.

Calvin leaned forward and stole another sip of Stef's coffee. Stef put the radio on and the rest of the journey passed pleasantly enough. She slowed to a crawl as near as she could get the car to Tweedbank railway station so they could jump out without the car registering a complete stop on her tracker, she waved as she pulled away, leaving them to walk to the station.

Calvin pulled up his hood and Colton donned a battered old baseball cap. Calvin lit up a cigarette which he stubbed out near the station grounds, they bought tickets from the self-service machine. They didn't say much while they stood waiting for the train, which arrived five minutes later. Both of them dozed on the carriage for the hour or so it took to arrive in Edinburgh. Once there, they transferred to a train going along the East Coast to Berwick-Upon-Tweed. They caught a Perryman's bus to Eyemouth, where they grabbed a bag of fish and chips, and a can of juice from the chip shop opposite the harbour, and walked along to the streets to where Calvin last knew his dad lived in a pretty run down area. They felt a little revived by the food and can of juice lining their stomachs.

"I dunno what state he'll be in mind, if he still lives here." Calvin said.

"No worries." Colton said.

Calvin knocked at the door, they could hear a television playing a football match, then there was silence from inside the flat. Calvin peered through the letterbox and saw a shadow move inside the hallway, "Da', it's me, Calvin, go an' let us in."

"Calvin? Is that you?"

"Aye, da'."

Steve Armstrong opened the door to the flat. He was wearing navy tracksuit bottoms with two white stripes running down the sides, navy trainers with white soles, a light blue t-shirt and he held a bottle of Becks beer in his hand. His eyes were deeply shadowed and his face filled with lines. A day's stubble covered his face, matching the length of his greying dark hair. The air from inside the flat was choked with the smell of cannabis.

"'Mon in son!" Steve exclaimed, putting his arm around his son, "Who's this y'got with ee?"

"Colton Cooper." Calvin said.

Steve glanced over at him, "Oh aye, thought he looked familiar. Come on in shut the door. Heck I thought ee was the Housing Officer coming to ask iz fir rent money!" he laughed, "Fancy a beer?"

"Aye do I." Calvin said, "Been a hell of a journey to get here."

Steve walked along the hall into a left hand doorway which opened to a small kitchen. Two crates of beer and a litre bottle of vodka sat on the table, "It's like I knew ee's were coming!"

Steve cracked open two beers and handed one each to them, he looked at Colton, "Christ look at ee, you're the spit of Aubrey, you look just like him at your age. What's the old man up to these days?"

"He's dead, Da'." Calvin said, taking a sup on his beer.

Steve's face fell, "What?"

"Aye."

"Then I'm guessing you're no' here for a social visit." Steve said, running his hand across his stubble, "Come into the living room, I need to roll a smoke to digest this news."

Steve grabbed another beer for himself and walked to the right of the kitchen through into a living room filled with the cloud of cigarette smoke. The curtains were closed, the dark wooden coffee table was covered with tobacco, cigarette papers, lighters, an overflowing ashtray, drink glasses, and other paraphernalia. Steve sat down in a single seater armchair, ripped and torn at the arms, which was within reaching distance of everything on the table.

Colton and Calvin sat on the two seater armchair opposite him.

"Aubrey's dead aih?" Steve said, shaking his head, "Fucking shit man."

"Sorry Da', I thought you'd have known." Calvin said.

"No, I didnae know that son, I'd heard he'd gone back to Hawick to try to make it up to June and be a dad to Colton, but that's as far as I'd heard. Bit out of the loop here, ken. Was even thinking of going across to visit him at one point, but it's that far and I cannae really afford it. Been a bit out of the loop now I don't have a mobile phone or that. They're always listening to those things, ken. You didnae tell onyone ee's were coming here did you?"

"No, but if anyone asks, I'm just visiting my Da'." Calvin replied.

"Aye, but niver let onyone ken yer business Calvin." Steve said, laying out a long cigarette paper, he sprinkled loose tobacco over it, then pulled out a bag of grass from a drawer hidden under the tabletop, and sprinkled that into the roll-up.

"Have you seen that in the paper?" Steve continued, "Microchips in our hands so we don't need to use money anymore. Zap zap, and there's credit on your hand. I mean hows that going to work for the likes of me? I never have any credit! There was talk of putting solar panels on the roofs here at one point, to give us free electricity and that, but now I think they're just going to knock all the flats down and start again, put some more expensive houses up, chuck the likes of me out. God knows where I'm going to end up. Might have to bunk up on your sofa till your mum gets out the jail."

"How did you know I was Aubrey's son?" Colton asked, wondering how other people knew he was the son of Aubrey Delaney and they all managed to keep it from him all these years.

"Oh aye, it was a secret aih? Yer maw asked everyone no to tell you. I just forgot as it was years ago now, ken." Steve shrugged, "What brings you boys to my door the day then?"

"The business of revenge." Colton said, "I need a man who can drive a boat."

"Revenge aih? Do you have a boat?" Steve asked, lighting up the rollie.

"No."

"I only drive diesel engines. Which, lads, remember, they destroyed. Every single one. I cannae drive these electrical ones. Even if I could, they've all got trackers in them, nigh on impossible to change course. The boys have tried everything to override the computers, they've not been able to so far. Unless you plan on rowing me somewhere while I steer, then you need to find yourselves a diesel boat."

"So we need a boat with a diesel engine." Colton said, supping his beer.

"And diesel." Calvin added.

"Dinnae worry aboot diesel, I can get old-school engines to run on vegetable oil out the chip shops." said Steve, "What's it for?"

"I need it to get to Spain and return with a small shipment of highly illegal substances." Colton replied.

"You going to deal? I'm no' wanting to get involved with any of that."

"No, this is a one off, I need to be able to frame someone." Colton said.

"Who?" Steve raised his eyebrows.

"The Alessi's da!" Calvin said.

"And the police." Colton added.

Steve whistled through his teeth, "Now you're talking business. How bigs the shipment?"

"Enough to fill a small car."

"Well, you don't need a big boat for that. I might know of a small one stowed away, but they've taken the engine. If you could get me a diesel engine, I could get you a working boat."

"I might know where we can get a diesel engine." Colton said.

"Where?" Steve asked, "They wiped all the engines out, clean out, there's literally not a single one left, even on the black market. They raised the price of engine scrap so high no one could resist. There were gang wars over engines. Then there were no engines left." Steve said, passing the joint to Calvin.

"I have a Black Mercedes C-Class hidden away." Colton said, interrupting Steve, who Colton surmised liked to do a lot of talking with his smoke.

"What? Colton! You didn't tell me you had a car!" Calvin exclaimed.

"Saving it for a rainy day." Colton shrugged looking at Calvin.

Calvin didn't know the half of what Colton now had in his possession, and Colton wasn't about to tell him, especially in front of Steve who didn't seem the most trustworthy sort. Colton had checked the garage and property at Buccleuch Road only briefly, during a time that Vivienne wasn't with him. Though she was desperate to see and move into the house, Colton was adamant he didn't want to live there, he wasn't ready, and she struggled with that fact, but accepted that living at The Abattoir with him was as good as she was going to get for the time being.

"Sacrilege." Steve said, shaking his head, "It would be absolute sacrilege to break up a car like that."

"Can you do it?" Colton asked.

"Aye. But, God, if people knew you had one of those cars, christ, you'd be a wanted man, it would fetch a fortune now." Steve said.

"Steve, I've got to know I can trust you. Like my father did. If you start talking about how much my car's engine is worth on the black market, I'm going to have to find me another boat driver. If you lynch on me for a two-bit deal over a couple of hundred quid for the engine, the whole thing goes up in smoke. And if you do that, it will come back to haunt you."

Steve raised his eyebrows, smiled and held up his hands defensively, "It won't come to that Colton, there's only one man I've ever been loyal to and that was your dad, still am, never told him any lies, never lynched on him, nothing, and I'll do what you ask because of that loyalty."

"Okay." Colton relaxed a little, taking a draw on the cigarette, "If I can get you a diesel engine then, do we have a deal?" Colton asked Steve.

"You paying for it? Will need to be cash up front" Steve said,

"I'll get you enough to cover your boat, and your time." Colton said.

Calvin shot Colton another look of amazement, which Colton ignored.

"And you think your plan will work? They'll kill you, you know, if they catch wind of any of this." Steve said.

"They've already killed me once, they're not going to get the opportunity to do it a second time." Colton said defiantly.

Steve looked at Colton, "There's an edge to you Colton lad, that I never see in anybody these days. They've all given up, ken, they've all gone comatose to the world around them, lost the fight. You, there's a fire in your eyes and guns in your hands, even though they're not there, I can see them. Yes, you might well be the one to finally bring an end to the Alessi's crazy rule."

"You'll have your solar panels once their grip on the Borders is gone, once they stop bleeding the place dry." Colton replied.

"Well, now, that would be something." Steve replied, reaching forward with his hand outstretched, "I don't expect you to change things that much, but you've got a deal."

Colton took his hand and they shook on it.

"Get the car to this location, get word to me, and within, hmm, a couple of months say, you'll have your boat." Steve drew a map on the back of a crumpled envelope on his table.

Chapter Forty-One

After a time, Colton and Calvin stepped out of Steve's flat onto the street which was covered in a thick dense cloud of sea mist, the air was cold and carried the smell of fish and salt on the air.

"Christ how much did we smoke, the whole streets gone foggy with it?" Calvin joked.

Colton was a bit unsteady on his feet, he held the wall briefly to regain his balance, "A bit too much." he replied.

"Christ we've got that whole train journey to do again." Calvin groaned, "and you've got a fucking car you told me nothing about you could have driven us here."

"And had the car impounded as soon as it left the garage? Or run out of diesel halfway here?" Colton replied.

"How you going to get the car to Eyemouth without it being lynched?" Calvin asked.

"Fuck knows." Colton replied.

They walked along the pier, "Look at that seal." Calvin said, "Just sitting waiting for tourists to feed it chips."

"I could go a bag of chips." Colton said.

"We've no long had some!" Calvin laughed a high pitched laugh, "You're a chip eating machine!"

"Let's get a carry out for the way home." Colton suggested.

"I think that's a wise idea."

They went up the street into town, buying beers and munchies for their arduous journey back to Hawick. They had a couple of cans on the Berwick to Edinburgh train but saved the rest for the train from Edinburgh to Tweedbank. On the train they received looks and glances from other passengers for drinking beers and rustling crisp packets, but they didn't care.

Forty minutes later they were nudged awake by the train driver at Tweedbank, "End of the line boys, off you get."

"Is it? Thank fuck for that." Calvin said, waking up.

"You taking your mess with you?" The driver asked, indicating the cans and wrappers strewn around them.

"Aye, of course we are." Calvin replied.

They hastily picked up their wrappers and cans under the scrutiny of the train driver, feeling like they were twelve again getting a row off a grown up, and stepped off the train.

Calvin sent a coded text to Stef notifying her they needed picked up. They walked out of the station and waited at the spot where Stef had dropped them off. They stood with their hands in their pockets, bracing themselves against the wind that was picking up strength.

"Sorry I shouldda text her on the train." Calvin said grimacing against the winter chill in the air.

"She definitely coming?" Colton asked.

Calvin shrugged, "Should be. She said she would finish her work for the day once I text her and head back to get us."

"What time's it?"

"Six o'Clock." Calvin checked his phone.

"Doesn't she usually finish at five?"

"Shit." Calvin said.

Just then a little white car came slowly round the corner, it flashed its lights at them.

"Thank God." Calvin said.

They jumped into the back of the slowly moving car and were met with a frowning sister's face, "What time do you call this Calvin? And you stink! Have you been drinking, I can smell you from here, God! I'm having to call this in as overtime Calvin, for you to just be drunk. And is that weed I can smell?"

"That was Colton." Calvin replied.

"Don't you bring him into this! You've got this car stinking if my boss smells it they'll take it off me! They'll take the job off me!"

"Stef, calm down." Calvin started, "We'll open the windows."

"Calm down?! Don't you tell me to calm down! I'm doing you a favour and you can't even say thank you!"

"Thank you Stef." both boys said in unison.

"We really appreciate you doing this." Colton added.

It seemed to ease Stef a little.

"Hows my dad doing? Did you see him?" she softened.

"He's looking well." Calvin said.

"Bastard." Stef said.

"Are you talking about me or our dad?" Calvin asked.

"Oh shut up, I hate both of you." Stef said.

Chapter Forty-Two

Colton cringed as he put the key in the lock at The Abattoir, waiting for Vivienne to appear at the top of the stairs demanding to know where he'd been. She did not make an appearance. He made his way upstairs and found a note on the office desk from her, "Gone to see Libby back tomorrow x" which must have been written some time yesterday. Nice of her to phone about it, he thought, but he was secretly relieved that she wouldn't know he'd been away.

Except maybe by the smell of his clothes if she caught a whiff of them, if she was to appear any time soon. He threw them off and jumped in the shower. The thought of getting grief from Vivienne made him the most stressed out he'd been all day.

Colton need not have worried about how to get the car across to Steve. Two weeks later, after revealing to the inner circle of Abattoir Boys his dilemma, and only the dilemma of needing to transport a car to Eyemouth as part of stopping the Alessi's, farmer's son Jimmy solved it for him.

"I'll take it across in my tractor and trailer." he said, "I'll put a tarp over the trailer, no one will know what's in it. I'll say it's a grain delivery or something for the farm tracker records. Its battery should hold all the way there, I'll need to find a charging point once I'm there to get home. My dad will probably kill me if he finds out, but what's new."

"It's a big risk Jimmy." Robbie whistled, "If you get caught, they'll have you slung in the jail and try and take your dad's farm off him too."

"We're already on the verge of losing it to the Alessi's anyway, what with them claiming their share of the income to 'keep the crops and livestock safe', and the taxes imposed on just about everything we do, its damn near impossible to run the farm." Jimmy said, "It's killing my dad. It's only a matter of time before they take it off us, so what if I bring forward the inevitable. It's worth a shot to be part of stopping them."

The movement of the car was arranged for the following week, as Jimmy's dad would be away to market. It had to be during the day as the tractor wasn't allowed off the farm after six pm, and early enough that Jimmy could return the same day without arousing suspicion.

Getting the car out of the garage and into a trailer without anyone reporting the odd behaviour of a tractor driver, as well as evading the curious mind of Vivienne was no mean feat. Above anything Colton was desperate to protect her, given her history with Marius Alessi, he didn't want to place her in danger by knowing too much of what he was doing.

The car was loaded up early in the morning, the tractor and trailer driven away, and Jimmy knocked at the Abattoir door two days later and reported that all went well. The message from Steve was to tell Colton he was an idiot for destroying a priceless car, that it would take him a couple of months to do what was asked, and to send word after that as to when he wanted Steve to leave, but not by telephone or car for fear of it being traced.

It was no mean feat what Jimmy achieved that day, he carried a new tilt in his chin, raised up a little with defiance and pride that he had played some part in bringing down the rule of the Alessi's, which would maybe be part enough to save his father's farm.

Steve would receive the car, and in the glovebox find his cash payment, as well as the written address of the secluded port he was to reach in Spain, with a handwritten letter from Colton to deliver to the people he would have to seek out once he was there.

It was risky, putting things in writing. Colton's written Spanish was not brilliant, and he was trying to write in a coded language so that the average reader would not understand the gist of what he was asking.

On receiving the directions from Colton, Steve laughed, as he knew the port in question quite well, having been there countless times before in his former life working for Aubrey. It was one of their favourite drop off and collection routes as it was relatively unmonitored by the authorities, he would be able to sneak a small British fishing boat into the docks without too much trouble at all.

Two months later, he was as good as his word, and set the little tiny boat running on its diesel engine sailing on the favourable wind. He maneuvered into the familiar dock with ease, and found the same faces that he had sought out in the past, who delivered Colton's hand written letter to the Baron.

Steve waited a month for the shipment to be ready for him, sleeping on the boat and spending days smoking, walking about the towns, hanging out in the small bars he used to frequent, and soaking up the sunshine. The shipment arrived in a small van, much to his surprise it contained something he didn't think Colton would ever have anticipated arriving, something that was to find its own way to Hawick, and cause its own storm on appearing in town.

Chapter Forty-Three

The storm was given directions by Steve, as to how to firstly get to Hawick, and secondly, how to find The Abattoir.

Sofia, for it was her who was stowed away on the boat going to Scotland, upon hearing it was sailing on behalf of her beloved Colton, walked the journey from Tweedbank to Hawick herself. She found herself at the open door of The Abattoir, taking a deep breath to compose herself.

The boys were not there, having went out for a run, it was Vivienne who was walking down the steps and saw the strange foreign girl standing there.

The girls knew instantly, as soon as they saw each other, that they were under threat by each other, no spoken words were necessary.

"Can I help you?" Vivienne asked icily.

"You will leave my Colton alone now, he is my prince, not yours." Sofia said in thickly accented English.

"Listen hen, I don't know who you think you are, but at my say so, Colton will have you killed. You'll disappear, poof, just like that." Vivienne retorted.

"Where I come from, the women learn to shoot guns as well as the men. We do not expect our men to sort our problems out for us."

Vivienne's eyes flickered, she was used to standing behind a tough man, and had never been challenged in such a way before. Looking gorgeous, charming people, fulfilling men's whims and desires, while she got as much as she could in return, that was her life. She realised she was physically out of her depth, the younger girl standing in front of her had a wild look about her face.

"You need to leave here, or I'll call the police." Vivienne said.

"Good, they will find your body then." Sofia said, "I am only going to say this one more time, you leave my Colton alone. I am giving you the chance to walk away now. Each time you contact him, I will come at you worse than before. First, I will chop your fingers off, wan by wan. Then I will shave off your thin limp hair and feed you the extensions so they twist in your stomach. Then I will sink a knife in your face so that you can no longer live off men for your looks alone. Maybe then you might grow a prettier heart. Do you understand me, white girl?"

"How dare you speak to me like that!" Vivienne snapped.

She stepped forward from the stairs and slapped Sofia across the face. Sofia's head moved with the impact, but her eyes registered no pain. She simply nodded, once, acknowledging the level Vivienne was preparing to play at, and adapted to it.

Sofia's arms were low down at her sides, she reached backwards then swung her arm full force with her fist clenched, impacting with Vivienne's chin. Vivienne went staggering backwards in her heels and fell onto the floor. She shook her head, dazed, never having been hit before in her life. But then she grew angry, adrenaline coursed through her body. She kicked off her heels, stood up and ran at Sofia with her hands outstretched like claws.

"You little bitch!" Vivienne screamed in a banshee like voice that wasn't her usual sweet tones.

They were dancing around the floor of the Abattoir now, the two girls, like some sort of awkward ballet scene, two beauties of different descriptions, hitting out at each other with venom in their eyes.

They fell into the ring, hands wrapped round each other's throats the impact driving them apart.

Fighting for breath, Vivienne laughed, "He will never leave me, he is in love with me!"

"You do not love him!" Sofia exclaimed, knowing it to be true.

The girls stood glaring at each other.

"I do not need to love him, I give him everything he needs. He is loaded now, rich, and gives me everything I ask for in return for his little lustful desires."

"Backstabbing whore! I know what you did to him. You covered it up with your lies so you would be the queen of this town."

"And he'll never hear it from you! He'll never know because I will have you killed for what you have done to me today! Marius Alessi is only a phone call away, you think I would leave someone like him for someone like Colton? I was sent to spy on him! Marius would never let me go! And later, Marius will have Colton killed, just like he did with his parents, and I will be able to go back to him and stop pretending! Most times I can shrug Colton off, but sometimes I actually have to let him fuck me, and it makes me sick."

Sofia leaped at Vivienne again, and the fighting continued in the ring. Hair was pulled out in clumps, faces were scratched, clothes were torn.

The boys arrived at The Abattoir from their morning run, all conversation stopping as they stepped through the door and took in the state of the two girls in the ring. Robbie and Jimmy instinctively strode forward, leaped into the ring and pulled the girls off each other. The others paused right in the doorway, Colton was the last into the room having to push past the other lads who were staring open mouthed at the scene before them.

Colton stepped toward the ring, completely taken aback that Sofia was standing there, being held back by Jimmy, and that both girls were covered in blood seeping from various cuts on their bodies.

"Colton, my love!" Vivienne whimpered, "This crazy girl just appeared and started attacking me, I have no idea who she is, I want her out of here!"

Colton moved towards Sofia, Vivienne saw this and let out a sob, feigning sudden faintness, "Colton, please can you take me upstairs?"

Sofia looked at Colton, pleadingly, "Colton I ..."

"I don't know why you've come Sofia, but please leave." Colton interrupted her, walking over to Vivienne to support her. Vivienne reached dramatically for him.

"She does not love you Colton." Sofia pleaded.

"I don't want to hear it." Colton said, "How could you just attack Vivienne like that? Please just go!"

Sofia's shoulders dropped, she climbed through the fight ring, picked up her travel bag and walked out of The Abattoir, finally defeated by the final blow coming from her Colton's dismissal of her, she was beaten, tears beginning to fall from her eyes.

Colton led Vivienne upstairs, leaving the boys downstairs muttering over what just happened.

"Colton's new lass is a psycho." Dave said.

"Yeah but she's hot." Robbie said.

"Colton's woman needs to be crazy to keep him in check." Jimmy said.

"Do you think he'll ditch Vivienne now?" Dave asked.

"It's about time he did." Calvin agreed, "She's no right for him."

"Wonder what it was all about." Robbie said.

"We have the whole fight on CCTV, awesome." Calvin said.

"Let's take a look!" Jimmy was already part way up the stairs.

The boys went upstairs to the office to replay the CCTV footage, while Colton tended to Vivienne in the bathroom, out of earshot.

"Turn it up, put the sound on, I want to hear what they're saying." Robbie said.

When they reached the stage where Vivienne stood in the ring and confessed to Sofia what was really going on, the boys grimaced.

"That's why the Spanish lass was beating the shit out of her." Jimmy said.

"We've got to tell Colton." Calvin said.

Vivienne was in the bathroom, which was a lot more ornate than it used to be, having had her designer tastes inflicted upon it over the time she had been staying there. She sat on the edge of the bath, while Colton cleaned her cuts. She deftly raised one of her legs, running her toes up Colton's thigh, luring him back to her completely, when there was a knock at the door.

"Colton can I speak with you a minute?" Calvin asked.

"Sure." Colton said.

Chapter Forty-Four

Sofia wandered along the high street, in a daze. She turned into the first pub that she came across. There were motorbikes and an electric car parked outside which she took to be a good combination. She glanced again at the bikes, noticing their engines were missing, undrivable homages to honour a time that was now over.

The barman raised his eyebrows as she walked in, "What happened to you? Do you want me to call the police?" he asked, concerned.

Sofia shook her head and bit her lip, tears escaping from her eyes once more.

"Bathrooms are through there if you want to clean yourself up a bit. First drinks on the house." the barman said gently.

"Brandy on the rocks, par favour señor." Sofia said, wandering through to the toilets.

She looked at herself in the mirror, blood was smeared across her cheeks, there was a bruise on one eye which was beginning to puff up, her hair was everywhere.

She sighed and looked down at the sink. What a mess. Her word against Vivienne's and Colton utterly besotted with the other woman, it was like he was enchanted.

She pulled a hairbrush out of her travel bag and smartened up her hair, the movement of brushing calming her a little. She washed her face in the sink, swishing the bloody water drips all away, then reapplied some makeup to her face.

She zipped up her travel bag, went back through to sit at the bar. The barman presented her with her drink, she looked at him gratefully, then burst into tears.

Colton walked through to the office with Calvin, the other boys had reversed the CCTV footage, Colton saw the two girls on the screen as he walked through the door, which Calvin closed behind them.

"Aw guys I don't wanna watch that." Colton said.

"No, this is something you have to see." Calvin said.

"You're a stupid bastard sometimes Colton." Jimmy said.

"Sofia's crazy." Colton said.

"She's got good reason to be, watch this." Robbie said.

"I don't want to watch them fight." Colton said.

"Shut up and listen." ordered Calvin.

They played the footage. The scene played back, Vivienne's voice spitting out those poisonous words once more.

"That's what happens when you think with your dick." Jimmy muttered.

"Or don't think at all." said Dave.

"My bets were on Sofia the whole time." said Robbie.

"I can't be with Sofia." Colton murmured.

"Why the hell not?" Calvin asked.

"Because, I've been with her mother." Colton said, staring at the screen.

There was the briefest silence, then the boys began to laugh.

"Colton you never banged her mother as well? First the Cougar then the kitten! Get you, you total stud!" Robbie laughed.

"Man, thats totally fucked up. Does she know?" Dave asked, trying to suppress a grin.

"It's not like that!" Colton said, he was still reeling from Vivienne's words on the screen, not properly taking in what the lads were saying to him.

"Vivienne told me that she'd come to warn me that day my dad got poisoned. But, she was part of it the whole time?" Colton said.

"Seems that way." Jimmy said.

Just then Vivienne's voice called from through the back for Colton.

"Oh, look out, you've spent too long with us and not given her enough attention." Jimmy said sarcastically.

"What are you going to do now?" Calvin asked Colton.

"I don't know, I need some time to think about all this." he replied.

"Do you want us to go, give you some space?" Calvin asked.

"No, I, um, if you could stay here and train like you normally do until she leaves? Keep an eye on her. Don't let her know we know anything, she's too dangerous. I think I need to get some air."

"Where do you want us to say you've went?" Calvin asked.

"I dunno. To get her some more bandages and wine or something." Colton suggested.

Colton walked out of the office and downstairs.

Jimmy watched him leave out of the large office window, then looked up at the sky, "He's going to get soaked, the storms about to break."

Colton walked with no purpose, out of The Abattoir, along the High Street, passed Blake's Bar, where a line of motorbikes were parked up, then crossed the road and went down a side vennel heading towards the river.

"Can I ask what happened to your face, or is it something you don't want to talk about?" the barman asked Sofia, "I'm Malcolm, by the way."

"Eet was a woman called Vivienne. She is a liar and a thief." Sofia said miserably.

"I only know one Vivienne like that in this town. The other ones are really nice. Is she a skinny girl with dark hair, wears expensive dresses?"

"Yes." Sofia nodded.

"Yeah, she's bad news. I'd stay well away from her in future. She goes with a bad crowd, her man's Colton Cooper, a bad guy to be around."

Sofia let out a wrenching sob at the mention of Colton's name. Malcolm didn't notice this, but the only other customer in the pub, the old man in the corner finishing his lunch noticed, and let out a large sigh.

"I can't help it, I love him, he breaks my heart. I am sorry for crying Malcolm I cannot help it." she reached for his hand, which was resting on the counter, and Malcolm didn't quite know what to do.

"I come all the way from my home in Spain to tell him that I love him, and he is with another woman. A woman that does not love him, and does wicked things to him and he does not know. But she makes him hate me. And my mother, I know about it, but it does not matter to me and he won't even talk to me."

Malcolm tried his best to look sympathetic, but was not following all of what Sofia was saying.

The old man in the corner glanced at the window as a shadow moved past outside, then he began to make movement and noises indicating he was getting up to leave.

"Alright there Tam?" Malcolm asked, "Do you need a hand?"

"No thank you son, I have somewhere to be." the old man said.

Tam picked up his two walking sticks and walked as quickly as he could towards the door.

"I'll get that for you." Malcolm said, walking under the bar he held the door open for the old man to walk through.

"Thank you Malcolm, you are kind to an old man." Tam smiled and made his way as quickly as he could down the street.

Chapter Forty-Five

The electricity in the air was setting off goosebumps of people on the street. The colour of the clouds with the dark hues and flicks of white through them, darkening the blue sky, sending it a brilliant white as the sun rays hit it and then turning the sky black as night, and the rain began to fall like the tears falling from Sofia's face where she sat in Blake's Bar.

Colton wandered along the street, drenched through to the skin in seconds. His hair clung to his head, drips poured down his face. The thunder rumbled nearby closely followed by flashes of lightning.

His feet took him along to the white foot bridge, which was lit up with purple lighting due to the lack of light in the sky. He walked out onto the middle of the bridge in a daze, smooth tarmac beneath his feet. He stopped in the middle of the bridge to watch the water rush by beneath him, it was mesmerizing, sending huge trees down with it despite it only just starting to rain in town.

He was close to giving it all up, everything. He couldn't possibly pull off his plan. Nor could he stand the pain in his heart from where the two girls tore at him with outstretched talons. Vivienne, the worst wound of all, for she played a part in the death of his parents. He was plotting revenge on the men involved, and now the woman he'd spent night after night with was part of that. She'd used him, she openly admitted that she used him and was intending to see him die at the hands of the Alessi's. And Sofia, oh how it hurt to think of her.

He just wanted a simple life and the world had thrown him into a battle not of his choosing.

"You chose it son, you finish it." he heard Aubrey's voice above the thunder and the roar of the river.

"I can't keep doing this." Colton said to Aubrey, "I'm not as strong as you were."

"You are twice the man I was. And you have an army now of your own making. You will not fail."

Colton waved the voice away and looked into the rushing water. Colton didn't notice in the downpour that a cloaked figure in a flat-brimmed hat shuffled quickly towards him along the pavement with the aid of two walking canes. The figure walked up the bridge and drew to a stop near Colton. Colton heard the old man muttering to himself but paid him no heed.

"Yes, I saw you." the man said louder now so he was audible above the wind and rain, "I was having my lunch and I saw you go past the window, and I said to myself, there goes a man with a broken heart, aye. I saw that look myself when my sweet Helena passed away."

The man wheezed a little when he talked.

"So I put on my coat, and I thought, where will this sad man go? And I saw you looking at the water like you are going to be jumping in. And I said to myself, 'Not on my watch'." the old boy puffed and wheezed, fighting to catch his breath.

Colton gazed at the man with a glaze over his eyes, barely taking in the stranger talking to him.

"Is it about the woman?" the old boy asked.

Colton looked back at the water.

"Ah it is. She was in the place where I was eating, she was most upset. Aye, she is very beautiful, she reminds me of my Helena. You are a cold fish though, with a cold cruel heart. I see it in your eyes, there is nothing there."

Colton turned and looked at the man. He had the cloudy haze of heavy glaucoma over his eyes so could probably barely see anything at all.

"I see things in here." Tam said, as if reading Colton's thoughts, pointing to his chest, "I am very old now. I have nearly lived all of my life. But if there is one thing you can do for me before I die, it is this - be with the woman who sits and cries at the bar for you now. Be a husband to her and you will live happily for the rest of your life. This I know. She loves you very much. If I am still alive then I will come to your wedding when you are married and have a drink of vodka with you."

Tam sighed and rested both his hands on the rail of the bridge, "My Helena, she died ten years ago. We had fifty-six years of blissful happiness, and children, such sweet children! I have very few breaths left in my body, and I'm wasting them coming to see you and set you right again. You have to realise how you have a precious thing, a chance with someone who loves you very much, and the gift of a beautiful life ahead of you. I have neither of these things now, just the memories of an old man. But, what memories they are!"

The old man reached out a little and Colton leaned forward and embraced him, racking back a sob in his chest, "Thank you." Colton said, "I think you just saved my life."

"Ach, what else is an old man to do to stop a woman from crying, ruining his lunch, aih?" the old man dismissed it, "Go to her." he added, "And marry her!"

Colton turned and ran over the bridge then stopped, "Wait! Where is she?" he called to the old man.

"Blake's Bar. Where I always have my lunch."

"Thank you!"

Colton ran up towards the High Street, his feet splashing through deepening puddles along the way.

Chapter Forty-Six

The door of Blake's Bar swung open and Colton walked in, evidently searching for Sofia. He waited in the doorway momentarily as he made eye contact with her. His hair and t-shirt were dripping wet, rain drops were running down his face and his hair stuck to his face in soaking strands.

"Is this the guy?" Malcolm said to Sofia, scowling.

She nodded.

"Oh." Malcolm said, then more loudly, "I can get rid of him if you like, hen, he's barred from this pub anyway."

"No, thank you Malcolm, I will hear what the idiot has to say." Sofia said.

"Just say the word, and he's gone." Malcolm growled and turned away as Colton walked over to stand next to Sofia sitting at the bar stool.

"I'm so sorry Sofia." Colton said.

She didn't move her face from staring straight in front of her. Colton fell back into speaking in his broken Spanish.

"The boys, they showed me the CCTV footage of what Vivienne said to you. I had no idea."

"You would not listen to me Colton, I told you she does not love you, that should have been enough. My mother told me why you would not be with me, I am not angry with her, it is in the past, and I do not care, Colton, you are my hero, you are my love. And I come here, and you hate me, you send me away from you like, like I am nothing to you!" Sofia replied in her native tongue.

Colton looked at the defiant yet vulnerable look in Sofia's eyes and his heart nearly beat clean out of his chest. He would walk over hot coals for the woman standing in front of him, if there was a chance that they could be together.

"I thought I'd never see you again." Colton said.

Sofia let out a small laugh, "Colton it is only three hours on the plane it is not the other end of the universe. A bit longer by boat."

Her light laugh and tone made Colton's heart lurch again. He longed for her to be near him all the time.

"I'm sorry, Sofia, please, forgive me. I was blind and foolish. You came all this way for me, and I didn't even let you speak."

"And why should I forgive you Colton, you break my heart into pieces all over again."

"Because ... " Colton looked earnestly into Sofia's eyes, "I want to spend the rest of my life with you, Sofia. Things are going to change, and I want you by my side through all of it."

Colton swept himself down onto one bended knee at the foot of the bar stool and looked imploringly at her, he took her hands in his, "Will you marry me, Sofia?"

Malcolm span round from polishing glasses to watch the moment in awe.

Sofia left out a sob from where she sat hand in hand with Colton.

"Colton, we have never even kissed each other."

Malcolm raised his eyebrows incredulously, not understanding what was being said, but understanding full well what it meant when a man got down on one knee.

"That didn't answer my question. It needs a yes or no answer."

"But …"

"Buts don't answer it either.

Malcolm gazed at Sofia, wondering who on earth this girl was to have Colton Cooper on his knees in front of her.

"You are crazy, Colton."

"Well, we go pretty well together then. Please, Sofia, how long do you want me on my knees for? I love you. Please marry me."

"Si." Sofia whispered, a small smile forming on her lips.

"What?" Colton asked.

"She said yes!" Malcolm said, completely involved in the moment.

Colton stood up, "I'll never let you go again." he said, and kissed Sofia long and passionately on the mouth,

Malcolm turned away, he didn't want to see the intimate details of the kiss. The first kiss, the shy kiss, the apology, the passion finally being opened up, the declaration of love finally being expressed. No, that was a step too far, he'd seen enough.

Colton asked Malcolm for a Brandy on the rocks, Malcolm poured three of them, one for himself, he had a feeling things were about to begin to unravel in the town.

Colton's phone buzzed in his pocket, a text message from Calvin, "V's gone out in a taxi to see Libby all good."

Colton picked up Sofia's travel bag, "Where are we going?" she asked him.

"Come with me." he smiled and took her hand.

They walked along the street, both of them getting soaked in the rain but not caring as they were together. They walked up past the street which led to the Abattoir, "Can you wait there for a minute? I'm just going to grab something." Colton said.

He ran into Abattoir and came out, holding something in his hand which he placed in his pocket.

They made their way up a hill. They said nothing to each other, both taking in each other's presence, comforted by it. Colton led Sofia to the top of the hill, where the public road ran out and walked up the final driveway on the hill, two stone pillars announced the entrance.

They crunched up a gravel driveway which rounded to reveal a beautiful sandstone house, with Georgian windows and a beautiful overgrown garden laced with trees.

Colton led Sofia to the front door, fished in his pocket and pulled out the set of keys he had retrieved from his safe at the Abattoir.

"What is this Colton?" Sofia asked.

"This is going to be our home, Sofia." Colton said, swinging the door open.

She looked at him, and he added, "I never let Vivienne step foot inside. I told her I didn't want to live here, I think I couldn't bear the thought of her changing it, filling it with gold and velvet. But now I know it was because it was meant for me and you."

The nervous expression left her face to be replaced with overwhelming joy.

"It's beautiful Colton."

They stepped into the doorway of the porch and Colton unlocked the inner door.

"Its freezing!" Sofia exclaimed as the cold air from inside the house rushed towards them.

"Ah, sorry." Colton said, laughing at Sofia's chittering, "I'll get the heating switched back on, it'll warm up for you in no time. There's a fire in the living room, I can set that going for you."

Colton led Sofia through to the large room that looked out onto the driveway. It was freezing cold.

"There's a smaller cosier room through past the kitchen. In fact, it's got a fireplace too. It'll warm up in no time." Colton picked up the dusty basket of logs from the fireplace in the living room and carried them through the kitchen to the snug room.

Sofia stopped in the kitchen and looked around, it was beautiful, laid out with dark wooden counters with blue tiles, and a large oak wood table, then she followed Colton into the snug. It was two steps down from the kitchen, a small room with long windows and a set of double doors that led out onto a low back patio and overgrown kitchen garden.

Shelves lined the walls, filled with books, Sofia ran her gaze along them as Colton bent down to light the fire.

"This was Aubrey's house. He bought it when he came back, if my parents had got back together I would have lived here. But now it's going to be our future instead." he said happily.

Flames made their way up the chimney and the kindling beneath the logs began to crackle. Sofia knelt down next to Colton on the rug, holding out her hands to take some of the heat from the fire.

He put his arm around her and pulled her close, "Let the rest of the world pass us by, let's take this moment as our own, just ours Sofia, before the world starts spinning again. This is ours and it will be waiting for us once the madness is over, to make a home, and our happiness together.

"I like the sound of that, Colton." Sofia murmured.

Chapter Forty-Seven

The next morning Colton left Sofia in the house and walked down the street to buy them something for breakfast after managing to switch the electricity back on and the heating. They had a feast of a breakfast together, complete with fresh coffee and a Spanish Omelette.

After breakfast Colton left Sofia, she proposed she was going to make the house more comfortable, already finding sheets in the cupboards for the beds, and make it her own.

It was the perfect day to set in force the motions for all out revenge. He had everything at stake now he had Sofia by his side, the same overwhelming protective instinct over her coursed through him as it had in Spain. It gave him enough drive to make the final push to setting the plan into action. It had been talked about for long enough.

He just had one loose end to tie up first: Vivienne.

Colton was the last of the boys to arrive at The Abattoir that morning. The lads cheered and wolf-whistled as he entered the training room.

"Late in this morning Colton, that's not like you!" Calvin smiled.

Colton's face flushed.

"Ah lads he's been getting laid look at the colour of him!" Robbie laughed.

"With that gorgeous Spanish bird. She's crazy, Colton, but gorgeous." Jimmy said.

"We're engaged." Colton said.

"What?!" All of the boys said.

"I asked her to marry me."

"God that's a bit quick is it not? She only just got here yesterday." Calvin said.

Colton shrugged, "Has Vivienne been back here?" he asked, looking around.

"No, she's not been seen since she went to visit "Libby", who coincidentally, was out with Stef last night and hasn't seen Vivienne for over a month, and said Vivienne's up to no good behind Colton's back, and she doesn't want to know her anymore. Stef came into my room at three am, off her face drunk, to let me know." Calvin said, yawning in perfect timing.

"What would I give to have Stef drunk in my bedroom." Robbie said.

Calvin punched him on the arm, "That's never gonna happen."

"Vivienne will be at The Prudential." Colton surmised, "She'll be keeping Marius busy till at least one o'clock, that's what time she usually gets back from 'visiting Libby'."

"For sure." Dave grimaced.

"Grassing us all up." Jimmy added.

Colton closed the door to the Abattoir and drew the bolt, "She isn't getting a sniff of what's about to go down."

The boys went quiet, "Are we actually going to do this Colton?"

"No time like today." Colton nodded, "Let's set this plan into action shall we?"

The boys cheered in agreement.

"We're going to get our town back!" Robbie said.

"It's not going to be easy." Calvin said.

"Who cares." Jimmy said.

"I want you to run the doors, like we have planned, get the townsfolk into the town hall by the back door, for twelve today."

The boys cheered in agreement.

They left The Abattoir separately, and made their way along the planned routes around town, they knocked on certain doors and entered certain shops, with the message to meet in the town hall. Word spread like wildfire.

At twelve o'clock, the town hall was filled with the murmur of anxious voices. They went quiet as Colton walked onto the stage.

He cleared his throat, and looked warily at the microphone, "Is this thing on? Okay. Hello everyone, thanks for coming along at such short notice. You'll be wondering why you've been summoned? I'm setting a plan into motion, which some of you thought I would do. I don't think you're all going to like it, but I need your help, and I sure as hell can't do this without you."

Colton looked about the crowd, there were a lot of scared, anxious faces staring back at him, as well as some angry ones. He floundered a little.

A man began to make his way through to the front and walked up the side steps to stand next to Colton on stage. It was Sam Turnbull, last year's Cornet. Sam threw off his outer jacket to reveal that he was fully dressed in his yellow waistcoat, high collar with a blue and yellow ribbon fluttering at his chest. It had the desired effect of drawing the crowd's respect and attention.

Sam stepped over to the microphone, "I know some of you weren't sure about what Colton is planning to do. That you're worried your homes and families are in danger if you help him."

"Aye, we've enough trouble as it is with the rates going up all the time" someone from the crowd shouted.

"And enough of my family are in the jail, I don't want to join them!" another shouted.

"And who was it who put the rates up?" Sam asked.

"Dreyfuss Alessi." someone shouted.

"And who put your families in jail?" Sam asked

"Marius Alessi and the police up his airse!" someone shouted.

"This is the first year since World War Two that that the horses have not ran the boundaries of Hawick. The first year that we have not chosen a Cornet. The first year that the men have not sung in the hut. There is no Common Riding this year. On whose say so?"

"The fucking Alessi's." someone from the crowd shouted.

"And the police." a woman's voice piqued up.

"Are we going to sit here and let this happen?" Sam challenged them, "Are we honestly going to say that it was on our watch that for the first time in almost a hundred years, we let outsiders stop our rideouts? That we just bowed down while they took our shops, our businesses, our families and our traditions away from us?"

"No." the crowd agreed.

"Well, this man, right here, is the only one with the ability to stop them." Sam turned to Colton, "I will follow this man to the ends of the earth, and I want you all to follow him, as you followed me last year. I'm going to take this moment, to elect Colton as this year's Cornet. It breaks with tradition, but I'm sure you'll forgive me, given oor dire situation. He is going to carry oor flag to victory and I want you all to rally roond him, because he stands for us, oor town, oor traditions and oor freedom!"

The crowd clapped and cheered in agreement.

Cornet Sam removed his blue and yellow ribbon from his chest and pinned it to Colton, "Three cheers for this years Cornet, hip hip!"

"Hurray!"

"Hip Hip!"

"Hurray"

"Hip Hip!"

"Hurray."

Sam stepped aside, motioning to Colton, "They're your people now." he whispered.

"Thank you." Colton's voice was hoarse.

Colton cleared his throat, and spoke a little more loudly, "Thank you, Sam, for bestowing this honour upon me. It means, well, it means an awful lot to me. They've taken everything from us, our identity and our freedom. We used to be a fearless people that were unable to be ruled by English or Scottish law. What happened to us? Are we going to cow down to these men? I for one, am not! It used to be called Reiver Justice, and by god that blood still runs in our veins does it not? We will make sure there will be hooves thundering in the hills of Hawick again!"

The people cheered. Colton waited for quiet before continuing,

"There are parts of this plan that I am not going to tell you all today, that is for your own protection. But I need you to trust me. And Sam is right, I am going to do something that no one else in this town is able to do. The only way to stop the Alessi's is to kill them, and please, if anyone here can see another way, let me know, by all means. But I've seen men like them before. They don't go away if they get put in jail. Their grip on this town won't stop. So I'm going to risk my own life to save this town. It's not a decision I've taken lightly. It won't sit comfortably with you all, but the bullets are being fired from my gun and will be on my conscience."

Colton paused to draw a breath, "And I'm going to get the corrupt police put behind bars too. With any luck, exposing their ring of corruption will lead to some, if not all of your families being released from prison."

There were murmurs in the crowd.

"And afterwards, if you want to see me put in jail for it all, that's fine. I can live with that. I'll not run and I'll not put up a fight. So, your part in this? I need riders, to get good-old hand written messages to people, out of range of the police's mobile phone scanners. Out of the eyesight of the drones. Out of the tracking ranges of the self-driving cars. You will be riding overnight, in the dark. Firstly, I need a rider with a horse strong enough to reach Eyemouth in as little time as possible?"

"I'll do it." a voice came quickly from the crowd.

"Pete." Sam said with appreciation.

Colton nodded, "I'll give you directions after this. Secondly, I need another rider to take a message to the press offices, the Hawick Paper, and the Southern Reporter in Galashiels, again overnight."

"I'll ride for you Colton."

"Andrew." Sam smiled, recognising another man who rode with him last year.

"Can you both find your way in the dark on horseback?" Colton asked.

"I can ride with my eyes shut, I've been riding our boundaries since I was five years old." Andrew said proudly.

"And thirdly, I need decoys. I want another three riders heading out in separate directions, so if you are spotted, they won't know who to follow."

Six hands from six separate people rose into the air.

"Or six. Six can ride, all the better." Colton said.

Several more hands shot up into the air. Colton felt a lump in his throat at the bravery of the people before him.

"Looks like we've got ourselves a midnight ride out Colton." Sam suggested to him.

"Okay, right. We can do that then. We meet tonight, at ten pm, for the first night ride out. We will ride the boundaries, just as we've always done, and we will see the two riders off into the night."

"Where will we meet you?"

"Where the riders have always met for the first ride out. The Alessi's will be tucked up in their beds. And if they hear us, so what? By the time they call their police, and get them out of their beds, we'll be long away into the night."

"They will find a way to punish us!" a woman shouted.

"No, they won't get a chance to, because in a couple of days, their lives will be finished." Colton replied.

"That's the most dangerous, crazy idea I've ever heard, riding at night time, in the dark, and killing these men!" a man's voice piped up.

It was Ronnie, Sam's Acting Father from last year. He pushed his way forward and stepped up scowling onto the stage to stand next to Colton and Sam. He looked out at the crowd, making sure they all knew who he was, before he added, "A cornet doesn't ride any boundary without an Acting Father by his side! Don't you be going off anywhere without me!"

Colton smiled, "We'll just have to pray for a cloudless night, it's a full moon coming up."

"The horses will find their way." Ronnie said confidently..

"Okay, so until tonight, don't breathe a word of this to anyone else, do not text, do not make phone calls, do not email, about it. This whole thing rests on keeping this to ourselves. See you all there. In the meantime, I need everyone to go about their daily business like nothings wrong. Don't show any hint of excitement or preparation. When the day comes that I take these men on, they mustn't know any of you are involved. That way, it's only my head on the line, and none of yours."

Sam looked at Colton, "When it comes down to it Colton, you'll see who the town stands behind.

Chapter Forty-Eight

The townsfolk left the town hall in small numbers and took the crooked little back lanes to their shops and houses to keep safe from prying eyes.

Colton hid the set of ribbons in an inner pocket and left the Town Hall taking the long way round the back streets back to the Abattoir.

Vivienne was standing outside the Abattoir pressing the call button when he arrived. She turned and met him with a smile, "There you are! You weren't answering your phone, the door's been locked with the code I can't get in with my key. I've not had a chance to speak to you since you left yesterday afternoon."

Vivienne reached for him, pulling him to her by his collar and kissing him on the lips. Colton fought to keep a calm expression on his face, yesterday afternoon, the fight between Sofia and Vivienne, it seemed like a month ago. And here was the loose end he had forgotten to tie up, Vivienne, standing in front of him like nothing had changed. He realised in that moment that it was imperative that Vivienne thought nothing had changed between them, as any change would raise the suspicions or anger of Marius Alessi, it was so intrinsically linked. Above anything he wanted to protect Sofia from them all.

"Vivienne," he smiled, "I've missed you so much! Sorry, I popped out and when I got back the boys said you'd went to Libby's. I didn't want to phone as I know you like to be left alone on your girls nights without any interruptions from me."

Vivienne smiled, and raised her face to his and kissed him again on the mouth. Colton felt a wave of revulsion shudder through him. He could smell Marius' aftershave on her. Funny, he'd smelled it on her before, but never realised what it was. A man claiming his territory.

"Well, we won't have any interruptions this afternoon Colton, why don't you take me upstairs and show me how much you've missed me?" she purred in his ear.

Colton pulled away from her to reach for his key and entered a code on the door.

"I wish you'd just tell me the code, it would make things so much easier, just think I could have been ready and waiting for you upstairs, to surprise you. Where have you been, by the way?"

She toyed with her hair as the door swung open.

"Oh, I went to see Calvin, we sat up and had some beers, watched the football. I crashed on his sofa." he lied, knowing full well Calvin had been at home that night and he could use him as an alibi.

Vivienne stepped through the door and stepped towards the staircase. She glanced at the fight ring, "What happened to that girl?" she sniffed.

"She's gone. The boys saw her off." Colton replied.

"Did you know her?" Vivienne asked, turning on the staircase to look at him. To scrutinise him. Colton made eye contact with her.

"No, not really. I met her once in Spain, in a bar, had a one night stand with her. God knows how she managed to track me down, she's off her nut." he said.

Vivienne smiled. Obviously the answer Marius was hoping for then. Vivienne walked through to the kitchen and put the coffee machine on.

"I'm going to have a coffee and a bath, then I think I might head back out." Vivienne said, any traces of wanting to sleep with him gone now that she was on safe terms with him again.

"Oh right." Colton said, scratching his head absentmindedly, "Where you off to?"

"Going to meet Libby she's going to drive us to Carlisle for some retail therapy. Then I might stop at hers for a glass of wine or two." Vivienne said, pulling a cup out of the cupboard.

Vivienne looked at him from the side of her eyes, expectantly. Colton played his role.

"I feel like we've not spent time together for days. Let's do something together, me and you, when we get back?" he pleaded, stepping towards her as if to embrace her.

Deftly she stepped away from him to tend to the coffee machine, "Wouldn't that be nice." she said to the machine, back to her usual cool demeanour with him.

Colton wandered through to the office, finally dismissed from Vivienne's attentions. He walked over to the counter and poured himself a brandy. He heard Vivienne going through to the bathroom, turning the taps on. He wanted her out of his place. Walking around like it was hers, all the while she'd been cavorting with Marius. He was tempted to drown her in her bubble bath there and then.

He glanced at the CCTV monitor as there was movement outside the front door, it was Sofia. He quietly walked downstairs and opened the door to her.

She stepped through the doorway and into his arms, "My love." she said.

He kissed her, on the mouth, a gesture which sent electric waves down his spine as he did so. When he pulled away from her, he motioned a finger to her lips, asking her to be quiet.

"Vivienne is upstairs, in the bath." he whispered.

"I know, I saw you go in with her, and I waited." Sofia said, with a hurt expression on her face.

"Oh no, no Sofia, it's not like that." he said, running his hand down her face to smooth the worried lines that had appeared there, "No, don't think like that. She was with Marius Alessi last night and is trying to get information out of me about you, to run back to him with. I need to keep her sweet over the next few days so she doesn't realise anything is going on. Please trust me, please, have a little faith in me."

She looked deep into his eyes, and smiled a small but accepting smile, what ever else she felt on the matter she did not reveal, "Will you be back at the house later?"

"Yes, I will, and I will explain everything when I get there." he said.

"Then I will see you then."

He cupped her face in his hands and kissed her again, "I never want to let you go." he said.

She smiled a little more, then her eyes flashed with a pained darkness, "I will go upstairs and stab her skinny flat chested bosom in the bath."

He laughed, "You will not!" he said, "now go, please, before she sees you here."

He opened the door again and Sofia stepped out, warily looking around her as she stepped away. He leaned his head on the door and watched her walking away, feeling protective over her and yearning to run to catch up with her.

He walked slowly upstairs to the office and poured himself another brandy. He felt the temptation run through him to down the entire bottle, so he picked up his glass and walked through to the kitchen to prepare some lunch.

His phone pinged, it was Calvin, "Libby's going out with Stef again tonight, if you want to come round to mine watch some football?"

Colton replied, "That would be great as V's away out with Libby tonight so I've got nothing on." then deleted the messages. The alibi was set.

Finally he heard the bath plug being pulled and the water beginning to drain down the pipes from the bathroom. He had only to play the charade a little while longer. He wondered if Vivienne thought she was playing Marius as well with the same games, or if she genuinely loved Marius. He shook the thought away. He ate his lunch and Vivienne came through, smelling fresh and looking radiant, but not for him.

"Well, Libby said she's going to pick me up on the High Street and she's on her way." Vivienne smiled, "We're going to go halfers on the self-drive and then have a lovely late lunch when we get there and a lazy afternoon of retail therapy to try to get that horrible girl out of my head."

Colton smiled at her.

"Could you possibly give…." she began.

"You're one step ahead of me, I was just going to ask if you wanted me to give you some money so you can really pamper yourself." Colton reached for his wallet and pulled out a wad of notes. Vivienne's eyes lit up, "Why don't you take a bottle of the good stuff for you and Libby for later on?"

He walked through to the office, unlocking a cabinet and handed Vivienne a bottle of brandy.

"Thank you, you are so good to me." she kissed him on the cheek.

And then she was gone. Colton waited a few moments, packed some clothes, food and his own bottle of brandy into a bag, and left the Abattoir, sealing it shut.

Firstly, he headed out of town, to the field to visit Becky. At his whistle, Becky lifted her head up from where she was grazing and pricked her ears. When he whistled again she snorted and came trotting over. He pulled her head collar on over her head and led her to the stable block, where he tacked her up. He rode her over the back lane to his house on the hill, where he dismounted at the gates, closed them behind him and walked her up to the house entrance.

Sofia came out of the front door when she saw it was him. Becky eyeballed her suspiciously, realised the lady in front of her wasn't Vivienne and sniffed the new lady.

"I'm going to leave Becky here for a few hours, I need her later on." he explained to Sofia.

"She looks very well." Sofia said, running her hand along Becky's arched neck.

"Watch her she doesn't really like women." Colton began, but he turned and Sofia had already lightly stepped up into Becky's saddle.

She walked Becky around the driveway, talking to her in Spanish as she went. Becky's ears pricked the whole time, listening to what Sofia was saying.

Sofia walked her back to Colton and smiled, "Have you just stolen my horse?" Colton asked incredulously.

"I think we share some things in common." Sofia smiled, jumping down and rubbing Becky's forehead, "We are both in a strange country for the love of the same man who drives us both crazy."

"Drive you *both* crazy?"

"Yes, thats what she told me, she said her Colton drives her crazy."

Becky snorted in agreement.

Colton unbuckled Becky's saddle, slipped off her bridle and let her loose in the garden, "She can make a start on getting the grass down." he said.

Sofia linked his arm as they walked inside. Sofia had made a huge dish of paella for their supper, and Colton told her of the plan while she cooked and they ate.

At nine o'clock pm, Colton began to get ready. He spent a bit of time polishing Becky's saddle, with a bottle of olive oil that was in the kitchen, and did the same with Becky, until her grey coat shone brilliant white.

He got changed into jodhpurs, black riding boots, a tan coloured waistcoat, and Sofia helped him set the prestigious ribbons and his tie correctly. They then walked Becky together down to the closed gates, which Colton opened. Sofia handed him a silver hip flask, engraved with the letters"AD" on it, filled with his brandy, "I found it in the cupboard." she said.

He looked at her, standing in the dimming light of the day, and brushed the strands of loose hair away from her face, "You are the most beautiful thing I have ever seen." he said.

She lowered her eyes, then looked at him again, "Promise me you'll be careful." she said.

He nodded and kissed her.

Sofia turned to Becky, and said, "and you, bring him home safe to me."

Colton raised himself up into the saddle.

Sofia looked up at him, "Prefiero morir de pie que vivir siempre arrodillado." she said.

"Thats beautiful, what does it mean?" Colton said.

"I'd rather die standing than live forever on my knees."

Colton raised his hand as a farewell and rode down the road. Sofia felt a lump in her throat and fought back tears as she walked back to the house. She was in love with a hero, and that meant her heart would get torn each time he risked his life to save other people.

Colton walked down the hill, the sound of Becky's hooves conspicuous in the quiet night. He rounded the corner and saw to his astonishment, a gathering of some forty people on horseback, waiting patiently and quietly for him. All of them were turned out in their finest Common Riding attire, riding boots polished, and their horses immaculate.

People quietly greeted him as he rode past them. He walked Becky to the front, she positively gleamed in the moonlight. Colton looked at the houses looming ominously around them. Some had their curtains shut. Others had them wide open, and people were waving silently at him as he rode past their windows.

Sam was waiting expectantly on his brown mare at the front, "There's more to come yet, it's not quite ten o'clock." Sam said nervously, "We're really doing this, aren't we?"

"I'd rather die standing than live forever on my knees." Colton repeated Sofia's words.

Sam set his mouth in a firm grimace, "Aye. Safe oot, safe in."

"Safe oot, safe in." Colton replied.

Ronnie appeared on a large sturdy grey hunter. He was carrying the flag, down by his side. He slowed to a stop and handed the iconic blue and yellow flag to Colton, "This flag is the embodiment of all the traditions that are our glorious heritage. Return the flag, unsullied and unstained, when our rides are done."

Colton took the flag solemnly from Ronnie.

"Malcolm from Blake's is bringing us all a shot of rum and milk, he should be here any minute now." Ronnie added, "To help us on our way, ken." his solemn face broke into a smile.

Sure enough, Malcolm and two members of staff appeared carrying trays of white coloured liquid, which they passed first to Colton first, then to every rider. As the drinks were handed round, the last two riders arrived, the messengers. They came to the front, where Colton acknowledged them, and felt a rush of adrenaline course through him.

Colton turned Becky to face the crowd. He raised his glass into the air, and downed the drink, and everyone followed suit. He then raised the blue and yellow flag into the air and waved it, challenging, defiant and brave.

"Riders of Hawick, follow me into the darkness, where the hooves of the horses of our fathers and their fathers rode before them, and we will ride as heroes. Tonight, we declare war on the Alessi brothers, and those who are in their pockets, and we will win, because this is our town! These are our streets, and these are our hills, and they shall not take them from us!"

The riders cheered.

Colton dug his heels into Becky's sides, she spun on the spot and broke into a trot. Together, they led the horses and riders along the street and round onto the High Street. People were standing at the top of the High Street, waving them on. Colton even saw Violet Lockwood standing among them. He raised his hand carrying the flag, waving at them all.

Down the street they went, as more of the horses trotted into the main street, the walls took up the echo of the pounding hooves, so that the whole street resounded with the cacophony of horse hooves.

"Well that's going to wake everyone up!" Sam laughed alongside Colton, "You're turning right up O'Connell Street."

They drew closer and closer to the Prudential building, looming larger than its stonework, like some deathly shadow over the street. Colton held the flag tighter in his hands. No curtains twitched from the main bedroom, and nor would they. Colton felt nothing as he rode past the building, he'd taken a leaf out of the Alessi's book and spiked the bottle of brandy he'd given Vivienne.

In the main bedroom of the Prudential building, two empty glasses sat on the bedside table. The last sound heard by Marius and Vivienne as they took their final laboured hazy breaths upon the earth before their hearts stopped beating was the roar of hooves thundering down on them from all around.

Colton urged Becky on, turning up O'Connell street and made a steady pace up the hill. More people waited for them there, raising their hands and cheering the horses. Not a single phone call was made to the police, nor did any of the henchmen hear what was going on from their houses several streets away.

The horses trotted along a road and turned left, it was not the usual route for the first ride out, but it led out of town towards the roads the messengers would be taking, and the first thing Colton wanted to do was see the messengers off before continuing the symbolic ride.

The group arrived on the outskirts of town, making their way down a thin single track road to the glen containing Hornshole bridge which spanned the river Teviot, where they stopped at the memorial cross. It was a usual stopping point for the Cornet and his followers to pay their respects to those who had gone before them. It marked the site of where the original boys of the town won the English flag. The cross was clearly visible in the moonlight, made of light sandstone, it was about eight feet tall, with a celtic cross and the year fifteen fourteen etched into it.

Colton waited for all of the horse riders to come to a stop, whereby he dismounted, walked over to the memorial cross, where he got down on one knee and kissed the stone work. He stood up and looked at the two messengers. They dismounted and walked towards him. Colton reached into his inner pocket and pulled out two white envelopes, which he handed to each man.

Colton said loudly, "We fight for the freedom of our town, just as they did over five hundred years ago. We remember their bravery each year, so that we too are as fearless as they were. We carry their blood in our veins."

Ronnie and Sam started singing the traditional song 'Teribus', and the other horse riders joined in.

The messenger going to Eyemouth wiped a tear from his eye.

Colton embraced them both, "May the souls of the first Cornet and his riders be with you tonight and protect you on your journeys."

The two riders mounted their horses again. Colton got back on Becky. They rode over the humpback bridge, past a lodge cottage, and up the single track road towards the small hamlet of Appletreehall. Ronnie and Sam guided Colton away from the hamlet and through the fields and gateways. At a certain point in the landscape, the group slowed to a stop, whereby the two messengers spurred their horses on. The group raised their hands in farewell to the two brave men.

Andrew, going to Galashiels, had a route that ran almost parallel with the A7 main road through Ashkirk, Selkirk and up to Galashiels. He would be back before dawn.

Pete, going to Eyemouth would navigate a route leading across the Greenlaw Moors, Duns and over to the coastline. He had over fifty miles to cover, sticking to the smaller roads where possible, he would also cover mixed terrain of flat fields, bog, and scrubland. He had mapped the route out that afternoon, already familiar with the area. He estimated that he would get there before dawn, where he would rest his horse before making the return journey at a slower pace over the next night. He had a hip flask and a bag of food with him. His horse was one of the fittest for miles around, it was a stunning beast some seventeen hands high, built of pure muscle, tan in colour with a black mane that glistened in the moonlight. He prided himself on the stamina it had, though it had never been pushed to travel fifty miles at such a fast pace. He was risking his life, and his horses life that night. He took a backward glance at the silhouettes of the riders waving him on, he knew they would all have ridden with him the whole way if they could, and that was why he was riding tonight, for his town, for his people and for his children to have a future without fear. He turned to face the night, gathered his reins, leaned forward and urged his horse into a canter.

Colton and the other riders turned and rode towards the village of Denholm, then rode around the bottom of Ruberslaw hill, and back into town through the hamlet of Kirkton. It deviated from the traditional routes, but still commemorated them as best they could. It was about two o'clock in the morning when they approached the street lights of town, all the riders were in high spirits, worn out, tired, with sweating, panting horses, steam snorting from their nostrils visible in the moonlight. All of them were happy, with smiles on their faces. They began to disperse round the separate stables and fields around the outskirts of town, rather than ride back into town as a group.

"This is exactly what we all needed." Sam smiled, taking a last swig out of a hip flask.

"It's been a hell of a ride!" someone shouted agreement from behind him.

"Even if they arrest us all tomorrow, it's been worth it, just for this!" someone else said.

Colton smiled at them all. Tomorrow was going to be another day entirely.

Chapter Forty-Nine

At three am Colton arrived back at his house, having stabled Becky for the night, scrubbed her down, fed and watered her. He entered the house quietly by the back door, discarded his mud-sodden clothes on the kitchen floor, took a quick shower, then crept into bed next to Sofia. She stirred only a little in her sleep, he reached to place his arms protectively around her, kissed the back of her neck and fell asleep next to her.

Colton awoke to the sound of his alarm ringing, it was eight am and he to be up and ready. The bed was empty next to him, but he could smell the aroma of coffee drifting up the stairs.

As Colton wandered into the kitchen, yawning, still in the daze of sleep, Sofia gave a yelp and ran up to him, splaying her arms round him and hugging him so tightly it took his breath away, "I am so glad you are safe."

He pried her arms off him and held her hands gently, "And I always will be if I have you to come home to."

Sofia spun round and gestured at the kitchen, "I made you breakfast, coffee and bacon and scrambled eggs and toast."

"Wow, thank you, I'm starving." he rubbed at his arms, "and a little bit saddle sore."

He sat down at the oak table, where Sofia laid a plate of food down for him.

"Amazing." he said, tucking into the breakfast.

"Made with love." she smiled, staring happily at him.

Colton had another shower, then made his way down to the Abattoir to open up. The boys arrived just behind him.

Calvin smiled at him, "No sign of Vivienne this morning?"

"No." Colton replied quietly.

The boys quietened down and looked at Colton for explanation.

"One down." Colton said.

Calvin nodded, suddenly understanding, "And one to go."

At that moment Calvin's phone pinged, it was a blank message from an unknown number.

"Looks like your message got through to my dad." Calvin said, showing Colton the blank screen.

"What do we do now?" Robbie asked.

"We go for our morning run." Colton said, "Nothing changes. The police are still out there, as is Dreyfuss."

They went out for their run, Colton looked about, he received eye contact from a few passers by, but no one said anything out of the ordinary to them.

The run did Colton the world of good, it loosened up his tight tired muscles, and cleared his mind, letting him think through what was about to unfold that day. He could feel an electricity in the air, this was the day, the day when it would all change completely. He'd set things in motion now, it had to all work. The only unknown factor was when

Dreyfuss Alessi would make an appearance. He knew without a doubt that he would. He just had to be ready for him.

The boys started their training circuits on returning to The Abattoir. Colton did a small workout, feeling the burn on his muscles. He then went upstairs to the office, and put the local radio station on. The broadcasters cut a song short, his voice had a sense of urgency.

"News has just reached us that after an anonymous tip-off, a Police Drone spotted an illegal car containing what is thought to be a vast quantity of illegal drugs on the A1 between Berwick and Eyemouth. Police arrived at the scene soon after and are in attendance. They have closed the A1 between Berwick and Eyemouth. Diversions are in place. That's just to let you know folks, that the A1 between Berwick and Eyemouth is currently closed due to a police incident."

Colton sat bolt upright. There it was. The messengers had reached their targets. Steve had positioned the car exactly where he was supposed to on word arriving from Colton, and the press sent their drone to grab the scoop.

Colton ran downstairs and grabbed the remote for the big screen television which was currently playing a music channel. The boys stopped what they were doing and turned to look at the screen. Colton flicked through the stations reaching the news channels. One of them had images of the A1 taken from the press drone.

"It's gone national!" Colton said.

The drone's camera zoomed in on the car, showing the black mercedes abandoned by the road, and hovered around the windows, zooming in to show the squares of brown substance wrapped in cling film badly hidden under a bin liner in the back seat.

The caption across the bottom of the screen read that the shots were taken at nine am that morning, before police reached the scene, after an anonymous tip off. Someone at the news offices informed the police of their find, after capturing the initial images.

The police drone was seen to arrive, whereby the news drone flew higher into the sky to avoid detection and being neutralised of power by the police drone.

The police drone hovered around the car, it could be seen hovering around the windows. The images cut back to the newsreader in the studio.

"If this is proven to be an illegal substance, this is the biggest haul of its kind in the South of Scotland. Police will also need to investigate how a banned car with no engine appeared mysteriously by the side of the main road."

The programme cut back to images of the drone filming the police arriving. Colton narrowed his eyes at this point, trying to focus the blurry image of the policemen on the screen. The drone zoomed in, and captured their faces. It was the men he had hoped for, the ones itching to line their corrupt pockets.

"That's Will Oliver, he's the one that killed my brother." Robbie said.

"And that's Frank Tate, the asshole who framed my uncle." Dave said.

More police cars arrived at the scene and the road emptied of passing traffic.

The spying press drone picked up two key phrases from the police over its microphone.

"Have you run the check on the car?"

"Yes, its registered to Dreyfuss Alessi."

"What? Why would he … This is part of something bigger, we'll have to talk to him before we do anything."

One of the police officers glanced up, a glint of sunlight reflecting on metal caught his eye.

"Shit, the press are already here, we'll have to take it back to the station."

The scene cut back to the newsreader who said, "It looks like the police are discussing taking the car back to the station, where they will examine it for evidence, fingerprints, they'll go over it with a fine toothcomb. They cannot leave it at the site due to the disruption closing the A1 route is causing."

Suspicious looks passed around the boys. Colton felt a strange wave of acknowledgement pass through him. The boys in the room knew what the police were discussing, even if the average watcher didn't. They were intending to keep the drugs themselves and re-distribute them.

"What is it you know that we don't know then Colton?" Jimmy turned and asked him.

"What?" Colton asked.

"You set this up, we know you did, it's the same car that I took over there for you in the tractor. This is part of your plan, isn't it?" Jimmy said.

Colton raised his head once in the slightest hint of a nod.

"So what's going to happen now?" Jimmy asked.

"Now?" Colton shrugged, "Dreyfuss will be alerted to the fact his name's been attached to illegal substances on the national news. He won't be best pleased with his police friends about that really, will he? He will ask them to get rid of the evidence."

Colton stretched, and continued, "The police might try to hold onto the cocaine themselves and redistribute it, as they usually do. But it might just be the hottest cocaine you can get. It might be cocaine that comes directly from Spain. From the source. And the source will know when someone is trying to sell his cocaine. I have heard that this source puts a tracking beacon in each brick of cocaine before it is sealed up, each tracking beacon happens to have a microphone in it which broadcast direct to chosen computers with a password log in. Maybe the local press offices now have access to that log-in as well as their tip off about the car this morning. The car may also be laced with its own camera, which will switch on at approximately eleven o'clock this morning with a direct feed to any computer logged in. If the police behave themselves, well, all is well, isn't it? The trackers will show the cocaine is sitting in their evidence room, won't it, and the microphones won't hear a sound. If the police do not behave, well it's up to the press how deep they want the police to land themselves in it before they call the big boys in to bring them down. And if the press don't do it, well, maybe someone else has a computer logged in, and is watching and waiting to turn things into an international incident if need be."

The boys were dumbstruck.

"And that my friends, is how you bring the Alessi's army down around them. Hopefully." Colton looked back up at the television screen thoughtfully, "Hopefully." he murmured again.

"Jesus, Colton, how in the hell's name did you figure all that out?" Calvin exclaimed.

"And where the hell did you get 'trackable' cocaine from? Who's even heard of that?" Robbie asked.

Colton continued to watch the screen, "I said that *might* be what is going to happen now. You know, if I'd dumped a car filled with drugs on the A1, that's why I might do that. You know, because it might help free some of the framed people from this town if the police are proven to be corrupt liars in it for themselves. Who could then take their word at any of the crimes they've arrested people for in the past? I didn't say that any of it was down to me."

"Jesus." Calvin said.

Jimmy and Robbie sat down to take it all in.

"You've got the bastards." Jimmy said, "You've actually got them."

"Maybe. Possibly." Colton replied calmly, "I'm also anticipating a visit from Dreyfuss Alessi today, so if you'll excuse me, I'm going to have a shower, get changed and be ready for his visit."

"Is he coming here? We'll not let him past the door!" Calvin said.

"I'm not sure where he'll find me. But I think, yes, I think he might try to find me today."

Chapter Fifty

Colton stepped out of the shower, dressed himself in a pair of jeans and a pale blue shirt, and calmly walked into Aubrey's old bedroom.

"I need your help now." Colton said, "I think they will intend to kill me today, and I'm not ready to die."

He opened Aubrey's wardrobe, looking at the clothes on the rail, and pulled out a long, lightweight black coat, which reached past his knees. Long enough to hide a gun from view. He secured the gun acquired from Violet Lockwood's safe to his side, and practiced drawing it from its position.

Satisfied, he went into the office for a shot of brandy, then there was a banging at the front door. Colton gulped. He checked the CCTV, it was Sam. Colton buzzed him in and walked downstairs.

Sam stepped through the door, breathless with a worried look on his face.

"Colton you've got to come quick, Dreyfuss is on the High Street going crazy, shouting for you. He has a lass by her throat, saying he's going to kill her if you don't show up."

Colton grimaced, but nodded, "I'll go." he said.

The boys walked behind him, and they all made their way to the High Street. There were people gathering on the pavements, all faces staring down towards the bottom end, where the Prudential building stood. Colton and the Abattoir Boys walked further down the street towards it.

"I've got her!" Dreyfuss could clearly be heard shouting, "I've your your little Spanish whore! I know it was you. You did this! Where are you?"

Dreyfuss was standing underneath the Prudential building on the pavement, he was holding Sofia round her throat. Her hands were scrabbling at his arm frantically.

Dreyfuss stood like a man possessed, his hair was wild, his eyes were white wide. He didn't care who was watching him, he was in a dark place, having just found the bodies of his brother and Vivienne, and was still under the impression that his police force would be able to protect him from whatever it was he wanted to do in the town to mete out his own justice.

"Thinking you got one over on my brother, lying about her, I know who she is! I will kill you myself, you wretched waste of nothingness, in front of them all!" Dreyfuss Alessi screamed, "Come out! Come out from where you're hiding you worthless piece of scum and watch your precious harlot die in front of you!"

Colton steadily walked closer.

"This is my town! I own this town!" Dreyfuss shouted, "Did you think, did you think you could kill my brother and get away with it?"

Sofia fought and struggled against his arm but she was held fast. She stamped on his heel, where he released her with surprise, but then he lashed out, striking her on the side of the head with his gun. She hit the ground with a thud. He grabbed hold of her head with a fistful of her hair, and hauled her body up to a kneeling position.

All this Colton saw, from where he was halfway up the High Street, and on he walked, his long coat tails flapping with his strides.

Violet Lochwood happened to be on the street, a rare occurrence for this old lady, but her prescription needed picking up and she liked doing that herself. She saw a young girl standing gawping at Colton, pulling out her mobile phone to film what was going on. Violet swung her walker frame at the girl with every ounce of strength she had and the phone flew out of the girls hand, smashing on the pavement.

Violet wobbled and lost her balance but a middle-aged man near her saw this and helped her steady herself on her walker again, "Not in this town, you don't betray your own people!" Violet shouted bravely to the girl, "Don't you dare film this!"

People turned to hear Violet, saw what had happened, and they followed her lead, snatching phones out of the hands of the younger ones, some even deleted the videos they found on the phones, others simply smashed the phones to pieces.

Dreyfuss dropped Sofia back onto the pavement, a wry smile suddenly played at his lips. He was filled with a knowing confidence that Colton wouldn't dare retaliate against him in front of so many witnesses.

Colton levelled himself, steadying his legs. He swept his coat to one side, and pulled out his father's gun from his side. Colton flicked the safety catch on his gun as he walked further on, Dreyfuss was just too far away for a clean shot, he'd never aimed at anything this far away before. Dreyfuss began to raise his own arm with his gun held in his hand.

Colton raised his gun, closed his right eye fractionally, aimed and fired.

Dreyfuss staggered backwards, dropping Sofia to grab his arm, dropping his gun to the floor. Colton's bullet had pierced his arm. Dreyfuss winced with pain, he bent down and picked the gun up with his other hand, releasing his grip on his arm made the blood soak through his clothes. He ran madly towards Colton. The people on the street swept away from him, terrified they would be caught in the middle.

Calmly, Colton raised his gun again, taking it in both hands, he levelled his eye along the barrel, aimed again and fired.

Dreyfuss went down, shot in the heart, clean dead.

Colton placed his gun back by his side, and ran toward Sofia, lying slumped on the ground.

Someone near him cheered, and others joined in.

"This is our town!" someone shouted, "And no one will ever take it from us!"

The crowd on the street roared, then the noise of sirens was heard coming closer, and a deathly silence fell over the High Street.

Colton lifted Sofia to him, he checked for a pulse, she was still breathing. Blood was drying as it caked the side of her face. He spoke soft words to her, she murmured a little and began to come round.

The sirens were there on the High Street now. Calvin was by Colton's side, urging him to run, Colton refused.

"I promised the town I wouldn't go anywhere once I'd done it." Colton said, "And I'm not leaving her like this."

Then Violet Lockwood was by his side, "Then you'll at least give me your gun you young fool!" she hissed in his ear.

She leaned forward and pulled the pistol out from his side, which she hastily stowed in her handbag and shuffled quickly away from him.

The blue lights came closer, the patrol car parked up and two men jumped out, sprinting towards the body of Dreyfuss Alessi. A small group of people crowded round to watch them.

"Did anyone see what happened?" one of the men shouted, "Can anyone tell us what's been going on?"

The crowd remained quiet, shaking their heads.

"Anyone? Did no one see what happened to Mister Alessi?" he insisted.

The crowd murmured their dissent.

"No one saw anything Officer." A butcher standing on the pavement in his apron said bravely, "We heard a gunshot and myself and my customers ran out of the shop to see what had happened and Mr Alessi was already lying there, isn't that right everyone?"

The group nodded agreement.

"Right, none of you are going anywhere, you'll all need to wait here while we call for reinforcements, then we'll need to question you individually. Someone must have seen something, a man doesn't just get shot in the head on Hawick High Street and no one knows anything about it!" the policeman shouted.

The policemen then noticed Colton on the ground with Sofia in his arms, the officers took in the blood streaked down her face and ran over,

"What's happened to her, son?" one of them asked Colton.

"We don't know we just found her like this." Calvin said for them both, following the example of the butcher.

"You just found her?" the policeman asked, "Right."

He lifted up the radio by his side and spoke into the mouthpiece, requesting an ambulance and police reinforcements. The person on the other end of the phone spoke quickly back at him, but it was too distorted for anyone else to make out.

"What do you mean, they're all busy? They're still at the scene at Eyemouth? Well they're needed here! We've had a shooting incident on the High Street we need to cordon off the street and get witness statements!" the policeman said abruptly.

The voice spoke to him again.

"I don't think it's advisable to call in the police from Edinburgh for assistance, no, they don't know the local people like we do."

The voice spoke once more.

"Okay, we'll just have to wait for them then!" the police officer was red in the face with anger.

The other one looked at him questioningly.

"They're sending down forces from Edinburgh as our guys are all still dealing with the incident on the A1. Unbelievable, that's the last thing we need them coming down and poking their noses into this. Marius will have a fit, how are we going to explain this to his brother? He'll be baying for blood and ours better not be part of it!"

The policeman realised other people were within earshot and went back into duty mode, "Is anyone else hurt?" he spun round looking along the street. People were already disbursing. The butcher was walking back into his shop,

"You need to wait here!" the police officer commanded the street, "You all need to wait here, you are needed as witnesses!"

But the people ignored him and walked away.

The ambulance arrived shortly afterwards, the ambulance men tended to Sofia, confirming she was concussed, but it wasn't serious. Sofia declined to be taken to the hospital, but the police advised her if she was well enough they would take her to the station, so she then consented to go in the ambulance, where the police would visit her in the hospital. The police made no association between her and Colton given that Calvin had expressed they did not know who she was.

"I'll come for you." Colton said quietly to her as they lifted her out of his arms and into the ambulance stretcher.

"I know." she smiled weakly.

All the while, Colton expected someone to tell the police it was all to do with him, he was the man who shot Dreyfuss, but not a word was spoken out against him. Calvin grabbed his arm and led him away.

"We need statements off you boys as witnesses." The police reminded them.

"Aye, we won't go too far officer, we just need a drink after seeing that body." Calvin said, "We'll be in the Waverley Bar, just across the road."

Chapter Fifty-One

The police from Edinburgh certainly did ask a few questions. They were specialists in gun crime. They knew a lying witness when they met one, and suspected each and every witness they managed to pull from the High Street was hiding the truth about what happened. But not a single person budged. They all stuck to the same story, that they'd been inside a shop or a building when they heard the gunshots and came running out to see what had happened.

The only videos of that moment that were able to be examined later by the city police reached the stage of Dreyfuss Alessi holding a girl who wasn't local by the throat, waving a gun in the air and issuing threats to kill someone, and striking the girl to the ground. Their videos reached no further, thanks to the vigilance and loyalty of the townspeople. The videos contradicted the witness statements, but there was nothing the police could do to get the people to open up to them. They couldn't trace the bullets lodged in the body.

Their suspicions were raised further when the body of Marius Alessi and Vivienne Cowbridge were discovered by Craven later that day after being unable to contact Marius. But no forensic evidence was pulled up at the scene of the second crime.

The mysterious foreign girl in the hospital said she couldn't remember what had happened to her. No recollection. She was visiting relatives in the town, and had left to go shopping and that's as far as she could remember.

The Edinburgh police surmised that it was possible that Marius was the one who shot Dreyfuss and for some reason, either Vivienne or Marius drugged each other, as all their deaths were evidenced to be roughly the same time. Close enough to suggest they could have been involved. Close enough, but not conclusive.

Closing the case did not sit comfortably with them. Their eyes had been cast over the Border town and they did not like what they saw there.

Then the newspapers broke with the story of how evidence was going missing from the local police headquarters. Drugs, in fact, that were being tracked and they had video evidence of policemen selling it on. The news team also demanded the investigation into hundreds of cases of crimes that were committed in the Border towns as they suspected police of framing innocent people to suit their own means.

The Chief Constable of Police Scotland was livid. He wanted heads to roll for the embarrassment of such a story hitting the headlines without his having any knowledge that such things were taking place. Then the First Minister contacted him directly in a very brief phone call to advise him that his head would be expected on a plate too, in a public press conference. His career, and his life, was over.

The Specialist Crime Division couldn't pinpoint exactly what had occurred in the Borders, they knew each incident was all linked, somehow, but now that it involved police corruption of this magnitude, their investigations were moved to internal suspects, and making sure their own heads were not in the firing line. Their attention fell away from the little town of Hawick and what actually might have went on at the shooting that day.

Colton collected Sofia from the hospital with the aid of Stef and her works car. Stef lied to her boss and said she had a 'female-related' hospital appointment to get permission to take the car. She parked in a space far away from the hospital then went into the building to collect Sofia. When they appeared round the corner, Sofia had a worried frown on her face, and evident bruising and stitches where she'd been struck. When she saw Colton standing next to the car waiting for her, her face lit up, and she ran into his arms.

"You are safe." she said happily.

"It seems that way." he replied, holding her tightly.

"Do we get our happy ending now?" Sofia asked.

"I really hope so." Colton said, leaning over to kiss her.

<u>The End</u>

Thank you for reading *Unfinished Business*.

If you enjoyed the story, I would be grateful if you could take the time to write a small review on the Amazon sales page.

You might also be interested in reading my other work, please visit www.gemmalubbock.com for more information.